The
Cat's
Pajamas

Gilbert Morris

HARVEST HOUSE PUBLISHERS

EUGENE, OREGON

Gilbert Morris: Published in association with the literary agency of WordServe Literary Group, Ltd., 10152 S. Knoll Circle, Highlands Ranch, CO 80130

Cover illustration © cocomartino / iStockphoto

Cover by Abris, Veneta, Oregon

THE CAT'S PAJAMAS
Published by Harvest House Publishers
Eugene, Oregon 97402

ISBN-13: 978-0-7369-1965-4

Printed in the United States of America

To Bobby Funderburk~
Thanks, partner, for all the joy your
friendship has brought into my life.

One

As the waves from the Gulf of Mexico made their sibilant sounds, the huge ebony cat with the enormous golden eyes gazed out the window of the glassed-in patio. He'd had a busy night prowling the beach looking for something to kill, making his way through the sea oats that line the shores of White Sands, Alabama. He had been rewarded by finding an Alabama beach mouse—a creature that was protected by law. But Jacques the Ripper, as he was grimly called, didn't acknowledge the laws of the state of Alabama, nor of the United States—nor of the planet Earth, for that matter. Jacques was his own law and bowed his sleek head to no legislature or court on earth. He had enjoyed the mouse.

Jacques stretched, his sleek muscles rippling under the glossy black coat, then turned and stared at his best friend, Cleopatra. Cleo was licking her fur, which was long and shiny in the nature of Ragdoll felines, and Jacques felt a wave of disgust sweep over him. He was pretty much contemptuous of everyone on two legs or four, and even though there was a special bond between him and Cleo, he often found her irritating. Nevertheless, there was a form of communication, not in words but in body language and strange feline telepathy—whatever it is that passes between Savannah cats and Ragdoll cats—that kept the two of them connected. Jacques growled in his throat.

You're going to get hair balls.

I can't help it, Cleo mused. *I've got to keep myself clean.*

Jacques was revolted.

Their Person, Mary Katherine Forrest—or Kate, as she preferred to be called—had remarked more than once to Jake Novak, who inhabited the upper floor of the large house perched on the Gulf of Mexico, "I know cats can't talk, not with words like we do, but they're almost mysterious the way they can communicate. You can just look at Jacques and tell how intelligent he is."

Jake Novak didn't share Kate's admiration for the big black cat, and he had merely grunted, "He's intelligent enough to kill or slash anything that comes within paw's reach."

Jacques rose and with that graceful, gliding gait that Savannah cats have, moved around the spacious patio room just as the sun was beginning to shine through the windows. Miss Boo, the flop-eared rabbit, hopped in and stopped dead still. She noticed Jacques and tried to turn around, but he was too quick for her. He made a lightning-fast slashing movement that caught Miss Boo on the flank. She hopped frantically away making imploring cries, and Jacques the Ripper found this hugely satisfying. Moving over to Cleo, he sat down in front of her and let her know his true feelings.

I'm sick of playing second fiddle to all of these mangy animals around here. Back when we lived in our last house we were the only ones our Person loved.

She can't help it, Jacques, she has to take care of the other animals. They came with the house. Cleo took another lick at the silky fur.

She's changed. She used to give us all her attention. Now she even forgets to feed us. Look, this bowl's empty. To prove his point Jacques went over to the bowl, gave it a blow with his paw, and sent it clattering across the ceramic tile floor.

She's busy, Jacques. She has important things to do.

Jacques had a way of expressing utter disdain with his eyes, his body language, and all that was in him. *Nothing is more important than me! I'm going to settle this right now.*

Cleo looked up in alarm. *You can't get in her room. She sleeps with the door shut.*

That's to keep out the riff-raff—not me!

Whirling gracefully, Jacques headed for the pet door, which was oversized to allow Bandit the coon and Trouble the muscular pit bull to come and go gracefully without squeezing.

Jacques paused long enough to give Trouble a quick slash, just to keep in practice. Trouble was sleeping, but came awake with a sharp yelp. He leaped to his feet and stood there staring at the huge black cat, who appeared ready for battle.

Trouble was a strange dog. He weighed seventy pounds and was all muscle. He wasn't afraid of a bull elephant and would have readily attacked one if his Person had told him to, but he *was* afraid of a few surprising things. Both Miss Boo, the rabbit, and Abigail, the ferret, seemed to bother him. But the animal in the house that put fear into Trouble was Jacques the Ripper. Trouble could easily have broken Jacques's back with one grip of his mighty jaws, but he wasn't able to overcome his innate sense of inferiority. Trouble backed up and watched as the two felines exited, then he walked over to his food bowl, saw it was empty, whined, and plopped himself down and waited for breakfast.

Cleo followed Jacques out to the deck. She sat down as Jacques went straight to their Person's sliding glass door. He paused in front of it, studying it and poking it with his paw.

Sometimes she leaves it open. Now it looks like it's shut.

You don't need to go in there and bother her anyway, Cleo protested.

Jacques ignored her, and set his sights on the Intruder—the name Jacques had given to Jake Novak.

The Intruder keeps his door open. I'll get him up.

He made one of those leaps that cats make so easily—not one fraction of an inch too high, just leaping and gliding in exactly right. Cleo followed, and they made their way up the stairs that led to the Intruder's deck, which was cantilevered out over the lower deck. He turned and gave Cleo a look of satisfaction.

He left the glass door open.

But the screen's shut.

I can fix that. With a few mighty rips, Jacques's powerful claws tore into the screen and he stepped inside, followed by Cleo, who entered with some trepidation.

Look, he's asleep. Don't wake him up, Jacques.

He's slept long enough. It's time for breakfast.

Jacques the Ripper advanced and picked his spot. The Intruder was slumped over his desk wearing a pair of shorts and nothing else, as he often did. Selecting a nice fleshy portion of the sleeper's calf, Jacques swiped it with his claws, not a bad slash—just enough to wake him up—and then backed a few feet away to enjoy the Intruder's reaction.

Jake Novak let out a muffled cry and threw himself back in the chair. He looked around the room in confusion for a moment, and then his eyes settled on the diabolic form of Jacques the Ripper.

"You sorry piece of trash!" Jake Novak grunted. Novak's coarse black hair was sticking out in every direction. His deep-set eyes were a startling hazel, and his wide mouth was framed by a wedge-shaped face and high cheekbones, plus a broken nose from his days when he was more than ready to throw himself into a fight. There was something ominous about Jake that frightened everyone—except the Ripper.

"I think I'll drown you in the Gulf, you mangy cat!" Jake advanced but Jacques held his ground, not backing up an inch. He reared up with claws extended and his amber eyes seemed to glow with incandescent fury.

Jake stopped abruptly, for he knew the damage those claws could do. He had never seen a Savannah until he had met Mary Katherine Forrest and her pets. A Savannah, he had discovered, was half serval, an African wild cat, and half domestic American breed. It made for an enormous exotic cat. Since it was partly a wild animal, it required a special permit to own one in most states of the Union. Savannahs were also terribly expensive, with a male kitten costing as much as three or four thousand dollars. Jake had suggested to Kate several times that she sell the monster cat and give the money to him so that he could use it more wisely.

Cleo—always the peacemaker—came sliding around Jacques and put herself against Jake's leg, rubbing sensuously.

Jake looked down and the anger in his eyes faded. He bent over, picked up Cleo, and held her in his arms.

"Well, sweetheart, don't tell anybody, but I've become a little bit attached to you." In truth, Jake had never liked taking care of animals. He'd wanted a puppy as a child but his parents had never allowed it, and as a result, Jake found himself developing a dislike of all types of pets. He supposed it was a defensive reaction.

When he and Kate had inherited the house in White Sands, he had been disappointed when he discovered that their inheritance was dependent upon keeping the pets of their benefactress, an old lady called Zophia Krizova, a distant relative of both him and Kate. Although he didn't relish the thought of living with animals, Jake complied with the provisions of the will. Simply put, Jake had no money and this was a sizable inheritance. He was also a wannabe writer and here was the perfect place to write a novel: on the shore of White Sands with the blue-green water sparkling, the gulls crying overhead, the dolphins swimming by in meticulous formation, and a beautiful suite on the second floor. How could a writer ask for more? In fact, he'd already finished one manuscript and sent it off to some agents and publishers and was now working on a second book while waiting for a response to his first effort.

"Why can't that black monster be sweet like you?" Jake asked Cleo.

Cleo purred at Jake's voice, and he put her over his shoulder as one would carry a baby. "I guess you're saying 'Where's breakfast?' Okay. I've done all the bad writing I can stand for one night."

Jake left his suite, which contained everything a man needed except a kitchen, and descended the staircase. A door at the bottom of the stairs separated the upstairs apartment from the rooms on the main floor, which made a single man and a single woman living together respectable—or so the theory went. Others in the community didn't see that door as justification for Novak and Mary Katherine living under the same roof. But that had been one of the conditions of Miss Zophia's will—they had to live in the house to take care of the animals. The living arrangements didn't bother Jake in the least, but he took devious pleasure in knowing it sometimes made Kate uncomfortable.

Jake entered the kitchen and opened two cans of tuna packed in spring water. The cats each had their own bowl. The Ripper's was red and Miss Cleo's was pink. As he straightened up and stepped back to watch the two cats eat, Jake noticed that Cleo ate daintily with good manners, while Jacques gobbled his down as if he hadn't had a meal in months.

Novak was startled by a sudden loud squawking of vile profanity, followed by a flutter in the air and two talons fastening on his shoulder. He twisted his head and saw Bad Louie, the parrot, clenching and unclenching his claws. Bad Louie had been raised by a houseful of construction workers and preferred their lewd language.

"You'd better not let Mary Katherine hear you talk like that, Bad Louie. She'll take you right off at the neck. You know she can't abide rude language."

Novak was always amused at Kate's efforts to reform Bad Louie. He had told her more than once that you can't fix a bad parrot.

Suddenly Jake felt something touch his leg and quickly he looked down, afraid that the Ripper had launched a second front. But it was only Bandit, the raccoon, who was seated upright and pawing at him. He looked at the animal and shook his head woefully.

"Little did I dream, Bandit," he said, "that when I was in that crummy apartment in Chicago I'd ever miss it. At least I didn't have to put up with a blasted menagerie."

He then fed Bandit, Trouble, and Miss Boo, thinking of how strange his world had become in such a short time. Up till now, his life had been one of nonstop action and violence. He had been a member of the Delta Force, where he'd learned many interesting ways of killing and maiming human beings. After he left the service he had become a homicide detective in Chicago—which meant seeing the worst of life on planet Earth.

Jake couldn't remember when he hadn't wanted to write, but it had never seemed a real possibility and thus always took a backseat to his military and law enforcement careers. He'd made several starts at a book, but it had proven nearly impossible to solve real-life murders and write a novel at the same time. Eventually he'd decided to drop out of the rat race for a while and give full-time writing a chance, and had been down to his last dollar...when out of nowhere the opportunity had come to inherit the house of this relative he'd never met. Of course, it also meant living in the house with two people he'd never met, Kate and her son, Jeremy, who were co-heirs with him. Nevertheless, he'd jumped at the chance. Now he didn't have to kill anyone in the line of duty or solve any crimes. All he had to do was write, but for some reason he was finding this difficult.

After all the animals were fed, Jake made coffee in the *real* way, the way God intended for coffee to be made. He carefully measured the beans and placed them in a burr grinder. Some people used blade grinders, which were less expensive, but the grind wasn't as consistent. He ground the perfect blend and then poured bottled water into the coffee machine. He'd had trouble over this with Mary Katherine, who wanted to use instant coffee, but Jake quickly threw out any of "that vile stuff" he found in the house. Kate had quickly learned that Novak was a purist where food was concerned.

When the coffee was ready, Jake went out on the deck and sat down on the steps. He savored these early cobwebby times of the morning alone. The old lady had bought seven lots on the beach and put the house right in the middle so that, unlike the other houses that sat elbow to elbow, there was the sense of isolation with this place—a privacy that Jake loved.

After a few minutes he looked up and saw a small figure trudging along the beach. He got up, gulped the coffee in his mug, and walked down enjoying the feel of the cool sand between his toes. This was the whitest sand he had ever seen and people came from all over the country to do what he did every day.

"Hello, Rhiannon," Jake said with a smile.

The small girl who looked up at him had a Welsh name and insisted on people saying it correctly—Rye-ANN-on. She was no more than ten years old and wore a pair of ragged cutoffs with a dingy, oversized, gray T-shirt. The shirt had a character called Animal on the front, straight out of *Sesame Street,* and on the back, faded so it was almost illegible, was the identification *Animal.* The girl was struggling with a five-gallon white bucket and Novak asked, "What's in your bucket?"

"Fish, of course." She put the bucket down. Jake leaned forward to see that it was full of fish just about right for cooking, not too small and not too large. "Red snapper," he said.

"I'm going to cook them for my grandpa."

"Well, if you cleaned them first, they'd be easier to carry." He noticed a grimy bandage on one of her hands. "What happened?"

"I cut my hand," Rhiannon said.

"Does it hurt?"

"That's a personal question." Rhiannon had a pair of sea green eyes, an ivory complexion, and black curly hair cut very short. She had a Mediterranean look and was extremely intelligent, more so than any child Novak had ever met.

"Sorry," he said now to Rhiannon. "That hand just looks like it might be painful."

Rhiannon gave him a look like she was considering whether he was worthy to know the truth. "Thank you, but the agony has abated."

Jake was amused. He knew that Rhiannon learned a new word every few days and he guessed that *abated* was her latest.

"Let's have some breakfast," Jake offered. "Then I'll help you clean the fish."

Rhiannon could be feisty at times, but was never shy about accepting invitations.

Jake picked up the fish and carried it up the steps and she followed him. He glanced back at her.

"Why are you so sad, Rhiannon?" he asked.

"I'm worried about Lucky, my dog."

"What's wrong with him?"

"He's sick."

"I'm sure it can't be that bad. Everybody gets sick sometimes." Jake led her into the house and began making Belgian pancakes, which were his specialty. As he made the batter, Rhiannon watched him with an air of considering whether to speak.

Finally she said, "Do you believe in heaven?"

Jake stopped beating the batter and gave her a curious look. There was something disturbing about the child that he could never quite identify.

"I don't know about things like that. There's enough going on in *this* life that I don't have much time to speculate on what's next...if anything."

"Only a fool doesn't believe in God and in heaven."

"Why would you say that?"

"It says so in the Bible. 'The fool hath said in his heart, there is no

God.' That's in Psalms, the fourteenth chapter, the first verse. In the King James translation."

Jake Novak was intimidated by very few people, but Rhiannon Brice was one of those few. She was a strange child living alone with her sickly grandfather. She was homeschooled by the old man, who had been a scholar and a writer in his day.

Jake continued to cook the pancakes and noticed that Rhiannon had picked up a *National Geographic* magazine and was turning the pages over fairly rapidly.

"Well, the pancakes are ready," Jake said. "One of them, anyhow." He gave her the first serving and set before her a jar of molasses bought at the Loxley Food Market. He also had pure maple syrup sent all the way from Vermont.

He watched as Rhiannon baptized her pancake first with the molasses and then a layer of maple syrup on top. "You're going to use *both* of those?"

"It's not genteel to talk about people's eating habits," Rhiannon said.

She began to eat the pancake and her eating habits reminded him of Jacques the Ripper. She was cramming it in her mouth and swallowing it as if she hadn't eaten in days.

"You're going to be fat like me if you keep on eating pancakes like that."

"No, Jake, you're not fat. You're muscular. And I'll never get fat. Only people who eat improperly and don't exercise get fat."

Jake couldn't argue with that and when she started on her second pancake, she looked up at him and licked her hand that was coated with either molasses or maple syrup.

"I'll never have heart trouble either." She sounded very sure of herself.

"How do you know that?"

"Eskimos have the lowest incidence of heart disease in the world."

Jake was accustomed to Rhiannon making statements that seemed to have nothing to do with the conversation. "What does that have to do with you? You're not an Eskimo. And how do you know Eskimos have the lowest rate of heart trouble?"

"It's in the *Encyclopedia Britannica* under Eskimo."

"Why were you reading about Eskimos?"

"I'm reading through the *Britannica*. I've gotten to page two-thirty-four in the J volume." She rattled off part of the article, apparently word for word, that had to do with Eskimos.

"Since I read that, I take fish oil pills that my grandpa buys, and I eat raw fish. If I eat just like an Eskimo, then I shouldn't have heart trouble."

"That ought to do it." Jake put his own pancake down, sliced it up, and took a bite. "These are the best pancakes in the world." He was still curious. "You've just gotten up to the J volume?"

"Yes."

"Okay. What's the annual rainfall in Brazil?"

"Forty-nine-point-six inches a year."

"You remember all that stuff, Rhiannon?"

"I have a phenomenal memory."

Rhiannon was on her third pancake when Kate and Jeremy came in sleepy-eyed and ruffled from just getting out of bed. Kate had a wealth of light auburn hair, which she kept very long. She had a widow's peak and gray-green eyes, an oval face and wide lips.

"How are you this morning, Rhiannon?" Kate asked.

"I'm eating pancakes."

"I see that. Jake makes good pancakes. How's your grandfather?"

Rhiannon didn't answer and, as if putting the question aside, she turned and asked one of her own.

"Jeremy, have you had any more bad dreams about dying?"

"What are you talking about?" Kate said, turning to her son. "I didn't know you had bad dreams."

"He has bad dreams about Derek Maddux getting murdered. I expect the memory hasn't abated yet." Jeremy had gone to school with Derek and had been a suspect in the murder for a while. The whole ordeal had been a shock to the entire town and had disturbed Jeremy terribly. It had been his first experience with the death of someone his own age, and it was little wonder he had bad dreams about it.

At the age of twelve, Jeremy Forrest was wiry, almost skinny. He had auburn hair and the blue eyes of his late father.

"Aw, she wasn't supposed to tell you that." He looked at Rhiannon and said, "Do you have to blab everything I say?"

"How long have you been having these bad dreams?" Kate asked.

"I don't know," Jeremy said. "It's not that big a deal."

Jake was taking all this in when suddenly he heard an odd crackling sound. He glanced across the kitchen into the living room and jumped up.

"It's Miss Boo again. She bit into another lamp cord."

Jake strode across the room, followed by the others, and pulled the plug from the outlet, then jerked the flop-eared rabbit's teeth out of the lamp cord.

"Is she going to die?" Rhiannon asked.

"I'm going to try CPR." Jake picked the rabbit up and began to massage its heart.

"I didn't know you could do CPR on rabbits," Rhiannon said, as she rattled off the encyclopedia description of CPR.

"Look, she's moving!" Kate said. She had knelt down beside Jake and now she reached out to smooth the animal's silky fur. "Oh, Miss Boo, I wish you wouldn't do that," she said. "You scare me to death."

The rabbit's eyes opened, and she gave two tremendous kicks with her hind legs. Jake handed her over to Kate and shook his head. "I never thought I'd wind up bringing stupid rabbits back to life."

"I think I can eat another pancake," Rhiannon said, returning to the kitchen table. She had been interested in the CPR performed on the rabbit, but that wasn't nearly as interesting as Jake's pancakes. "Did you know they're making a movie here?"

"Making a movie where?" Jeremy asked.

"Right here in White Sands." Rhiannon pointed out the window. "They've rented the Blue House, at the end of the beach."

"The party house?" Jake said. "I never see anyone there—except every once in a while it's mobbed with people and cars and loud music."

"That's the one." Rhiannon pushed her chair back. "Time to go. I've got to cook some fish for my grandfather."

"Jeremy, why don't you go help her clean those fish?" Kate said.

"All right, Mom," Jeremy said. The two left, Rhiannon giving Jeremy instructions on how to clean the fish properly. "You have to do it right or I won't let you help," she said as they left the room.

"I swear that kid is an alien," Jake said with a shake of his head. "She's not from planet Earth."

"She's a strange child," Kate agreed. "No telling what her IQ is. More than mine, I'm sure." The two finished their own breakfast, and Jake started to clear the table.

"I'll do the dishes, Jake," Kate said quickly.

"You don't know how."

"I don't know how to wash dishes?"

"Apparently not. If I weren't here, this place would be hip deep in dirty dishes—and dirty laundry."

Kate felt a tiny bit insulted, but she knew Jake was right. She was a terrible housekeeper, while he was an excellent one. She had often thought they were like Felix and Oscar, the Odd Couple in the movie. Sometimes she felt guilty that Jake did so much of the housecleaning, but she reminded herself that she took primary responsibility for the care of the animals.

"Let me put it this way then: If you can deal with my inferior methods, I'll do the dishes. You fixed breakfast, it's only fair," she said.

"Okay, fine. Just don't let me find any dried crusties on the plates later. But," he continued, "the only reason I'm agreeing is because I need to go to Gainesville today."

"Florida? What for?"

"To visit a guy."

"What guy?"

"Pete Yastremski."

"Who in the world is that?"

"A guy who nearly killed me. I cornered him in an alley and made the mistake of turning my back on him."

This was part of Novak's life that Kate had difficulty understanding—a world of violence, murder, assault. "So you're going to the prison."

"Yep."

"Why are you going to see him?"

"He's reformed. I used to write him once in a while when I was in

Chicago. I met his mother. Nice lady. So...I'm trying to give Pete some, you know, moral support. Encouragement. It's not easy going straight once you're in the slammer."

"That's nice. God will bless you for it."

"Sure He will," Jake said with a touch of sarcasm. "So what are you going to do?"

"I'm going with Beverly to a concert in Mobile."

Beverly was a thirty-five-year-old English lawyer—Beverly Devon-Hunt—who had been helpful when Jeremy had been accused of murder. Bev had a law degree from Oxford and had plunged into the case with great enthusiasm. He was wealthy, with a title, but to Jake he was just a strange British guy with a strange name.

"You watch out for that guy, Mary Katherine," Jake warned. "You can't trust a guy with a girl's name."

Kate glared at Novak. "Bev's a perfect gentleman." She started washing the dishes, slamming them around, and Jake grinned at her and left. He went to the fish tank and watched at the tropical fish. One of them began making O's with its mouth. Jake leaned over and tapped on the glass, drawing the attention of several of the fish. When they came to him, he said, "You know, I think I'll get a few piranhas to put in there with you. That'd cut down on a few mouths to feed around here!"

Two

Kate turned around slowly, studying herself in the full-length mirror for a moment—and was pleased with what she saw. She was wearing a pair of blue linen capri pants and a white tank top covered with a short-sleeve flowered linen shirt, which she left unbuttoned. As she slipped on a pair of white pearl earrings, suddenly a thought came to her: *Am I dressing up because the minister's coming to see me?*

The idea brought a wrinkle to her brow, and for one brief moment she considered taking off the outfit and replacing it with something more casual. She had noticed that good-looking ministers—and even those not so good-looking—seemed to attract women like flies to honey. She wondered, *Will Pastor Bates think I'm one of those women who's out to trap a man?*

She pushed the thought from her mind and smiled at her foolishness. She looked down at Cleo, who was sitting a few feet away, sleepy-eyed, watching her dress.

"We females have to be careful, Cleo. We wouldn't want to be thought of as man-chasers, would we?"

Cleo yawned hugely, revealing a red mouth and sharp white teeth. The conversation bored her and she turned to a rumpled sweater Kate had tossed on the floor, padded it for a few moments, and then curled up and closed her eyes.

As Kate studied herself, she was pleased to see that she had kept her figure at the age of twenty-nine. She remembered that when she was seventeen, she had thought a woman of thirty was old. Now she herself was on the threshold of that, but she didn't feel old, even with a twelve-year-old son to attest the passage of time. Turning, she walked to the closet and chose her new Marc Jacobs sandals. They had cost more than she'd ever paid for a pair of shoes, but she had fallen in love with them and splurged.

The doorbell rang at that moment and after a quick look at her hair Kate hurried out of the bedroom and moved toward the front door. When she opened it, Elvis Bates, pastor of the Seaside Chapel, nodded and said in a Southern drawl as thick as day-old grits, "Well, hello, Sister Forrest."

"Good morning, Pastor. Come on in."

Elvis Bates was a tall, lanky individual with a craggy, sunburned face, out of which beamed bright blue eyes. His straw-colored hair looked as if he had cut it himself. Bates had been a major league pitcher for three years, breaking records right and left. When he had left his baseball career after hearing the call of God, the groans of his fans could be heard from coast to coast.

"Sure is hot out there, ain't it?" Elvis said, tugging at his collar.

"Come into the kitchen. We'll have something cool to drink," Kate offered.

Kate led the way, seated him at the island, and said, "Go ahead and put your things down. You want a Coke or some lemonade?"

"Got any root beer?" Elvis asked as he set down his rucksack.

"I believe we do. Jeremy loves root beer." She opened the refrigerator door and nodded, "Yes. Let me fix you a glass."

"On, no, right out of the bottle will do."

Kate placed the tall brown bottle of A & W in front of the pastor and got herself a lemonade squeezed from fresh lemons. She had tried to use a commercial mix and Jake had thrown a fit. "That's *not* lemonade," he had said. "That's slop. You gotta start with real lemons." As with every other kind of food, Jake Novak demanded only the best.

"This sure is good. I wish—" Elvis Bates turned, for Jacques the Ripper's nap had been disturbed. He had been sleeping on top of the refrigerator and now came down with a single bound, looking for all the world like a black panther right out of deepest Africa. His amber eyes gleamed, and as he advanced, Elvis leaned down and held out his hand.

"Last time I was here, he seemed to like me."

Jacques looked up at Bates with disdain, then stalked away.

Kate laughed. "He's fickle, I guess. Usually he doesn't like anybody but me. Even Jake's afraid of him."

"Can't blame him. He's a fearsome-looking critter."

The two sat and talked, and soon the table was littered with notes concerning the youth beach ministry. It had been the dream of Mary Katherine Forrest, since she had been converted, to do something like this, but while she'd been in Memphis there had been little chance for it. After her husband's plane had gone down over the ocean, she had been forced to work a double shift, one at Wal-Mart and one at McDonalds. When, through her inheritance, the doorway had miraculously opened for her to come to the Gulf Coast, she had jumped at the chance. The legacy provided enough money that she didn't have to work full-time, so she'd finally been able to be the mother Jeremy needed. She'd thrown the rest of her energy into taking care of the animals and doing ministry work for Seaside Chapel, and had already grown to love the church and the fellowship.

Finally she gathered the papers up and put them into the folder. As she did, Elvis took a sip of his root beer and studied her face. He talked like a caricature of a Southern bumpkin, but he had a keen, analytical mind and knew the Bible better than any man Kate had ever known.

"You look all tuckered out, Kate," he said. "Is something bothering you?"

Kate hesitated, then shook her head. "I'm worried about Jeremy."

"What's the matter? He's not sick, is he?"

"Not physically, but I found out he's having nightmares. Bad dreams about all that trouble with the murder."

"Well, that was a rough go, and it was just a few weeks ago, so a little fallout is normal. But he's a strong boy, got good people here supporting him—he'll come out of it. I'll tell you what," he said. "Why don't you let him do a few things with me? Maybe he could be my assistant coach for the peewees. He's a good baseball player himself. The kids would like that."

"That would be so great, Pastor," Kate said quickly. She knew that Jeremy missed having a father and this seemed like a good solution. The two sat there, and from time to time the Ripper would go by on patrol, daring the pastor to mess with him.

"That cat sure is a scudder," Bates grinned. "He reminds me of my ninth-grade algebra teacher for some reason or other, mean and lean and hard to get along with."

Kate laughed and then went quiet for a moment.

"Pastor, has there been any gossip...that you know of?" Her voice was hesitant.

"Always gossip in a small town," the minister replied. "Anything in particular you worried about?"

"Well, about me and Jake. Living in the same house. Of course, he stays in the upstairs apartment except when he cooks down here, but I expect some people think our situation is a little odd."

"Well, Miss Birdie has some ideas." He grinned and winked at her. "That woman's got a tongue long enough to sit in the living room and lick the skillet in the kitchen."

"That's the kind of thing that worries me," Kate confessed. "We have to stay here in order to collect the inheritance, but I've thought of moving out. My reputation is important to me."

"Don't worry," Elvis said. "Appearances aren't everything, and you'll never please everybody. Jesus said in the seventh chapter of John, verse twenty-four, that we're not to judge by mere appearances but make a *right* judgment. Anyone who knows you and Jake knows the truth."

Elvis leaned forward and studied her face carefully. She was an attractive woman, not beautiful in the Hollywood sense but tall and well formed, shapely in a way that would strike any man. And he had noticed that in her eyes lay something flexible but carefully controlled—as though she feared to fully reveal herself. There were ways about her that Elvis had never noted in another woman.

"I know Jeremy's having trouble, but what about you? How are *you* doing? Kind of hard to relocate from the big city to the boonies."

"I'm fine, I guess," she said. "I just—well, I do get lonely sometimes."

Kate's marriage hadn't been good, but at least she'd had somebody. A man to share life with. "I guess I miss being married," she said simply.

Bates thought, *Not many women would say a thing like that out loud.* He admired her for it and said warmly, "A lot of women make a mistake when they lose their husbands. The loneliness can make you jump into a new relationship too quickly. I think it's better to be alone than to be with someone that's not right for you."

"Well, what about you?" Kate ventured. "Are you ever lonely?"

"Sometimes."

"Have you ever thought about getting married?"

"I think about it a lot," the pastor admitted. "Nothing I'd like better than to have a good woman and six or seven kids running in and out of the house, but I—" He suddenly stopped, for a loud bang had drawn their attention. They turned and saw that Trouble was on the sand just below the deck and had picked up what appeared to be a fence post. It was at least eight feet long and he had grasped it in the middle and was attempting to climb the steps to the deck. The post was too wide and both ends struck the rails with such force that he sat down in momentary frustration. He didn't release his hold, however, but started trying again.

"Trouble, you can't bring that thing up here," Kate scolded. "Now go away."

Trouble dropped the fence post, gave her a reproachful look, and then turned and walked off with his tail between his legs.

"Well, I guess I hurt his feelings," Kate said.

"I didn't know a pit bull could have feelings."

"Trouble does. You know, I think pit bulls have a bad reputation. And undeserved."

"You're probably right. Some of them are mean because they've been trained to fight. If they were let alone, I reckon they'd be like all other dogs," Elvis said.

"He's always trying to bring things in the house, but he should have had better sense than try to get that long post up the steps."

Elvis Bates laughed suddenly. It gave him a youthful look. "I guess I was like Trouble, Kate, when I was younger. I always tried to do the wrong thing, it seemed like, and got knocked flat just like he did." He rose and gathered his things. "We'll meet with the youth leaders Wednesday night after prayer meeting. It's going to be a hoot, this youth ministry!"

Kate escorted him to the door and told him good-bye. She watched him get into the old fifty-two Studebaker he had restored and go roaring off. Turning, she walked into her bedroom and changed into shorts and a pink top that was worn but comfortable. She stood in the middle of the room and looked around and reluctantly told herself once again that she wasn't the world's neatest person. Jacques had come in and sat watching her cautiously.

"Well, Jacques, I'm going to show Jake that I can be a good house-keeper, as good as he is or even better." She flew into cleaning the room, and when Cleo came in and joined Jacques, he looked at her as if to say, *Our Person lost her mind, I think.*

What's she doing, Jacques?

She's going to show the Intruder that she's as good as he is. Jacques licked one forepaw judiciously and opened his mouth in what appeared to be a grin. *Pathetic.*

• • •

For a moment Kate stood in the bathroom and looked around feeling extremely virtuous. She had scrubbed the tiles on the walls and the floor and had thrown away every bottle that had cluttered up the vanity. Everything was gleaming and fresh, and as she opened the medicine cabinet, she admired all of her cosmetics and medications lined up perfectly. She shut the door and then walked into the bedroom. Cleo and the Ripper were in the middle of her bed. She said with a playful sternness, "Don't you mess up my bed, you hear me?" She turned and marveled at her bedroom, which was neater and cleaner than it had been since she'd lived in it. She had worked all morning and was exhausted and sweaty. "Now we'll just see what Mr. Squeaky Clean Novak has to say. He thinks he's so much better than me—but I'll show him."

The sound of the Gulf—and a chance to relax in its waters—called to her, and she slipped out of her clothes and put them into the hamper and then donned a bathing suit. She went outside and made her way quickly to the water. Trouble was following but she turned and admonished him. "No, Trouble, you can't go. You can't swim far enough." She watched as he turned and walked away with a despondent air. "I wish he weren't so emotional," she muttered. She turned and made a run at the waves that were coming, hit the water at a flat, shallow dive and, pumping hard, swam until she was at least a quarter of a mile out. She was always a little shocked at how the Gulf tapered off so slowly. You could walk out almost half a mile when the tide was out, but now she began swimming in earnest. She had always been a fine swimmer, especially at long distances, and now there was a great joy as the warm water washed over her and she slipped across the surface. This far out the waves were mere undulations lifting her gently.

Suddenly she saw a group of dark figures to her left and for one moment her heart seemed to skip a beat—sharks had been known to travel in the area. But then she realized these weren't sharks but stingrays. They were supposed to be placid creatures but they looked frightening up close, their long tails barbed with a poison tip. Kate had heard of a famous animal wrangler being killed by a stingray, and now she took a deep breath and went below the surface. The sun lit the clear waters above her, and she saw the rays as they moved like birds flapping wings, flying through the water. They were an amazing sight, graceful and ghostly. Some of them were as much as six feet across, others no larger than a dinner plate. They paid her no attention at all, but from time to time one would go down and skim across the sandy bottom, coming within inches of her.

When her lungs demanded air, Kate broke the surface, took some deep breaths, and then continued her swim. She reached the Florida line, which was indicated by a saloon called the FloraBama that had been featured in a book by John Grisham. He'd made it famous enough so that every night it was packed. Now, however, it was the beach that was packed, and curiosity got the best of Kate. She swam ashore quickly and almost at once was accosted by an overweight man in his late twenties. He was pale and starting to burn, and she couldn't help thinking that if he didn't get out of the sun, he'd soon be a crispy critter. As he approached, the man came close enough that she could smell the alcohol radiating from him.

"Hey, doll, you here alone?" he asked.

"Yes."

"Well, this is your lucky day. So am I."

Kate eyed him with disgust, but her curiosity got the best of her. "What's going on here? What are all these people doing?"

"It's the Annual International Mullet toss."

"Mullet? You mean mullet like the fish?"

"That's right, doll. The one that throws the mullet the farthest wins some kind of a prize. Don't know what it is. Don't matter. What this really is," he confided, his speech slurred, "is a good excuse to party."

"Well, you'll have to excuse me. I'm not throwing any fish." She tried to leave and he jerked at her arm but she gave him a shove. He fell flat on his back and had to struggle to get up. Without another glance, she turned, went back into the Gulf, and began swimming toward home, this time staying closer to the shore. She got a shock when a dark dorsal-finned form went by headed in the opposite direction.

It swam past her not five feet away—and then she gave a sigh of relief. *It's a dolphin.* There turned out to be six of them all in tandem, and she admired them as they swam by.

I've got to stop being so scared of everything that swims by, she thought. *The "creatures" on the beach are much more dangerous anyway!*

● ● ●

As she came out of the water, Kate saw Novak's Harley and knew he was back from the prison at Gainesville. She couldn't imagine what would drive him to make that trip on a motorcycle. She suspected he just liked to ride and had gone to get away from the menagerie. It grieved her that he didn't like the animals—but that was his misfortune, not hers. She washed the sand off her feet at the faucet outside on the deck, dried them, and then walked inside. She heard a noise and walked over to where Romeo and Juliet, the two lovebirds, were having a disagreement. They were pecking each other and uttering cries of anger.

"I thought you two were supposed to be lovebirds," she scolded. "Now kiss and make up!" She had started toward her bedroom when

Bad Louie, the parrot, squawked out a profanity. Kate went to him and saw he was trying to get into the big glass cage next to the wall. She picked up the bird, who looked at her innocently.

"You crazy bird. You better stay away from Big Bertha." She looked down at the six-foot albino Burmese python. "She'll have you for lunch if you give her a chance. So scoot!" She lifted her arm and Bad Louie flew off toward the kitchen. She paused for a moment admiring Big Bertha, and a smile touched her lips. The night they had moved into the house, the python had gotten loose and ended up in Novak's bed. It had scared him witless, and she'd found out his biggest fear—snakes. *If Jake ever makes me mad enough, I can always put Bertha in his bed.* She smiled at the thought, even though she knew she'd never do a thing like that.

Kate headed for her room and heard the music coming faintly from Novak's apartment upstairs. She recognized it as Glenn Miller's classic, "In the Mood." She had known little about the music of the forties, but Novak insisted on educating her. He never ceased to confound her with his eclectic tastes in music, books, and food. One minute he was playing rock music, the next he was listening to the big bands. He regularly prepared gourmet meals but insisted that certain truck stops had the best food around. In all truthfulness she was learning quite a bit from Jake and enjoying expanding her own interests—but she'd never admit it to him.

Entering the bedroom, she gave a look of satisfaction at the neatness of it and determined she would keep it this way. Moving toward the bathroom, she opened the door, stepped in—and then stopped dead still. She look around almost wildly.

"Bandit! What have you done?!" she yelled.

Bandit, the raccoon that shared the house with the other animals, was perched on her double vanity. He looked at her calmly but all around him all was havoc. He was holding a box of expensive powder and he was covered in it. The vanity and the floor were littered with bottles and boxes and shredded tissue. There were lipsticks extended, first-aid bandages torn apart, and bottles lying open with the contents poured out. Suntan lotion was all over the floor, and the sharp fragrance in the air brought another scream from Kate. The bottle of perfume that she'd bought for herself after saving for months lay in a small pool on the tile.

Bandit's clever little paws were like hands, and no amount of destruction was beyond him.

Kate wasn't a screaming woman, but she was furious and yelled at the top of her lungs, "Bandit, I'm going to barbecue you!"

A calm voice interrupted her rant. "What's wrong?"

Kate whirled to see Jake with a gun in his hand and a tough look on his face.

"Look what he's done, Jake."

Jake looked at Bandit who was staring at him with a pleased expression. He shook his head and stuck the gun in his belt. "I don't see anything wrong. The bathroom looks about like it usually does."

Anger flooded through Kate like a tide. She turned and glared daggers at him. "You get out of here! I spent all day cleaning this, and now *look* what this monster has done. All my cosmetics—everything is ruined."

"Hey now," Jake said in sympathy. "No big deal. I'll help you clean it up."

She looked up at him through tears of anger. "I wanted to show you I could clean house as well as anybody."

Jake put his arm around her. "I know you can. I shouldn't tease you so much. Tell you what. You go for another swim. When you get back, this room will be all cleaned up and then I'll grill you the best baby backs you ever had in your life. I'll even make a salad with some of my special Uncle Jake's salad dressing. It'll be all right."

Jacques and Cleo had come in along with Trouble, Abigail, and Miss Boo to watch the action.

What's that running down her face? Jacques said to Cleo.

Tears, you moron. She gave him a furious glance and added, *It's a female thing. You wouldn't understand.*

Three

The sun had gone down leaving a strange glass-colored light in the air. Kate sat on the deck watching the last flecks of sunlight as they seemed to meld with the flashing waters of the Gulf in the distance. The silence of the beach was broken only by the breaking of the waves and the raucous cries of a few seagulls fighting over a bit of something on the sand.

She looked at her watch and saw that it was nearly seven o'clock. A thought crossed her mind, bringing a smile to her lips. She was going out with Beverly Devon-Hunt, and she was aware enough of her own shortcomings to realize that she'd prepared as if she were going out with the son of the Queen herself. "I must be crazy," she muttered, "getting excited about a date with Bev. I'm like a high school sophomore going out with the star quarterback."

The thought somehow disturbed her that she would get so excited about a date with Beverly. She liked him well enough but wondered if they could ever really connect. He was from a completely different background—one with money and privilege. He had a British title and that peculiar hyphenated last name.

Getting up out of the chair, she went inside. The house was quiet except for the bubbling of the huge aquarium, and Romeo and Juliet having some kind of tiff as usual. She stood and watched them, wondering if this was also what love really looked like in humans.

Jake had taken Jeremy to Mobile to see the BayBears in a baseball game, and she was grateful for the attention Jake was paying to him.

She knew her son missed his dad, more than she did as a matter of fact, even though Jeremy had been so young when Vic died that he barely remembered him. She usually kept her thoughts away from her marriage. Except for a brief period of ecstatic joy when she'd thought the whole world rose and set on Vic, their marriage had been nothing but a trial to her. Thank heavens she had Jeremy to show for it.

Turning aside, she went over and watched Jacques, who was eating the last of the food she had put in his bowl. Cleo lay beside him watching him devour the food as if he hadn't eaten in a month. "You're a glutton, Jacques," Kate murmured and then let her eyes run over the spacious living room, the cathedral ceiling, and the expensive and comfortable furniture. She felt a deep gratitude to Zophia Krizova for being a distant relative and leaving her such a beautiful place to live. She thought of the many awful places she had lived with Jeremy after Vic had died. One place still gave her the creeps. It had been a candy factory and had been divided into apartments by the owner. She had moved in early one Thursday morning, but all that night the rats that infested the place came boldly out. She remembered with startling clarity getting Vic's baseball bat that had hit a home run in the hands of Mickey Mantle, and getting Jeremy into bed with her. She had fended off the rats all night and had moved the next morning after dressing down the owner in no uncertain terms.

Pushing the memory away, she began to walk back and forth. Finally she sat down on the couch, and Cleo came up to be petted. The cat leaped up on Kate's lap and purred like a small engine as Kate stroked her ears. "What's wrong with me, Cleo? I'm a bundle of nervous energy waiting for that Englishman to get here. I guess I'm excited to be dating anyone at all."

Cleo agreed with everything that was said as long as her head was being stroked. She flexed her claws in sheer ecstasy and listened as Kate spoke aloud.

"I feel so...so odd, Cleo. Living in this house with a man who's not my husband. I must have been out of my mind to let myself get into this."

Jacques came over and sat down in front of her, his eyes glowing. He licked his chops, savoring the last bits of his meal.

Listen to her, Cleo. She's like all females—always thinking about men.

She's not like that at all, Jacques.

Sure she is. You just watch. The Intruder will catch her at a weak moment. He'll find her when she's lonely and crying. He'll be there for her and she'll fall, just like all females do.

The doorbell rang just then and Kate shoved Cleo off her lap and quickly moved over to the full-length mirror beside the bar. She was wearing a slim skirt two inches above her knees in a brilliant aqua color. She smoothed down the embroidered white tank top and glanced at the pair of white wedge shoes that she'd bought just for this date, noticing how her tanned legs set off the outfit. Then she shook her head, suddenly disgusted with herself. "When did I get so vain? I don't know why I'm going to all this trouble for someone who is so out of my league."

When she went to the door and opened it, she found Beverly standing there looking as if he had dressed to grace the cover of *Esquire* magazine. He was wearing a pair of pleated khaki trousers with a short-sleeved burgundy silk shirt and a cashmere sweater thrown over his shoulders.

Stepping inside, Bev nodded his approval. "You look absolutely beautiful, Kate."

"So do you, Bev," Kate said.

"Well, we're a matched set then. Are you ready?"

"Yes." She followed him out to the Rolls, waited for him to open the door, and then got inside. He walked around the long sleek car, got in and started the engine.

"Aren't you a little...embarrassed to be driving a car like this? It's so...ostentatious."

"Well, people drive cars to be noticed."

She turned and looked at Beverly, admiring his aristocratic manner and fine looks despite herself. He turned and smiled at her, his eyes blue as cornflowers, and she asked suddenly, "Do you really want to be noticed so much, Bev?"

"Not really. I'm used to it. But mostly, it's a pain in the patella."

"Patella?" She couldn't help laughing.

"That's a kneecap. Truthfully, I'm going to get rid of this car. I think

I'll buy a used Volkswagen, then I'll be a nice humble chap like everybody else. So, on to more important matters. Where would you like to eat?"

"You pick."

"I thought we might go by the Sonic," Bev said. "We could sit in the car and order foot-long chili dogs and you could spill down your gorgeous front side."

"Never mind my gorgeous front side. You'd never go to a place like the Sonic anyhow."

"Oh, you underestimate me, Kate. Like the king in Camelot, I like to know what the common folk are doing. But actually, I thought we'd go to the Original Oyster House."

"You like oysters?"

"I can't stand them, but they have other things on the menu." Bev kept up a chatter as he wheeled the Rolls toward Interstate 10, where he turned left and headed for Mobile. Kate settled back in her seat and listened to him, fascinated by his quick wit. He had traveled the world over and so she listened with envy and fascination as Bev spoke about his adventures. His company wasn't so bad after all, she decided.

● ● ●

The meal at the Original Oyster House had been excellent and afterward Beverly took Kate for a drive on Highway 65, headed north. He let her drive the Rolls, and although she had driven it once before, she found it a delightful experience. He had told her once, "When you're driving sixty miles an hour, the loudest noise you'll hear in this car is the ticking of the clock in the dashboard." She was amazed that it was true.

Bev had driven back and now he pulled up in front of her house. The moonlight was bright, shedding its silver flecks over the Gulf, and for a moment Beverly sat there, then he turned to her.

"Would you rather sit in the car and be kissed or would you rather that take place at your front door?"

"Neither, thank you," Kate said with a grin.

"Pity," Bev said as he got out and came around to open the door for her. They walked without speaking to the front door, and when she turned to thank him for the evening, he reached out in a move so accomplished that she knew it must have taken years to perfect it. She was unprepared for his kiss despite the fact that this wasn't the first time. She'd thought she had said good-bye to things such as this—left them to her teenage, starry-eyed past. But deep down she understood that there was a need in her for someone special in her life. She didn't think it would be this Englishman, but for the moment he held her, she felt a strange sense of completeness.

Suddenly a light came on, and she pulled away from Bev just as Jake opened the door. Humiliation flooded her, although she couldn't quite figure out why she was embarrassed in front of Jake.

"There, that's the one kiss you've been begging for. I hope it made you happy." Bev turned to Jake and said, "She's been putting the moves on me all night, Novak. You know how she is. Good night." He turned and walked away with a wink.

Now Kate was furious. "You—that's not—!"

"You better come inside," Jake said, his voice noncommittal. He held the door open as she stepped inside.

"I'd think you'd have better sense, Mary Katherine, than to be making out with that Brit where everyone can see you."

Kate was flooded with embarrassment. She felt like she had when she was fourteen years old and her father had caught her kissing Bradley Timmons on the front porch after a basketball game. That was fine for a girl of fourteen, but for a woman of her age to be feeling this way was foolish.

"You're not my father, Jake. I'll go out with anyone I want and I'll kiss anyone I want."

"No, I'm not your father. If I were, I'd give you a good spanking."

Jacques and Cleo had come out to watch the fun. Jacques studied the two Persons and swished his tail.

I told you he'd get her, didn't I?

What are you talking about, Jacques? They're having a fight.

It's part of the act, Cleo. He's got her all stirred up. It's just one step away from what our Person calls "love." They'll fight. She'll cry and he'll put his arms around her, and that'll be when she gives in to him.

She's not like that.

She's a female, isn't she? She's a goner, Cleo!

● ● ●

A flight of gray pelicans flew over as Jeremy reached the Brice house. He looked up, admiring them as always, wondering how they knew so much. He had watched them ever since he had arrived at White Sands. Sometimes they gathered in large flocks, and when they found a school of fish, they folded their wings and fell like dive bombers, hitting the water and coming up with silver fish flopping in their beaks. Other times they simply floated out on the Gulf placidly and seemed to be having a communal meeting.

Turning toward the house, Jeremy found Rhiannon sitting on the sand. She was wearing a nauseatingly green T-shirt and a pair of ugly purple shorts, both too large for her. She always looked like she had gone to a yard sale and deliberately picked up things that didn't match. Jeremy sat down.

"Hi, Rhiannon."

She looked at him but didn't speak. He saw that there was sadness on her face, which was surprising—usually there was something like pride or anger. "What's the matter with you?" he asked.

"Nothing."

He reached into his pocket and pulled out a candy bar. "Want a Snickers?"

"No, that would be insalubrious."

Jeremy stared at her, but he was used to her using pretentious words. "What does that mean?"

"It means not conducive to good health. If it were good for you, it would be *salubrious*."

"You're just showing off. Don't you ever get tired of that?"

"Go away, Jeremy."

Jeremy knew she liked Snickers bars, and he reached out and tossed it in her lap. "You can eat it later." She picked it up and studied it.

"What's the matter? Are you sick?" Jeremy asked.

"No. It's Lucky. He's sick. He's going to die."

Jeremy frowned. He knew she was attached to the dog, a nondescript stray she'd rescued from some adolescent hoods who were going to hurt him. She had scared the boys with the sawed-off shotgun she sometimes carried in a beach bag. Jeremy had asked her once if she really would have shot them if they had harmed Lucky. She'd looked at him as if he had asked a stupid question. "That's what I carry the gun for, to take care of things like that." Now Jeremy looked at her with a mixture of pity and bewilderment—the response she usually elicited from him.

"He'll probably get better."

"No, he's going to die." Rhiannon seemed convinced.

"Well, if he's sick, we need to take him to Dr. Stern. You know, the vet lady."

"I don't have any money."

"Dr. Stern's nice. I'll bet she'd let us clean her cages out or something. Let's take him."

"How would we get him there?"

"You wait here. Tell your grandpa where we're going. I'll get Jake and we'll borrow Mom's car. She won't mind."

"Jake doesn't like me. Besides, he looks mean."

"That's just a façade."

"A what?"

"A façade."

"What's that?" She reached in her beach bag, took out a notebook and a stub of a pencil. "How do you spell it?"

"F-a-c-a-d-e." She took out a small dictionary and thumbed through it. "Façade—it means the front of a building. It can also mean a false, superficial, or artificial appearance." She closed the notebook, stuck it back in the bag and said, "I know lots of people who have a façade and seem to be something they're not."

"You can do psychology stuff later. Wait here. I'll go get Jake. I bet Dr. Stern can fix Lucky right up."

● ● ●

Dr. Enola Stern looked more like a movie star than a vet. She was tall with a spectacular figure, olive complexion, and sensational blue-green eyes. Her father was Jewish and her mother was a Sioux, which made for a striking combination. Jeremy was fascinated that her mother was a direct descendent of Crazy Horse. He'd never known anyone with such an interesting heritage.

"Is he going to be all right, Dr. Stern?" Rhiannon asked anxiously.

"He'll be fine. He's just got worms. I'll keep him here for a couple of days and he'll be a new dog by the time I get through with him."

"I don't have any money," Rhiannon said.

"Don't worry about it," Jake interjected. "I'll take care of it."

"No, Jake—it's okay," Jeremy said. "Is it all right if we work it off, Dr. Stern? We'll clean up the cages and things like that."

"That's a good deal," Enola smiled. "You can start right now."

"It will be salubrious for Lucky to get rid of his worms, won't it?"

Jake shook his head. "Where do you come up with these words?"

Enola smiled. "She's just bright, Jake. I was like that myself."

"I wasn't," Jake said, "but I was cute. I charmed teachers all the way through school."

Enola took the two youngsters back to where the animals were kept and instructed them on how to clean the cages. When she came back she found Jake sitting at her desk, eating a peppermint stick. She kept them on top of her desk for young people who came in with their pets.

"Jake, have you ever wanted to meet a celebrity?" she asked.

"Can't stand celebrities. Except maybe Ozzy. Why?"

"I got an invitation to a lunch. I doubt Ozzy Osbourne will be there, but it'll be packed with movie stars. Bjorn Kristofferson invited me and said I could bring a guest."

"Never heard of him."

"He's a movie director—or an assistant director, I think. He's working on that movie they're going to film here. Did you hear about it?"

"Yeah, I heard about it. It'll probably be a clinker."

"The luncheon's for Aaron Tobin. It'll kick off production of the film."

"Who's Aaron Tobin?"

"He's the owner of New Leaf Motion Pictures. The producer of the movie. Should be a good party. Would you like to go?"

Jake shrugged. "Sure. Could use a break from working on the novel." He paused, then appeared to think of something. "Can I bring Mary Katherine?"

Enola studied Jake as if he were a specimen under her microscope. "You got something going with her?"

"We share the same house. We're friends. I've explained all that."

"Oh, yeah, you explained real well how you have to live together."

"We just do it for the money."

"She's pretty cute."

"I know it. She's passionate, too. She's after me all the time. I have to keep my door locked at night to keep her out."

"I'll bet." Enola's eyes sparkled. "Well, bring her along."

"What time do we leave?"

"We can't all three go on your Harley, so I'll pick you up about eleven."

"Maybe somebody will stop me and want me to be in the movies. It's about time for me to get discovered."

"Well, that's why I'm bringing you, of course. So I can say I knew you when."

He winked at her. "Don't be surprised when I'm the next Tom Cruise."

Four

Jake had never ceased to be amazed at Trouble, who was, no doubt, one of the strangest pit bulls he had ever seen in his life. For one thing, Trouble had a strange mixture of bravado and timidity. Jake had seen him struggle and strain to get at a matched set of huge Dobermans walking along the beach. Either of them would have been vicious, but it took all of Jake's strength to hold Trouble back from doing battle.

Despite this foolhardy courage, some things frightened Trouble for no apparent reason, and he was absolutely timid when it came to some of the animals in the house. Abigail, the ferret, who weighed less than two pounds, had her bluff in on Trouble. She loved to run at him in the comical sideways gait that ferrets have and for some reason this terrified the dog. All Abigail had to do was head toward him and Trouble hit the doggie door full speed. He also seemed fearful of Miss Boo, the flop-eared rabbit. When she tried to come close to him, he would back up and look for an escape hatch as if she were a fearsome sight.

The other thing that puzzled Jake and amused him at the same time was Trouble's habit of dragging things home and trying to bring them in the house. He had enormous, powerful jaws, and now as Jake sat on the deck eating from a huge cluster of concord grapes, he watched as Trouble dragged part of a crate home with him. It had probably come floating in from a ship off shore and was made, as far as Jake could tell, of solid oak. It must have been terrifically heavy. For the past hour Trouble had been struggling to drag it through the sand toward the deck, with the obvious intention of bringing it inside. It was so large and heavy the dog could only move it a few feet at a time before he had to stop and rest. His efforts were Herculean, and Jake shook his head, muttering, "If I could harness that energy into something useful, it would take care of all the work that has to be done around here."

Jake's reverie was interrupted when he felt a touch on his leg. Looking down he saw Bandit, the coon, sitting there waving his paws in the air, his eyes bright as he silently pleaded for a grape.

"You're nothing but a beggar, Bandit." Jake broke off a grape from the cluster, extended it, and watched as Bandit took it in his paws. He never ceased to marvel at the paws of the coon, which were as handy as fingers. Bandit popped the grape in his mouth, lifted his head, and slowly chewed as he drank the juice. When he had finished it, he immediately pawed again at Jake's leg for more.

"Why are you such a greedy glutton, Bandit? Why can't you be like me—nice and sweet?"

Talk didn't carry much weight with the coon. He was mostly interested in food, and any leftovers were always siphoned up at his first opportunity.

"You're in hot water, boy. After the mess you made in Mary Katherine's room it's a wonder she didn't throw you out. She probably would if it weren't for the agreement. You're lucky we're required to take care of you."

Jake continued to carry on a one-sided conversation with Bandit, somehow finding it humorous the way the coon would take the grapes, hold his head up, and eat them daintily. Finally all the grapes were gone, and Jake tossed the empty stalk out into the sand. "That's all there is, you bottomless pit."

Bandit scurried away just as Mary Katherine came out on the deck. Jake turned to look at her and saw that she was wearing a pair of ratty old shorts and a T-shirt much too large for her. It was faded but he could make out the letters across her chest. *Property of Athletic Department—University of Tennessee.* He grinned and had a rude remark framed when he decided that, for once, he'd keep it to himself. She had been making cookies and the fragrant aroma came out of the kitchen just as she did. "I like your outfit," he said. "Real neat."

Kate gave him a look that would have curdled milk. She was still upset with him for criticizing her for kissing Beverly. She wanted to explain to him that her clothing—and her life—were none of his business, but she didn't have the nerve. Now she said shortly, "This shirt was my husband's. He played for the Volunteers."

"What position?"

"Fullback."

"Tough guy. Did you go to the university too?"

"No, I had Jeremy instead."

Jake studied her for a moment, noting that for an almost thirty-year-old woman she still had the figure of an eighteen-year-old girl, which even her crummy outfits couldn't fully conceal. "What kind of a guy was he, your husband?"

"What do you care?"

"If we're going to live together, I need to know things about you."

"We're not living together!"

"Well, everybody thinks we are. We're under the same roof. Of course, I have to keep my door locked at night to keep you out, but most people don't know that."

"You say the most awful things!" She sat down on the deck chair beside Jake, and for a while the two of them were silent. He studied her, and she kept her eyes fixed on the Gulf. She was watching a sailboat that was skimming across the horizon, and finally he said, "Why don't you like to talk about him—your husband, I mean?"

"It's not any of your business, Jake." She hesitated, then added, "Jeremy misses him."

"That's natural enough, I guess."

Kate turned to him but remained silent. She wasn't ready to explain that her husband, Vic, had always been a good father but a terrible husband. He had spent every free moment at home with Jeremy, very little time with her. He had been unfaithful to her, too, and it had hurt her worse than anything else. Before he died she had lost her first illusions of love, and now she was in the stage of life where she was wondering if there was such a thing as true faithfulness in a relationship. She watched married couples carefully and most of the time was convinced that a happy marriage was something that only took place in a romance novel or a Hollywood chick-flick.

Jake interrupted her thoughts. "I don't know why you're wearing yourself out making all those cookies."

"It's for the youth group. They're doing some evangelism on the beach this afternoon."

"No sense cooking all those things for kids. What a waste. Just go buy some Little Debbie's or Ding Dongs."

"This from the guy who makes everything from scratch?"

"Kids don't taste anything anyhow," he complained.

"I'm almost through with them now," Kate said. "I can't cook like you, but I'm going to learn. I can do cookies anyway."

"Well, I've got us an invitation to a fancy lunch."

"A lunch? What kind of a lunch?" She listened as he explained how Enola had invited them to a luncheon given by the crew from Hollywood.

"You might meet the star and he could fall in love with you, and the two of you could make beautiful music together," Jake teased.

Kate laughed. "I doubt that, Jake. You enjoy it, though. I don't want to go to a thing like that."

"Oh, come on. It'll be fun," Jake insisted. He continued to try to persuade her, and finally when she agreed, he said, "You can just wear that nice outfit you've got on. It's informal."

She looked down at her shabby outfit, swatted at him, and went inside to get the cookies from the oven.

● ● ●

Enola picked up the two of them in her Hummer. She was wearing a black sheath dress embroidered with roses and Jake couldn't help noticing it fit her like a second skin.

"I like your dress," Jake said with a wink. "It looks like you saved a lot of money on material since there's not much of it."

"I thought about what you said," Dr. Stern said. "I'm hoping to catch the producer's eye. Maybe I'll get discovered, too, and you and I can do a remake of *Gone with the Wind*."

"Frankly, my dear—"

"What are you two talking about?" Kate interrupted as they loaded into the vehicle.

"Our future movie careers, of course," Jake informed her. "By the way, your dress is nice, too, Mary Katherine. Maybe you'll marry a movie star after all."

"Oh, stuff it, Jake." They continued bantering as Enola drove down the beach highway. It was only a couple of minutes before she pulled off into the driveway of an enormous three-story beach house painted a pastel blue. The parking area was filled with cars, mostly Jaguars and BMWs. There were also equipment trucks lined up as far as they could see.

"What is this place?" Kate asked.

"It belongs to the Dallas Cowboys, the football team. They come here to party two or three times a year," Enola said. "Everybody calls it the Blue House."

Jake was intrigued. "Why can't we get invited to one of those parties?"

"I could but you couldn't, Jake," Enola said. She parked the car and when they walked inside, Kate was overwhelmed by the opulence of the place. Everything about it said *money* and she thought, *What a waste. This would pay for a whole mission project in a Third World country.*

But the people she saw obviously weren't interested in mission work. There were white-jacketed servers moving around with trays full of canapés, and the bar was doing a brisk business.

"Not much like McDonald's, is it?" Jake said. He reached over and put his arm around Enola. "Hey, I don't see Ozzy here like you promised."

"Is he going to be here?" Kate asked with disgust.

"No," Enola said, removing Jake's arm. "That's just Jake's dream."

"Well, *here* you are, Enola." The speaker was a tall man with fair hair and sky blue eyes.

"Let me introduce my friends, Mr. Kristofferson," Enola said. "This is Mary Katherine Forrest and Jake Novak. This is Bjorn Kristofferson, the assistant director of the movie."

"Glad to meet you both," the director said. "Is this the one you told me about having the cats that might do for a role in the movie?"

"She's got two dandies."

"What on earth you talking about?" Kate asked quickly.

"We need a cat to be in the movie. Pretty important part," Kristofferson said. "I don't know as I've ever auditioned a cat before, but Enola here tells me you've got two beautiful animals."

"She's got *one* beautiful animal. The other's a monster," Jake said. "His name is Jacques, but we lovingly call him Jacques the Ripper. He wants to tear the flesh off the bones of everybody he meets."

Kristofferson grinned. He had a boyish look about him and a slight Swedish accent. "I don't think we could use Jacques. What about the other one?"

"She's a beautiful cat—a Ragdoll," Enola said, "and very placid. She loves to be picked up and carried around."

"I'd like to have a look at her," Kristofferson said. "All right if I drop by and take a gander?"

Kate nodded. "You could look, but I don't know if she's what you want."

Suddenly Kate's attention was taken. "There's Erik Lowe," she whispered. "He's my favorite movie star."

"Well, I hope a million women feel the same way," Kristofferson said. "You want to meet him?"

"I'd like to," Enola said. "I want to ask him a few questions about what he said on *Letterman*."

Kristofferson called, "Hey, Erik, come over here."

The man who came over had crisp, brown hair and warm brown eyes. He had the Hollywood pretty-boy look and seemed at least five years younger than his thirty-eight years. He smiled crookedly as Kristofferson introduced him.

"I'm glad to know you all," he said. "You'll have to come and watch us do some shooting. Have you ever seen a movie being made?"

"Never did," Jake answered for the three of them. "When will you be shooting the juicy stuff?"

Lowe laughed. "To be honest with you, I hate all that."

"Well, maybe I can be your stand-in." Jake volunteered. "We look pretty much alike."

"Don't be a fool, Jake," Kate said, embarrassed. "You look like a thug, which you are."

"A real thug, huh?" Kristofferson asked curiously.

"He was a cop in Chicago, and before that he was in the Delta Force," Enola said.

"Well, let's talk to Aaron," Kristofferson said. "Maybe we need an extra who's a thug."

"I've had lots of practice," Jake grinned. "Who's Aaron?"

Kristofferson gave him an odd look. "Aaron Tobin. You don't know about him?"

"Nope."

Enola interrupted, "Jake, I told you about Aaron. He's the producer."

Erik was grinning. "You obviously don't keep up with the Hollywood scene much."

"Well, I think the last movie I saw was *Robin Hood* with Errol Flynn."

"He's lying about that," Kate said. "He loves movies."

"Well, you can meet Aaron now. This party is actually for him. Come on." Bjorn led them over to where a short man, overweight, with the florid complexion of a drinker, was sitting in a chair. He had his arm around a sexy-looking starlet, and he had the large hooked nose of a falcon. Kate had read about him and knew that starlets were snacks to him. Bjorn bent and whispered something in Aaron's ear, nodding toward the group. Then he straightened and introduced the three.

Aaron looked up and studied them as Kristofferson ended by saying, "Miss Forrest has a cat we can use, Aaron. Haven't seen her yet, but from what Dr. Stern says, she may be just what we need."

"You were in the Delta Force, Novak?" Aaron asked.

"Yep."

"Pretty tough outfit."

"Oh, we all were just a bunch of sweethearts," Jake said. His manner made it clear he'd taken an instant dislike to Aaron. He said nothing about it, but stood listening as Aaron told them about the picture they were making. "The title of the movie is *Roses All the Way*."

"Must be from the Browning poem," Jake remarked.

Aaron Tobin gave him a hard look. "What poem? What're you talking about? A friend of mine came up with that title."

"Mm-hmm. Original." Jake quipped.

Aaron ignored Jake. He had his eyes on Enola, and he got to his feet and reached over to put his arm around her. She attempted to lean back, but Aaron held her tighter and laughed. In the struggle he spilled his drink down the front of his shirt, and immediately his temper flared.

"Jesse! Jesse, get over here!" A man was instantly at Aaron's side. "Jesse, get me another shirt."

"Sure, Dad." Jesse Tobin was no more than five-eight. He had mild brown eyes, a thin face, and a body to match. There was a shyness about him that one didn't expect out of a Hollywood crew. He hurried off quickly and Aaron shook his head. "The kid is no good except for a gofer."

"He's a good boy, Aaron. You should be proud of him," Bjorn said.

"Kid wants to be a poet. Can you imagine in this day and age?"

"Have you ever read any of his poems, Mr. Tobin?" Kate asked. She was fascinated by the man. He had a distinct aura of power about him despite his rather ugly appearance.

"Who's got time to read poems? I read screenplays, babe. That's all." Aaron got up and tugged at Enola's arm, dragging her away almost by force.

"I think Enola's made a conquest," Jake muttered.

"You better tell her to be careful around Aaron," Kristofferson said. "He's got a pretty bad reputation with women." He leaned in toward Jake and Kate. "Actually, Jesse's the director of the movie. But we'll see if Aaron actually lets him direct. I'll probably end up doing most of it."

He took them around, introducing them. Kate stood a moment talking to Dontelle Byrd, the director of photography, as Jake and Bjorn drifted away. Dontelle was a handsome black man, but there was a bitterness that seemed to lurk just beneath his calm exterior. Curious about Aaron Tobin, she asked, "His son's not much like him, is he?"

"Not at all."

"Does his father always treat him that way?"

"Usually worse."

"Too bad. I don't think I'd get along with Mr. Aaron Tobin."

"Well, the rest of us have to. He treats some of us worse than he treats his son."

"What about you?"

"Me? He thinks he's funny. He once sent out for food and had them bring a watermelon back for me. Fried chicken, too."

"How awful! Why do you do it?"

"I do it because it's my job. Besides, if I can handle Tobin, I can work for just about anybody in this business."

Jake was meeting Lexi Colby, a minor actress, and another named Callie Braun. Lexi had a hardness despite her good looks. She cursed Aaron's name in front of Jake, in no uncertain terms. "He's been promising me a leading role for years. He's a liar. I don't know why I ever believed him."

Callie Braun was a blonde with blue eyes. She was a likable girl, soft where Lexi Colby was hard.

"Do you like being in the movies, Miss Braun?" Jake asked.

"Well, it's all right for now. It pays the bills, but it takes me away from my family and my real future."

"Your real future?"

"I'm never going to make it big in acting. I'm just a stand-in for the star on this picture anyway. I want to start a real estate company with my sister." There was a light in the woman's eyes as she talked about her dream, and Jake thought she seemed out of place in the Hollywood bunch.

He was still talking to the two women when Kate came over. Jake introduced her to the two women, then Lexi Colby said, "Look out everybody. Here comes Her Majesty."

Kate turned to see Avis Marlow entering. She had seen her in several movies, but there was something about the woman in person that came across differently. She had a magnetism on the screen, but it was nothing compared to the power of her real presence. She had a squarish face and a wide mouth, too wide for real beauty, but there was something sensuous about everything she did.

Kate turned to comment to Jake, but she didn't speak. Jake was standing transfixed and was absolutely pale.

Avis Marlow had come right toward them. Without hesitation she approached Novak. "Hello, Jake," she said. "It's been a long time."

Kate was watching Jake's reaction. He was clearly deeply disturbed. Finally he said, "Hello, Avis."

"I'm surprised to see you here." She had a slight mischievous grin.

"Of all the gin joints in the world, you had to walk into mine." Jake's face was expressionless.

"*Casablanca*. It was always your favorite. You still do a good Humphrey Bogart."

Enola was watching this and said, "I take it you two have met."

"A long time ago," Avis said. "You haven't changed, Jake. Who are your friends?"

Jake introduced Enola and Kate, then turned without another word and left the room. Kate turned to look at Avis Marlow, who was watching Jake go with an unfathomable expression.

Kate frowned. "I've never seen Jake act like that."

"How do you know Jake?" Avis demanded, her eyes fixed on Kate.

"Jake and I are in business together."

"What kind of a business?"

"We take care of a house on the beach."

"What does that mean?"

"I live downstairs, he lives upstairs. We're co-owners."

Avis put Kate under a microscope and studied her. "Does he still talk in his sleep?" she asked.

"I wouldn't know about that."

Avis studied her carefully, then said, "That must be convenient, living with Jake." She turned and walked away, and Enola moved closer to Kate.

"Hmmm, the plot thickens. That woman reminds me of a tiger."

"I don't think she has the tender mercies of a tiger," Kate commented. "Did you see Jake's face?"

"I saw it. It was like he had been hit in the stomach. They must have had quite a history."

Suddenly Kate could take it no longer. "Let's get out of here. I don't like this place or these people." She turned and walked away and Enola followed her. Kristofferson met them at the door. "You have to go? You just got here."

"I'm not feeling too well," Kate said.

"Still okay if I come and look at the cat? Or have somebody come?"

"Of course," Kate managed, eager to leave.

When the two of them were outside, they found that Jake was gone. "He's gone," Enola said. "I was going to ask him about his relationship with that woman."

"I don't think he wants to talk about it, Enola, and I don't either. Come on. Will you drive me home?"

Five

Enola tried to look into Trouble's mouth, but the pit bull wouldn't be still. He kept moving closer to her, his weight shoving her until she was off balance, and then promptly sat down on her feet.

Kate was smiling at the friendly dog. Despite the reputation that pit bulls had, in many ways Trouble was the most affectionate animal in the place—except for Cleo, of course. Kate looked over at Cleo, who was sitting beside Jacques. Jacques was watching the two women with a cold, calculating look in his eye.

Enola was making her way through the monthly examinations of all the animals in the house—as required by the will. She finally managed to look into Trouble's mouth, and then—her examination finished—she moved over and sat down on the couch. Before she could speak, Trouble made a wild leap and landed sprightly in her lap. "Oof!" Enola said. "Get off my lap, Trouble. That hurts!" She shoved at Trouble but made no headway toward removing him. "He must think he's a Chihuahua."

"He's the oddest dog I've ever seen," Kate said. "He'd tackle an elephant, I think. He could protect us, but he's scared to death of Jacques."

"I don't blame him," Enola said. "That's one mean cat. I'll check him for you, but it's like checking a mad Bengal tiger."

"I appreciate you seeing Cleo and Jacques along with the rest of the bunch, Enola. I'll hold him for you."

"Get down, Trouble. I can't hold you. You're too big." Enola shoved Trouble off her lap and got to her feet. Trouble at once sat down on her toes. With a grunt Enola pulled away and then laughed. "I think he's got a fetish for feet. I had a boyfriend like that once. I'd dress up and do everything I could to make myself attractive. Spent hours on my face and doing my hair, and you know what he liked? My feet. Isn't that an insult of some kind?"

"To each his own," Kate grinned. "Guess you should have spent time on the pedicure instead." She walked over and stood looking down at Jacques, who looked back at her.

She's going to pick me up, Cleo.

Don't you dare claw her, you hear me, Jacques?

I wouldn't hurt our Person. She's our meal ticket and you got to take care of your resources, but that other Person better watch out. She starts trying to take my temperature in that awful way they have, she's going to get what she deserves.

They're just doing it for your own good, Jacques.

They're doing it because they don't know what else to do. How'd she like it if I took her *temperature?*

Kate was careful as she picked up Jacques. She had learned to carry the big animal, who weighed over thirty pounds, by supporting his body with both arms. She sat down on the couch, holding him tightly. She stroked the silky fur, black as the darkest thing in nature, and said, "He's a beautiful animal, isn't he, Enola?"

"He's the most exotic cat I've ever seen. You know there's something about the big cats—they're majestic."

You hear that, Cleo? I'm majestic. Jacques began to purr. *Maybe this chick isn't so dumb after all.*

Enola continued, "Of course part of their beauty is in their ability to kill. Beauty and power, an unbeatable combination. I think all the great courtesans in history had it. All the great movie stars, too."

Enola, moving slowly, advanced toward Jacques. She put her hand out, ready to draw it back, but Kate was holding Jacques firmly.

"You be still, Jacques," Kate soothed. "Even we humans have to go through this when we see the doctor."

She better not be probing me with anything or I'll put stripes on her arm.

Jacques made a low growling noise but permitted the vet to examine him. "I don't think I'm going to take his temperature," Enola said. "You remember what happened the last time. You would have thought I was pulling his claws out." Enola reached out to stroke Jacques, but the big cat growled deep in his throat and she pulled her hand back. "Well, they need a cat for that movie they're making, but I don't think they'll want this one."

"No, Cleo would be wonderful though. She's so photogenic." Kate let Jacques go, and he jumped off her lap to the floor.

Photogenic! Have you ever seen a picture of me that wasn't impressive, Cleo? Jacques struck up a regal pose.

You always look like you're about to claw somebody—which you usually are. Cleo turned away and continued grooming herself.

You heard the lady talking about power and the ability to kill. Females love that stuff—they can't help it. That's what the Intruder has, you know. Jake fascinates our Person because he's strong and quick. Of course, he's not as good looking as I am, but there's something dangerous about us that makes us irresistible to women.

Cleo looked at Jacques with what could only be a grin. *I notice you weren't irresistible to that tiger-striped female who lives in the house across the way.*

That mangy animal? Who cares about her? There are other felines on this beach. Jacques gave Cleo one last disgusted look and stalked from the room.

Enola reached for Cleo, who loved being examined. She lay on her back, and when Enola rubbed her stomach, her eyes closed with ecstasy.

"She loves to have her tummy rubbed." Kate couldn't disguise the motherly pride in her voice.

"Well, so do I," Enola laughed. "This is a beautiful cat. You'll probably get a call from Kristofferson. Watch out for him. He's got Hollywood morality—or the lack of it."

"I don't think I'm in any danger. He has eyes for you, Enola, not me."

Enola continued to stroke Cleo's stomach. "Where's Jake?" she asked.

"I don't know." Actually, Kate had been worried about Jake. She hadn't seen him since he walked out of the party. When they had gotten home, they had found that his Harley was gone, and now she shifted nervously. "He didn't come home after the party yesterday and he's been gone all day today."

"That was some reaction he had to Avis," Enola mused. "He took one look at her, and it was like he stuck his finger into a live electrical outlet."

"Yeah, it was strange, like he froze. I've never seen Jake act like that."

"She's definitely an old flame." Enola grinned, studying Kate carefully. "No telling if there's still a spark, though." She hesitated, then put Cleo down. Looking right at Kate, she asked, "Are you jealous of Avis Marlow?"

"Don't be ridiculous," Kate answered. "Why should I be jealous? Jake's nothing to me."

At that moment they heard the sound of an approaching motorcycle outside and before they could say anything, they heard a tremendous crash.

"Jake!" Kate cried and ran for the door. Enola was right behind and so were Trouble and the two cats. Jacques passed Bandit, who was dozing near the door. He reached out and gave him a slash across the rump, which brought Bandit up, turning wildly, disoriented from sleep.

As soon as Kate stepped outside, she saw that the nose of the motorcycle had plowed into the garden shed, where all the tools were kept. The fork was bent and the rear wheel was up in the air with the engine still racing. Jake was getting up from a prone position with a dazed look in his eyes.

Enola quickly moved over and shut off the motorcycle. Jake stood but was swaying like a sapling blowing in the wind, and Enola grabbed his arm.

"We've got to get him in the house," Enola said. "That's a bad cut he's got there. Probably has a concussion, too."

The two women helped Jake into the house. He appeared to be barely conscious at first, but when they sat him down in a chair and Enola started examining the cut in his hairline, his eyes came to a focus and he said belligerently, "Well, Mary Katherine, I suppose you think I've been drinking."

"Well, haven't you?"

"I ain't had a drop," Jake slurred.

Enola laughed and said, "You smell like a distillery, Jake. I don't think you need any stitches in this cut, but it needs to be pulled together."

"I haven't had a drop, Doc."

Jake sat there protesting he hadn't touched so much as a single beer, but he was so drunk he could hardly sit in the chair while Kate and Enola got him cleaned up.

"Well, we're going to put you to bed," Enola told him.

"Not going to bed."

"You've got to go to bed and sleep it off."

"I don't want to go to bed. I'm fine."

● ● ●

It had taken the two women quite an effort to get Jake up the stairs to his room, but finally they'd managed to get him under the covers, where he promptly passed out. They came back down, and Kate made some coffee while they chatted about this latest episode.

"Well, I guess we were right. Seeing Avis Marlow had quite an impact on him," Enola said.

"I knew he had a past, Enola, and there was a woman who broke his heart. I never imagined it could be a famous celebrity." Kate shook her head. "Still, I'm surprised he went out and got drunk. He's always so in control."

The doorbell rang and Kate rose to her feet. "Who could that be?"

She went to the door and opened it and was surprised to find Erik Lowe standing there. He was dressed casually in a pair of tan cotton chinos and a white-and-blue-striped rugby shirt. His hair was crisp and a curl hung down over his forehead, and for one instant Kate wondered, *Does he fix it like that so he looks cool and casual or does it just happen?*

"Sorry to bother you, Kate, but Bjorn asked me to come by and see if I can get along with your cat—that is, if you decide to let her be in the movie."

Kate smiled and stepped back from the door. "Of course—come in. Let me introduce you to Cleo. You remember Enola?"

Lowe entered the house, nodding at Enola, and glanced around. "Nice place." He looked embarrassed. He had none of the attributes usually associated with celebrities, and there was a shyness about him. He cleared his throat before saying, "I'm not all that great with animals."

Cleo had come into the room, and now Kate reached down and picked her up. "Oh, don't worry," she assured Erik. "Cleo loves everyone. Why don't you sit on the couch."

Erik looked hesitant as he sat, and Kate placed Cleo over his shoulder. "Wow, she's pretty big, isn't she?" Erik observed.

"Just rub her back. She'll get used to you." Cleo began to purr and Lowe smiled and, after a moment, said, "Looks like Cleo and I will get along nicely for the picture."

Enola had been standing by, and now she said to Erik, "So what about this movie? Is it going to be a good one?"

Erik continued rubbing Cleo's back as he responded, "It could be. Aaron Tobin's made some blockbusters. He's a talented guy—behind the camera at least."

"What about when he's not behind the camera?" Kate asked.

The question seemed to make Lowe uncomfortable. He rubbed Cleo absently, but his eyes were far away. "Let's just say he's my boss and I've gotten into trouble for criticizing people in the biz."

"Don't worry, Erik. It's not like we're undercover reporters for the *Enquirer*." Enola paused, then continued, "I've heard a few stories abut how hard Tobin is to deal with. Is he like Jekyll and Hyde?"

"If he's two men, it's Hyde and Hyde," Erik said slowly. He lowered Cleo to the floor, and she sat at his feet. Anger flickered in his mild eyes and his lips grew tense as he drew them together. He seemed to be struggling to keep his own counsel, but he began to speak in a low voice, almost gritting his teeth.

"He's a...monster. That's the only word I can think of. There are some people that are just pure evil. They don't have to have a motivation. They don't do it because they want something. It's just in them."

"He must be terrible to work for," Kate said sympathetically. "Do you have to do it?"

"This is a plum role—I couldn't afford to turn it down. If this movie goes well, I could be up for a lot more starring roles. But if I'd turned it down, I'd probably end up playing the hero's best friend for the rest of my life." Erik bent over and petted Cleo again, who resumed her purring.

"So you put up with Tobin to keep your career alive," Kate said.

"He's horrible, but he can make or break actors. He insults everybody in his sphere. Of course, he knows how to turn on the charm, but that doesn't last long once he gets his hooks into someone."

"But it's like that everywhere," Enola said. "All over the country, people are taking their lumps from somebody like Tobin. I had to kowtow to pretty low characters to get through vet school."

"Most of the other actors feel this way about him?" Kate asked.

"Even his own son does. You saw the way Tobin treats Jesse. He's a very sweet guy. His father forced him into the business although he has no talent for it."

At that moment Jacques the Ripper appeared in the doorway. "Whoa!" Erik exclaimed. "That's your other cat?"

Kate looked over at Jacques. "You stay right there, buddy." She turned back to Erik. "That's Jacques the Ripper, the one we told you about."

"I think I'll pass on that one," Erik said nervously.

"Good decision," said Kate, smiling. But she wasn't ready to drop the subject of Aaron Tobin. "What about the others?" she wanted to know. "The rest of the cast and crew—how do they get along with Tobin?"

"You met Lexi Colby?"

"Yes, she didn't keep any secrets about how she felt about Tobin. She hates him."

"Tobin promised her a big role. I thought Lexi was smarter than to believe him. He's made that promise a hundred times."

"What about Dontelle Byrd?" Enola asked. "He's the guy in charge of the camera, right?"

"Sometimes I think Dontelle has it worst of all. You'd think today racial prejudice was pretty well gone, but it just goes underground in a guy like Tobin. He can't get away with being openly racist, but he finds ways to stick it to Dontelle. I can understand why he hates Tobin."

"Well, is there anybody who doesn't hate Tobin?"

"Thad Boland. I don't guess you've met him. He's a stunt man and he doubles for me. He seems to get along with Tobin all right."

"What about Avis Marlow?" Kate said. "How does she stand with Tobin?"

Erik paused and shook his head. "Avis is a different breed. She's big money—she can open a picture. She's the one person that would never let him get away with anything, and he doesn't try much. He needs her more than she needs him." He suddenly laughed shortly, and as he stood up he said, "Well, I've washed all our dirty linens in public. I don't know when I've talked this much. Cleo will be perfect. Got to run now."

Erik started for the door but halted abruptly. Jake had appeared at the bottom of the stairs, swaying unsteadily and looking like a war casualty with all his bandages.

"You have an accident, Novak?"

"What are you doing out of bed?" Kate demanded.

Enola grabbed Jake's arm and attempted to steer him back up the steps, but he wasn't having any of it and shook both the women off.

"What are you doing in my house, Lowe?" Jake looked like he had the attitude of a fighting bull about to charge a matador and impale him in the tender part of his anatomy.

Erik looked stunned. "Uhh...I was just..."

"Jake, be quiet," Kate interjected. "You need to go back to bed."

"I'm not going to bed. I'm going to stay here and protect you from this lowlife. You can never trust an actor, you know that, right?"

Enola laughed. "That's a lot of wisdom coming from a man who just tried to ride his motorcycle through a house."

Jake steadied his gaze on Kate. "Why...is...he...here?"

Kate responded quietly and slowly as if talking to a small child. "Remember they wanted to use a cat in their movie, Jake? Erik just came by to make sure Cleo would be a good fit."

"Wahoo!" Jake cried. "I got just the cat for you, buddy." He moved quickly, reached down, and caught the surprised Jacques around the middle. He whirled and tossed the big cat at Lowe. "There he is. See if you can get along with him."

Jacques crashed against Lowe's chest, let out a penetrating howl, and made a wild slash with his claws. They caught in the front of Lowe's shirt and for a split second the cat couldn't get loose.

Jacques was spitting and hissing, working himself loose. The two women grabbed Jacques and pulled him free. Jake was laughing wildly. "There's your co-star, movie actor. Just the cat for you."

Lowe was grimacing. He pulled up his shirt and saw there were scratches on his chest and stomach.

Kate was carrying Jacques to the door to put him outside, but she looked at Erik, mortified.

"I'm so sorry, Erik, oh my goodness..."

Enola said, "I need to disinfect that."

Erik looked at Kate. "Does he always act like that?"

Kate threw Jacques out the door, then turned back and rolled her eyes. "Who—Jake or Jacques?"

"Well, both of them, actually."

"They both seem to be a little out of sorts today," Kate said apologetically. She turned to Jake with a glare and said, "You're making a fool of yourself. Now go up to bed."

Jake gave Lowe one last ferocious look. "Actors are despicable creatures." Moving very carefully, he found his way out of the room, slamming the door behind him.

Erik Lowe had been watching Novak with something like incredulity in his eyes. He turned and shook his head. "And he was in the Delta Force?"

"Believe it or not," Kate said.

"I don't see how he made it."

"I've never seen him like this before," Kate said slowly. "He's...different. Ever since he saw Avis yesterday."

"What's the story on him and Avis Marlow, Erik?" Enola asked abruptly.

Erik rubbed the back of his neck. "I didn't know anything about it. I still don't. You think they had a thing going? They seemed to know each other all right, but Avis is pretty close-mouthed. Of course, she's had lots of—how do I say it?—male friends."

"I'll bet she has." Enola smirked. "Are you one of them?"

"Are you kidding?" Erik seemed revolted by the idea. "I may be dumb, but I'm not *that* dumb."

"Why not? What's so bad about her?" Kate said.

"Same thing with all big stars. They've got to have the spotlight. They'd sell their own mothers to get ahead in the business."

"You're a big star," Enola said. "Would you sell your mother?"

Erik stared at Enola for a moment. "I can see you don't know much about Hollywood. I'm not a big star."

"You've made a dozen movies," Enola said. "Doesn't that makes you a star?"

"There are writers who have written dozens of books but nobody's ever heard of them. Same way with actors. I haven't been in any huge hits except one."

"I know what that was," Kate smiled. "*In Tune with the World.* I saw that movie half a dozen times. You should have won the Academy Award for it."

"It wasn't a good year for newcomers," Erik said, "but thanks for the endorsement. Listen, I really have to go."

"I'm glad you came by," Kate said. "And don't be mad at Jake. He's really not himself."

"Well, if he had a thing with Avis, I can understand it. He's not the first guy that took to a bottle over her. I'm surprised he walked away in one piece."

Kate walked Erik to the door, but abruptly he turned back and faced her. "By the way, you know a man named Morgan Brice? I heard he lives here."

Kate furrowed her brow. "Yes, he lives with his granddaughter right down the beach. Why?"

"Somebody needs to give him a warning." Erik's tone sounded ominous.

"A warning about what?" Kate asked, puzzled.

"Did you know he wrote the novel *Honor in the Dust*?"

"Oh my! I read that book, but I never put it together that he was the author! It must be twenty years old by now."

"Yes, but it's still in print. Won about every prize a novel can win, I guess," Lowe said. His eyes grew warm. "I loved that book. Every producer in Hollywood has wanted to option it."

"I've often wondered why they didn't make a movie out of it," Kate said.

"Morgan Brice is stubborn. He doesn't like films, especially films made from novels. He says they ruin them—and I guess that's true."

"What are we supposed to warn him about?" Enola asked curiously.

"Tobin has offered the old man a bundle for the rights, but Brice has turned him down. That's a dangerous thing to do."

"What do you mean?" Kate asked.

"Aaron doesn't like to lose. He's a powerful man and he gets what he goes after. So, if you're a friend of Morgan Brice, give him a warning. He can negotiate for more money, but he's going to get blown out of the water if he doesn't sell to Aaron Tobin." Erik went out the front door, then turned one more time. "I'll tell Bjorn about Cleo. Thanks, ladies."

As soon as Lowe left the house, Enola gathered her things. "I've got to go as well. The animals are fine—except for Jake. They didn't teach us in veterinary school how to fix his problem. See you later."

Six

The sliding doors to Jake's upstairs kingdom were pulled open, and the warm salty sea breeze blew off the beach, bringing the scents of the Gulf with it. Jake lay flat on his back on his bed. His eyes were closed, his mouth was open, and he was breathing heavily. From time to time he would mutter, "No, I haven't been drinking," or "Leave me alone, Mary Katherine. I don't need a keeper."

Cleo and Jacques had made their way upstairs and now sat on the bed next to Jake, peering down at his flushed face, and it was Cleo who manifested the curiosity for which cats are so well-known.

What's he doing, Jacques?

Being human. Haven't you noticed how little judgment our Persons have?

Well, what's wrong with him? Is he sick?

He's what human beings call intoxicated. Jacques assumed an air of wisdom. *They drink stuff that makes them throw up. Nothing clean and pure like a hair ball, just awful stuff. You wouldn't catch a cat eating or drinking anything that would make them so sick.*

Well, you ate that snake. Remember? It made you sick and you almost died.

That's different. An indignant look assumed possession of Jacques's face, and he leaned forward to sniff the inert man's breath. *Boy, that really smells bad. The Intruder is dumber than I gave him credit for.*

Cleo advanced across the bed until she was looking directly down into Jake's face. *He needs to wake up.*

She reached out and, with her claws retracted, gently touched one of his closed eyes. When he didn't respond, she tapped harder, and their Person came awake with a loud grunt and sat up, throwing a startled look around the room. His eyes fell on the two felines, and he tried to speak but found his throat was raw. Clearing his throat, he muttered, "What are you two looking at?" Jake stared at the Ripper who seemed to be laughing at him. He reached back, grabbed a pillow, and threw it at Jacques, who dodged it easily. Slowly Jake sat up on the edge of the bed and put both hands up to his temples. He waited until the throbbing had lessened. Slowly he arose and made his way to the bathroom.

As he stood under the cool shower, letting it soothe away the outward signs of his degradation, he felt like a fool. Glancing out of the shower, he saw Cleo and Jacques had been joined by Bandit and Abigail.

"I don't need an audience. You guys get out of here." They didn't move, and Novak breathed a few impure words and shut his eyes and ignored them.

"A man should know better than to put himself in a shape like this. It's something a high school junior might do." The muttered words seemed to make him feel worse, but finally the water worked its magic, and he began to think he could rejoin the land of the living. He stepped out of the shower, ignoring his audience, dried off, and put on a clean pair of khaki shorts, some flip-flops, and a white T-shirt. It had a small white and red square on it, and he shook his head at the expensive memory. "That dumb emblem cost me fifty dollars. I could have got the same shirt at Wal-Mart for twelve. Pride was the devil's downfall, and the rest of us are following right along in his footsteps."

He made his way downstairs and felt like he was being followed by the four horsemen of the Apocalypse—the animals that seemed so fascinated by his every move—and found Jeremy eating toasted frozen waffles.

"You got a hangover, Jake?" Jeremy asked.

Jake hated frozen waffles. He hated frozen anything. He eyed Jeremy's plate with disdain.

"What do you know about hangovers, Slick?"

"You look terrible."

Jake glared at the boy. "Your mother should have taught you better than to make personal remarks about other people." He moved over, ignoring Jeremy, and began squeezing juice from a pile of oranges. He poured it into a cup, and when he picked it up and drank it down, his hands weren't quite steady.

Jeremy got up and took another waffle from the Munsey oven, put it on his plate, and baptized it with Log Cabin maple syrup. He cut it into four huge pieces, stuck one of them in his mouth, and chewed it with obvious pleasure.

"That'll make you sick. It's bad stuff," Novak warned.

"Not as sick as you. Why'd you get drunk?"

Jake glared at him. "Why are you so nosy?"

"You tried to ride your Harley into the house."

"Didn't your mom ever tell you it's impolite to make personal remarks?"

"Sure, Jake, lots of times."

"Well, you ought to pay attention to her."

Jake began fixing oatmeal, thinking it was about all his stomach could stand. Jeremy watched him and said, "Mom and I are going over to save Rhiannon's grandfather, Mr. Brice."

"Save him from what?"

"That movie star came over and told us some stuff—Erik Lowe. I think he's cool."

"No actor's cool. If they were real people, they'd get jobs like everybody else. They're hypocrites, that's what they are! Pretending to be something they're not."

Jeremy stared at him. "Well, shoot, Jake—that's what acting is."

"No job for a grown man."

"How's it different from writing a novel? Aren't you writing stuff that's not real?"

Jake glared at Jeremy. "What's wrong with Morgan Brice?"

"He wrote a book that Mr. Tobin, the owner of the movie company, wants to make into a film. Only Mr. Brice won't let him do it."

"Good for him. All Hollywood's ever done is take good novels and ruin them."

"Well, if Mr. Brice doesn't let Aaron Tobin make a movie out of the book, he's going to be sorry. I guess Mr. Tobin has ways of making people do what he wants—or making them wish they had."

Jake finished cooking the oatmeal and sat down. He laced it with sugar and pure cream and began to eat.

"What are you and your mom going to do?"

"I don't know. Why don't you come with us?"

"One thing I've learned is to mind my own business, Slick." He finished the oatmeal and rinsed the dishes, then without another word turned and walked outside toward the Gulf.

"Morning, sweetheart," Kate said as she walked into the kitchen.

"Mom, I always thought Jake was smart," Jeremy said.

"I suppose he is smart," she said. "Don't you think so?"

"Smart people don't get drunk, do they?"

"Sometimes they do." Kate moved to the refrigerator and took out a carton of milk. She poured a glass, sat down, and began to sip it. "There's a difference, Jeremy, between being smart and having wisdom."

"What's the difference?"

"The Bible says, 'Wisdom is the *principle* thing, therefore get wisdom.' Wisdom is knowing the wise thing to do."

"Do smart people know that?" Jeremy asked.

"Not always."

"So Jake is smart, but he doesn't have much wisdom."

"Wisdom comes from God, Jeremy. There's no place else to get it. Remember we were reading in James the other day? There was a verse that said, 'If any of you lack wisdom, let him ask of God, who gives to all men liberally.' So you're right, Jake is smart, but he doesn't have wisdom. Are you through with breakfast?"

"Yep."

"Then let's go see Mr. Brice."

"You think we can help him?"

"We can warn him. That's about all a friend can do. Let's go."

● ● ●

Rhiannon had propped up the J volume of the *Encyclopedia Britannica*. When she read she closed out the rest of the world so that all that existed were the words on the page. Somehow, in a mysterious way her grandfather hadn't been able to understand, the words seemed to come off the page and troop into her brain, where they took up permanent residence.

Morgan Brice sat watching her now, and pride washed over him. He had taken Rhiannon when her parents had died, and of all the things he had done in his life, he was most proud that she had survived. She was an unusual child, as he had also been an unusual child. He knew the dangers of being different, for peculiar people are not welcome in most segments of society.

She looked up from the encyclopedia and said, "I'll fix you something to eat. What would you like?"

"How about some cold-water cornbread?"

"You always want that. I'm not sure it's salubrious."

Morgan grinned at her use of the word. "It's salubrious enough for me."

"All right." She got up and began to fix the cornbread, which simply involved mixing cornmeal and water and frying it in grease. It made a rather tasty cake. She liked it herself.

When she brought the plate to her grandfather, he said, "Do you want to say the blessing?"

"Sure." She bowed and began, "God, thank You for this cold-water cornbread, for the cornmeal that's in it, and the water, and for the salt and pepper and for the grease that it was cooked in. Amen."

"You forgot to bless the milk that we're going to drink."

"Thank You, God, for the milk and for the cows that gave it. Amen."

Morgan laughed. "I'd hate to be there when you bless the Thanksgiving dinner. It'd take you an hour just to get through the basic elements."

"It's a good thing to give thanks unto the Lord. That's what you always say."

"You never forget anything, do you? Where are you now in the encyclopedia?"

"Still working through the J volume."

"Well, what's taking you so long, girl?" He gave her a wink and a grin.

Rhiannon said, "I was interested to learn that the Jain religion of India relies on the doctrine of *ahimsa*. The word is usually translated as *noninjury* or the imperative *do no harm*."

"I think I've heard of that," Morgan nodded.

"Ahimsa absolutely forbids the killing of living things."

"*Any* living things?" Morgan asked. He leaned back in his chair and sipped at the milk that seemed to soothe his stomach.

"That's what the article says. They can't burn candles, Grandpa, because a moth might fly into them and die. They can't use fire for heating or cooking because it might kill some bugs in the wood."

"That'd be a pretty hard religion to follow."

"I don't see how they do it. It says here they can't cut their hair because their lice might be injured by the scissors."

"Well, now that's going a bit too far."

"I think so, too."

"What else did it say?"

"Well, they can't plow in the fields because they might cut a worm in two." She looked up and made a face. "I don't think I want any of that religion. We couldn't even eat red snapper, could we?"

"I'm sure we couldn't—not if we were sincere Jains."

"Why do people believe things like that? Why don't they just believe the Bible?"

"Most of them in that part of the world never read the Bible."

"Well, we ought to send one over there," Rhiannon said. She looked at his face and said, "You don't feel so good today, do you?"

"Oh, I feel fine."

"Have you got your nitroglycerine pill?"

"I left them on the dresser. I don't need one."

"I'll go get them. You need to carry them with you. If you have a spell, Grandpa, you don't need to be running around hunting for pills."

Jumping up from her chair, she ran into his bedroom and came back with a small bottle. She put it in his shirt pocket and said, "If you need it, there it is." A thought came to her then. "I thought nitroglycerine was for blowing things up. Why do you take it for your heart?"

"Well, I think it can be used for both. I understand that these pills open up the arteries so that the blood can flow more freely and prevent a heart attack."

Rhiannon sat down and studied her grandfather. "I was reading in the Bible last night. It says in First Samuel 10:9 that God gave Solomon a new heart."

"That's what it says."

"Well, why can't He give *you* a new heart?"

Morgan Brice marveled at the ten-year-old's question. It was a simple matter to her. Her religion was of the most basic kind. "I suppose He could if He wanted to."

"I used the concordance and in Ezekiel 18:31 the Bible says, 'Cast away from you all your transgressions whereby ye have transgressed; and make you a new heart...' You see, Grandpa, you *can* have a new heart. The Bible says so."

"Well, sometimes, honey, when the Bible says *heart,* it doesn't mean the physical heart that's in your chest."

"But people do get new hearts," Rhiannon insisted. "It's in the H volume. I remember when I was reading it. It said that they started giving people hearts. In December of 1967 South African doctor Christiaan Barnard gave patient Louis Washkansky a new heart. He survived eighteen days."

Morgan Brice looked at this granddaughter who had become, to a large extent, his world, and smiled. "I hope it won't come to that."

● ● ●

Kate and Jeremy arrived at the Brice house and were admitted almost as soon as they knocked.

"I saw you coming down the beach," Rhiannon said. "Come in."

Morgan got up from the table to greet them. "Well, we're sure glad to have visitors. Join us for some fresh-squeezed juice. You can have orange juice or orange juice. Either one you like."

Kate smiled at Morgan. "I think I'd like some orange juice. Wouldn't you, Jeremy?"

"Sure, thanks. Jake says anybody who drinks concentrated orange juice is killing themselves."

"Mr. Novak has strong opinions," Morgan said.

Five minutes later they were sitting around the table. After listening to Rhiannon explain the principles of Jainism, Kate asked, "How do you remember all that stuff? I can't even remember my own name sometimes."

"I don't know," Rhiannon said. "It just seems to stick. I don't want to be one of them though, one of them Jains."

Kate hesitated, then said, "We had a visitor, Mr. Brice. One of the people with the movie company, Erik Lowe. You've heard of him?"

"I read a story about him in the paper," Morgan answered. "What kind of a fellow is he?"

"Very nice, but while he was at our house he asked if we knew you, and when I said we did, he asked me to drop you a warning."

Morgan's eyes flew wide open. "A warning? About what?"

"Well, it's about Aaron Tobin. He wants to buy the film rights to your book, I understand."

"Yes, he does. Most of the major studios have made me an offer, but I don't want to see the book at the mercy of Hollywood."

"Well, Mr. Lowe says that Aaron Tobin can hurt people. I think he's right. You can see it in him."

"He can't do anything to us, not to Rhiannon and me. I've got a clear title to this book. It's about all I *do* have. Now, don't you worry about it." He changed the subject suddenly saying, "It's good for Rhiannon to have a friend like Jeremy. That's a fine boy you have there."

"Jeremy isn't as smart as I am, but that's all right," Rhiannon said. "He's nice."

"That's not a nice thing to say," Morgan admonished.

"She's right," Jeremy said. "She is smarter than I am."

"Why don't you let Jeremy stay here with us for a while?" Morgan said to Kate. "He and Rhiannon can go fishing and swimming later on."

"Sure we can," Rhiannon said. "We can catch some fish, and I'll cook them. They're quite salubrious."

"I think you've got that word down pretty well, Rhiannon," Morgan Brice smiled. "Why don't you start on a new one?"

"All right, Grandpa. Do you have one for me?"

"Why don't you work on *sesquipedalian*."

"Ooh, that's a good one!"

"It won't be too easy to work into a conversation."

"What does it mean, Grandpa?"

"A sesquipedalian is one who likes to use big words. When you put 'anti' in front of it, it means being against the use of big words."

"That's not me," Rhiannon said. She grinned. "But I'll bet Jeremy's an antisesquipedalian. Come on. Let's go swimming."

Jeremy looked at his mom. "I didn't bring a suit."

Rhiannon rolled her eyes. "Just swim in those shorts."

Kate nodded at Jeremy, and the two kids left. Morgan shook his head ruefully. "She's a little bit unusual, Kate."

"Yes, she is, but she's a precious child. I know you're proud of her."

"She's all I have left," Morgan Brice said simply.

Kate felt a chill. Aaron Tobin was a strong man, powerful through the use of his money and influence, and this elderly man with a weak heart and this innocent child would be at his mercy. She made a silent vow. *I'm not going to let that man hurt them.*

"Well, I've got to get going," Kate said. "Send Jeremy home if he gets in your way."

"It won't come to that. He's a good boy."

● ● ●

Kate was cleaning out Big Bertha's glass enclosure, when the doorbell rang. When she found Avis Marlow standing at her door, she was taken completely aback. She couldn't speak for a moment, but then she managed to say, "Good afternoon, Miss Marlow."

"Call me Avis. Do you have a few minutes?"

"Sure—come in," Kate said.

Avis entered the room and then stopped, looking at the fish tank, the birds in the various cages, and Big Bertha in the glass case. She gasped when the huge pit bull came and sat down on her feet.

"Get off of her feet, Trouble. I'm sorry, Avis. He likes to sit on people's feet."

"You've got lots of pets."

"You haven't heard about that?"

"No."

"Well, come have something to drink and I'll tell you our story."

"That would be nice."

"We don't have anything too exciting. Milk, soft drinks, and juice. Oh, and I've just learned to make real Southern sweet tea."

"A glass of iced tea would be nice."

Kate was flustered by the woman. She had seen her in several movies and there was an odd, eerie feeling about a famous movie actress idolized by millions sitting down in her kitchen. She busied herself with the tea, then sat down.

"It's really simple. I lost my husband some time ago, and I was raising my son, Jeremy, alone. He's twelve. A bit of good fortune came my way when a distant relative who built this house died. She left it to her heirs with very rigid restrictions."

"What sort of restrictions?"

"Well, the heirs would have to live in the house and take care of the animals. She was a lonely woman, apparently, and loved her pets like children. We have to have the veterinarian come once a month to certify that they're all being cared for. I was living in Memphis in a terrible place, and of course this is heaven after that."

"But what about Jake? He lives here, too, I understand."

"Yes, he was the other heir that the lawyer found. I guess we're cousins several times removed. Neither of us knew the lady that left the place. And we knew nothing of each other."

"An interesting situation."

Avis was going to say more, when suddenly the parrot flew across the room and lit on her shoulder, at the same time uttering a particularly vile curse word. She let out a short cry of alarm.

"That's Bad Louie," Kate said with resignation. "You can see why we call him that. Now, Louie, say something nice. Nice Louie. Good Louie."

"Hallelujah!"

Avis laughed. She waited until Kate lifted the parrot and tossed him into the air. "I've heard you're religious, aren't you?"

"You could say that. I'm a Christian."

Avis said nothing for a time, then she said, "I came by to see the cats. They've decided to use both of them in the picture."

"I doubt if that'll work out with Jacques," Kate said. "We call him the Ripper for a very real reason."

"So Erik told me. But Bjorn thought it would be a good idea. They would be sort of symbols in the picture. Good cat, bad cat. Could I see them?"

"Of course. They're probably asleep out on the deck." She led Avis outside, and the two cats, indeed, were sprawled out soaking up the sun. They got up at once, and Jacques examined the visitor with a steady gaze.

"There's a good cat," Avis murmured. She stepped forward and put her hand down.

"I wouldn't do that if I were you. He scratches."

Avis slowly lowered her hand. Jacques was absolutely still, which amazed Kate. Avis stroked his silky, black fur and said, "He's a beautiful cat. And so big."

"I can't believe he's letting you pet him like that. He usually claws anybody who gets close to him—except me or my son."

"Well, I get along well with tough characters. This is the other cat?"

"Yes, this is Cleo. You won't have any trouble with her. She's the sweetest cat I've ever known."

Avis picked up Cleo, and Kate showed her how to hold her over her shoulder. "She is a sweetheart. They're quite different, aren't they?"

"As different as night and day."

Avis put the cat down, then gave Kate a straight look. "Is Jake here?"

"No, he's gone. I don't know where he is today."

"How long have you two been living together?"

Kate didn't like the way that Avis put it. "We're not really living together, not in the way that term is usually used. He has his own apartment upstairs."

"I see. Has he ever said anything to you about me?"

"No, he's never mentioned you."

"I guess you saw the way he acted when we saw each other at the party. It was quite a shock to both of us." She turned and looked out over the Gulf and didn't speak for a while. When she did speak, she kept her eyes on the sparkling, blue-green waters. "We were in love once. We were going to get married."

Kate was surprised. "But you had such different lives."

"Well, my career wasn't much back then. I was working on a movie in Chicago, and I was just one of a thousand starlets. I would have given up acting for him." She turned to face Kate and there was somehow a shadow in her eyes that didn't go with the rest of her features. "But then I got a couple of big breaks, and it looked like my career was going to take off. It was what I'd always wanted. I couldn't get married."

"How did Jake take that?"

"He'd never been in love before. I guess it pretty well destroyed him. You know how the toughest guys have the softest hearts." She turned quickly and said, "Maybe that's why I like Cleo—but my favorite is Jacques."

"He might be difficult on a movie set."

"No, he'll be fine, won't you, Jacques?" She reached down, caressed the cat's big head, and then straightened up. "Tell Jake I came by and I'll see him later."

"I'll—I'll tell him."

Cleo was staring at Jacques with amazement. *You didn't claw her.*

No, Cleo, she's a lot like me.

What do you mean?

She's got claws, Cleo, and she'll use them when someone crosses her. She's my kind of Person.

She seems nice.

She seems that way, but look in her eyes, Cleo. Our eyes are the mirror of the soul. Look into her eyes and you'll see a carnivore.

Seven

The rising sun sent pale brilliant bars of light through the sliding glass doors, and for a moment Kate stood looking out over the Gulf. The weather was fine and people were walking along the beach. There was no way to have total privacy since the beach was public domain. The set of seven lots that she and Jake had inherited enabled them to keep people from having parties or picnicking in front of their house, but not from walking along the shoreline.

A bell went off, and walking over to the oven, she opened it, pulled out a cake she had been baking, and saw that it was burned to a crisp.

"Oh, fudge!" she uttered in disgust. "You'd think anyone could bake a cake. I don't want Jake to see this." She quickly slid the burnt item off into a paper sack, wrapped it, and stuffed it in the trash. It was somehow embarrassing that Jake Novak, a tough guy in every way, could cook and she couldn't. Glancing up at the clock, she went to Jeremy's room and said, "Jeremy, get up and take your shower."

"Mmm-kay," came the muffled reply.

Walking back through the house, she stopped to check the aquariums. The tropical fish took more attention than most people realized. Pausing before a small tank with a separator down the middle, she studied the fighting fish. She was often tempted to take the partition out, just to see what would happen. But she knew she probably wouldn't enjoy the results.

Hesitating for a moment, she walked over to the door that led to the upstairs—Jake's realm. Straightening her shoulders, she opened the door and called out, "Jake, are you up?" She heard something that might have been, "Yeah, I'm up," but it might have also been, "Get away from here."

"Can I come up?"

Again there was a mumbled reply, which Kate took for an affirmative. She mounted the steps, and when she stepped into Jake's apartment, she saw him sitting at his desk staring fixedly at the monitor, which glowed with the white of a blank page. Walking over to him, she said, "How's it going?"

Jake turned toward her, and she saw that he had missed a night's sleep again. His coarse black hair was mussed up where he had run his hands through it, and she had an urge to trim his heavy, black brows. He looked at her with a scowl but she ignored his attitude. "Come on down and I'll fix breakfast."

"You can't cook."

"I'm getting better, aren't I?"

"Leave me alone, Mary Katherine. I'm enjoying my misery."

She looked at him more closely. "What are you miserable about? You ought to be thankful you're not living in that little dump of an apartment in Chicago."

"I was able to write there. Writers need to be miserable. Happy writers never produce anything."

"The book's not going well, I take it."

"It's not going at all."

"But Jake, that's what you kept saying about that last novel. You finished that one, didn't you?"

He looked at her like she'd uttered the dumbest thing he'd ever heard. He slapped at the computer and the screen went blank. "Maybe I'm using the wrong method. Hemingway may have had the right idea."

"What did he do?"

"He wrote with a pencil, Faber No. 2, and he stood the entire time. When he had gone through two pencils, he quit."

"What if he wasn't finished, or was in the middle of a good part?"

"He always quit when the last of the pencil ran out. There was another writer named Anthony Trollope. He would put his watch down, take his goose quill, and begin writing. He wrote for six hours nonstop, not even getting up to take a bathroom break or get a drink of water, and when his clock showed him that six hours had passed, he quit. He did the same thing every day."

"It doesn't sound like a very good way to write."

"Well, it worked for Trollope. So, what do you want, Mary Katherine?"

"I want you to go out to the movie set with Jeremy and me."

Jake groaned.

"They're shooting some scenes at the new pavilion. You know they finally finished building it after Hurricane Katrina took the old one out."

"No, I don't want to go," Jake said flatly.

Kate wanted to reach out and shake him. He had a stubborn, mulish look on his face. "You've got to get out of the house."

"Don't want to."

"Jake, you don't seem like a man who would run from trouble, but I see you're just like everybody else, after all."

"What trouble?"

"Avis Marlow trouble."

Jake glared at her. "That's all ancient history," he spat out.

"You remember what you told me about Faulkner?"

"No, I don't."

"You told me that Faulkner said one time, 'The past is not dead. It's not even past.'"

"It sounds like psychobabble by some psychiatrist who wants to say that everything we do is because of something in the past. I'm a bad boy because my mama didn't change my diaper often enough."

For all his size and strength, at this moment there was something pathetic about Jake. Stepping forward, she looked into his face and said gently, "I know seeing Avis threw you for a loop. But you're right—it's ancient history. Maybe going down there and seeing her again will help you put it in the past."

Jake glared at her, then a vulnerable expression touched his hazel eyes. "Maybe you're right, Mary Katherine. I've been reading Heraclitus this week."

"Who was he?"

"He was a Greek philosopher in the sixth century BC. He lived in Ephesus near the coast of Asia Minor. He wrote one book and, more or less, put it where nobody could read it. The book itself was finally lost, and there are just a few fragments left. One of them you've probably heard. He said, 'You cannot step twice into the same river.'"

"What does that mean?"

"It means that the river changes all the time, and what you step into today will be a hundred miles downstream tomorrow. He was right."

"Come along and go with us."

"I might as well. Is anybody else going?"

"Bev said he might stop by, and Enola's going. She'll drive us."

"Why does she have to be there?"

"Because we're taking Cleo and Jacques. They're going to be in the movie, and there has to be a vet on hand. Hurry up and get dressed."

● ● ●

Enola pulled her Hummer to a halt in front of the new pavilion. "Looks like they're here," she said. "Takes a lot of people to make a movie."

"Too many people," Jake muttered. He glanced back at the two carriers where Cleo and Jacques stared back at him. "Serve them right if the Ripper slashes somebody today. What idiot decided to put him in the movie?"

"I think they wanted them for symbols," Kate said. "Movies are big on symbolism these days."

"I hope you negotiated a good price," Enola said as she turned the engine off and opened the car door. "If they're going to star in a movie, they deserve big time money."

Kate smiled. "Don't worry. They're paying these two more for a day's worth of acting than I used to make in a month."

The three got out, and Jake picked up Jacques's carrier. Jake grunted and said, "Jacques, I'm going to put you on a diet."

You're not putting anybody on a diet, Intruder.

Cleo put her face against the wire and stared across at Jacques. *Why don't you be nice, Jacques? We're going to have a good time. We're going to be in the movies. You'll be a movie star!*

I know what'll happen. They'll make me the bad guy and you'll be the good guy.

Well, isn't that true to life?

No, it isn't. I only hurt people who deserve it, and when the Intruder opens this door, I'm going to get a piece of him!

The two cats carried on their wordless conversation commenting on the human condition all the way to the pavilion. Jeremy was excited. His eyes gleamed and danced, and he said, "I always wanted to see a movie being made."

"Don't make any friends with these people, Slick—they're scum," Jake said.

"That's a pretty broad generalization," Enola said.

"Yeah," Jeremy nodded, "movie stars are always helping others."

"They get a cause like ingrown toenails, start a program, and get their picture in the paper. Then a week later they're off on to something else. Inverted belly buttons or something really important." Jake didn't bother to hide his disdain for the Hollywood types.

A large section of the beach, which included the pavilion, had been roped off. Spectators stayed behind the rope, waiting eagerly to see the movie stars. Kate and her entourage were greeted at once by the mayor of White Sands, Devoe Palmer. Palmer was a small man who wore lifts to put himself a little closer to heaven. He also owned a successful real estate firm and was smiling broadly as he welcomed them. "Well, you brought the stars, I hope."

"Hello, Mayor," Kate said. "Yes, the cats are right here."

"It's wonderful what this is going to mean to White Sands."

"It's going to put us on the map, is it, Devoe?" Jake's voice was sarcastic, but the mayor didn't notice.

"Sure it is," Devoe answered excitedly. "Just like when John Grisham put the FloraBama in one of his books. It was just an out-of-the-way run-down dump when he discovered it."

"It still is," Jake stated flatly.

"But it's famous now. They're going to rebuild the thing since the hurricane messed it up. But just think, this movie will be seen by millions of people. They'll be flocking into White Sands, Gulf Shores, and Orange Beach just to get a look at the place where the movie was made."

"Yeah, I suppose the place will become a mecca for rude tourists. That's what we want."

They were interrupted by a roar. "Uh-oh, it looks like the boss is mad," Enola said.

They all turned to watch as Aaron Tobin shoved himself right into the face of the cameraman Dontelle Byrd. Dontelle stood silently meeting the producer's eyes with a gaze that should have warned Tobin.

Tobin suddenly gave Dontelle a poke in the chest. The cameraman's eyes went down to his chest, then back up at Tobin in an unflinching gaze. It seemed to anger Tobin even more, and he cursed Dontelle as he turned and saw the group that had just arrived. He came over and went through an instant metamorphosis.

"Glad you're here. Those cats ready to go?"

"Right here, Mr. Tobin." Kate gestured to the carriers that they'd set on the ground beside them.

"That's good. Let me see them." Tobin knelt to take a look.

"Don't open their carriers. Cats aren't like dogs," Enola said. "They don't come when you call them."

Tobin was looking at Jacques. "That's the biggest cat I've ever seen. He looks like a panther."

"He's a Savannah," Kate said. "Half wild cat."

Tobin grinned. "Sounds perfect. What about this one?"

"That's Cleo. She's a sweetheart," Enola said. "She won't give you any trouble, but you have to watch out for Jacques there."

Jake added, "His name is Jacques the Ripper for obvious reasons."

Tobin stared at the cats and then nodded with satisfaction. "The cats are going to be symbolic."

"Good and evil?" Jake asked.

"Yeah," Tobin nodded. "So, this black one here, what's his name? Jacques the Ripper? I like that. He's going to be the villain." He suddenly lifted his head and said, "Hey, Byrd, the black guys are always the villains, right?" He turned and was laughing, a sadistic look twisting his lips. "Rastus there thinks he's the greatest cameraman ever lived, but I ain't seen it yet. Anyhow, we'll use the cats as symbols."

Enola slipped away and walked over to where Dontelle Byrd was making adjustments on the camera. "Hello. I'm the cat woman," she said.

"Sure. I remember you. You're the vet," Byrd said.

Enola studied the man, who was fine-looking and well-built. There was a sensitivity in his features that made Enola curious. "Is it worth it, Dontelle? They must pay you a lot of money to put up with a man like Aaron Tobin."

The name seemed to trigger something in Dontelle Byrd's face. "I could kill him some days."

Enola almost took a step backward, so vicious was the light in the man's eyes. "Why don't you just quit?"

"Because I don't allow small men like Aaron Tobin to control my destiny. I'm good at my job, and I choose the movies I want to do. I'm not gonna play the poor black sharecropper to Simon Legree over there, and I'm not going to let him get the best of me either."

"Couldn't Tobin hurt your career if he wanted to?"

"He could try. But it's not like I'm some starlet who wouldn't come across for him. He's famous for his treatment of those girls—he can bury an acting career in a second. But I've worked with plenty of other directors. I'll get work, with or without Aaron Tobin."

"Well, it seems most everyone hates him."

"You're right. I don't see why someone hasn't killed him already."

"Well, who knows. Could happen."

"I guess that's true. Anyway, to kill Aaron Tobin, I'd have to get in line and take a number." He laughed. "Don't pay any attention to this talk. Everybody talks about Aaron when he's not around."

"What's going down, Dontelle?"

Enola turned to see a tall, well-built man she had missed before. He was almost a dead ringer for Jean Claude van Damme and Dontelle said, "Have you two met?"

"Don't think I've met the lady," the man said.

"This is Thad Boland," Dontelle said.

"Everybody calls me Bo," the newcomer said in a deep voice.

"This is Dr. Enola Stern, Bo. She's the vet for the cats that are going to be in the movie."

"Glad to know you." There was a rough handsomeness about the man. "I don't know how you're going to get those cats to do anything."

"They're pretty independent," Enola said. "But I think we'll do okay. What do you do here, Bo?"

"Oh, I'm a man of many talents," Bo said. "I'm a stunt man for the action sequences."

"He's Aaron's bodyguard, too," Dontelle added.

"How do you get to be a bodyguard?" Enola asked. "Is there a school you go to with a major in guarding bodies?"

"Let's just say I've led a rough life. Learned my trade on the streets."

Enola was fascinated by Thad Boland. She had always thought Jean Claude van Damme fascinating, and this was somewhat like meeting him in the flesh. "What does that mean?" she asked. "How rough?"

"You mean you haven't read about my sordid past in the tabloids?" Bo asked with a sarcastic edge to his voice.

Enola shook her head. "I'm not usually into celebrity gossip, sorry."

"Good for you. Well, I was a bit careless in my youthful days. Did a little time. I was even arrested for murder, but I was innocent. You can't believe everything you read in the papers." He glanced over Enola's shoulder and said, "Well, looks like the queen has decided to grace us with her presence. We can get this scene put together."

Enola nodded to Boland and said, "Nice to meet you."

"You, too. Hey—" He leaned in and said quietly, "Catch up with me after we wrap today. We can go grab a beer."

"Maybe."

As Enola walked away, she overhead Bo say, "Dontelle, you'd better watch what you say about Tobin. He's got ears everywhere."

"Don't I know it, bro."

● ● ●

Kate was fascinated as Bjorn Kristofferson took charge.

"Okay, people, I'm gonna direct the first scene today. Jesse'll be here in a bit." His voice carried well over the sound of the surf.

"All right, here's the scene. Avis comes out wearing a robe. She's going swimming in the Gulf, so she drops the robe and starts for the water. Erik, you let her get halfway there, then meet her. There's the dialogue, the kiss, and then out."

Kate was watching along with everyone else as Avis Marlow approached wearing a white robe. Kate shifted her glance to Jake next to her and saw that his eyes were fixed on Avis.

Bjorn called, "All right. Action!"

Avis left the pavilion and walked on the sand toward the Gulf. Even dressed from neck to feet in a beach robe, there was something sensual and almost predatory about the woman. She dropped the robe and kept walking, and Kate felt Jake tense like everyone else who was watching. Avis was wearing a white bikini that set off the golden tan of her body. There was a raw sexuality in her as she continued to walk, and glancing at Jake, Kate saw that he was transfixed.

When Erik came up and spoke his first lines to Avis, Aaron Tobin's coarse voice broke the air.

"CUT." He cursed loudly and came plowing toward the two, kicking sand. "What's the matter with you, Lowe? You've just seen the best-looking woman since Monroe. You got a look on your face like you're constipated, you idiot!"

There was something embarrassing about seeing a man verbally crucified in such a cruel way. Tobin continued to berate Erik Lowe, and finally he whirled and came back growling, "Shoot it again, Kristofferson!"

"Why don't you take it easy, Aaron?" Kristofferson said. "He's doing pretty well."

It was Kristofferson's turn to take the abuse. Tobin raved at him, shouting, "You're not directing a home video here! This is the real thing. Shoot that scene again."

They went through the scene again, and just then Jesse Tobin hurried onto the beach. "Have your beauty sleep, Jesse?" Aaron said sarcastically. "Sorry to disturb you."

"I was taking care of some business on the phone, Dad. We talked about this."

"Get over here and shoot this scene," Aaron commanded.

Jesse had the two actors go through the scene four more times, and in each instance Aaron was unhappy. Finally he said, "Take a break. Come on, Jesse, I want to explain a few things about this movie to you."

Avis walked over toward the edge of the crowd where an assistant stood waiting with her robe. She slipped into it, then lit a cigarette. She stood there aloof, ignoring everyone, but staring across the sand at Jake. Kate could see there was something possessive about the way she looked at him. Finally Avis walked over, her eyes constantly on Jake.

"Like what you see so far, Mr. Novak?" Her voice was sultry.

"Oh yeah. The beach looks awesome. Great location."

"Touché," Avis responded with a slight grin, still gazing directly into Jake's eyes.

Erik Lowe joined them, dispelling the tension. "Hey, guys. This movie's gonna take forever if Aaron keeps backseat-directing every scene."

They bantered for a bit until Aaron came over shaking his head. "Nobody seems to know what's going on here."

"What's the problem, Aaron?" Avis asked.

"There's more going on in this picture than what's on the surface, okay?" Aaron said gruffly. "This is a heavily symbolic film. It's gotta come through in every scene."

"We know, Aaron," Erik said. "It's about a woman who hits the top and then goes downhill. The public turns on her."

Jake interjected, "Sounds like the theme of the poem."

Aaron looked baffled. "What are you talking about?"

"'The Patriot,'" Jake said. "It's the poem with the line, 'Roses, roses all the way.' Same theme—a guy at the top, then goes downhill."

"I don't know about any stupid poem," Tobin growled.

Avis suddenly laughed. "Jake probably knows it." She put her hand on Jake's arm. "Say the poem for the man, Jake."

Thad Boland had come over and joined the crew. He laughed loudly, "He's a soldier boy. He don't know anything."

Jake had determined to say nothing, but something about the arrogance of Tobin and the grin on Boland's face stirred an anger in him. "Pretty well-known poem," he said.

"I bet you've got it memorized. Let's hear it," Avis said.

Jake began to quote the poem:

> It was roses, roses all the way,
> With myrtle mixed in my path like mad:
> The houseroofs seemed to heave and sway,
> The church-spires flamed, such flags they had,
> A year ago on this very day.

Every sound had stopped as Jake quoted the poem, and Jake saw the anger on Tobin's face. He knew there was nothing worse for a man in Tobin's position than to be shown wrong about anything.

"It's by Robert Browning—about a man who entered a city in triumph, and a year later was brought back on the same street, this time to be executed." Jake's voice was low and confident.

Aaron Tobin's face grew red. "I thought you were a tough guy. You're like that worthless son of mine. No good except for spouting worthless poetry."

Jake suddenly grinned and winked at Kate. "I wouldn't call Robert Browning worthless."

"Get off the set," Tobin said.

"I can't think of anything I'd rather do." Jake stood glaring at Tobin, and Boland stepped forward and gave him a shove. Jake caught his balance and turned. "I don't need your help, Boland."

"Get rid of him! Throw his rear off the set, Bo!" Aaron demanded.

Bo advanced and reached out and threw a hard punch at Jake, who simply drew his head back. He went at once into a strange-looking crouch such as Kate had never seen, and instantly Boland went into the same crouch. It was martial arts, she knew, and the two men circled each other striking out and kicking.

Avis watched with amusement. "You're going to let them fight, Aaron?"

"Novak thinks he's such a tough guy. Let him take care of himself. See if he can do anything besides recite poems."

The fight had become a focal point and a circle was formed. Jake and Boland went around each other slashing, and Jake caught a hard blow that reddened his cheek. He stooped down and before Boland knew what he was doing, threw a low punch straight to Boland's gut. Boland doubled over, and Jake grabbed him and easily put him on the ground. He held Boland's wrists and put his heel right on Boland's neck. "I could break his neck, Tobin. Would that show you I'm a tough enough guy?"

Aaron Tobin was staring at Jake, then looked down at Boland. "You're supposed to be the tough guy, Bo." He suddenly laughed, instantly changing his mood. "Why don't I fire Boland and have Mr. Delta Force be my bodyguard?"

Jake stepped back. "No thanks, Tobin. Don't need a job." Boland got to his feet and gave Jake a poisonous glance. "I'll see you around, poetry lover." He strode stiffly away from the group.

"I don't think anybody has ever put him down like that," remarked Avis, turning her admiring eyes on Jake.

Jake watched Boland retreat, then shrugged his shoulders. "You know, there's this scientist who studies animals. He says he never trusts anything that slithers on the ground and has a poisonous bite."

Everyone stared at Jake for the statement seemed to make no sense at all. But Avis was delighted. "You always did that. You've got a crazy mind. What does all that have to do with anything?"

"The scientist was talking about snakes. Wrote a great piece about it. Said there was something scary about anything that glides along the ground silently and attacks with no warning. I decided he had the right idea, so I made a decision not to be afraid of anything except snakes— not even phonies like Boland."

Avis moved closer and whispered. The others had drawn back and were watching, but no one could have heard the soft whisper.

"You were always afraid of me for some reason, Jake."

Jake stared at her, and for all his strength, quickness, and power, there was something vulnerable in the way he looked at this woman. "I was afraid I'd lose you, Avis—which I did. Now I've got two things to be afraid of—snakes and getting close to a woman like you."

Eight

The cast and crew had broken for lunch and returned to work with the morning episode safely behind them. They filmed a couple more scenes and were now in a lull between shots. Bev had arrived a few moments earlier and was standing next to Kate. "I say. Did you see that?"

Kate had seen what the Englishman spoke of. Jesse Tobin went up to his father, and Aaron seemed displeased with what he said. He lifted his voice so they could hear his curses, and then Jesse looked at him for a moment and turned silently and walked away.

"There's a real father-son relationship," Enola said. "I haven't talked to a single person on this set who doesn't want to murder Aaron Tobin."

"Yeah, he's a piece of work, isn't he?" The three of them hadn't noticed the woman who had approached from their left. Callie Braun stood with them, and she continued, "Most people don't like Mr. Tobin, but he gave me a job when I needed one."

"How does one qualify to be a stand-in for Avis Marlow?" Bev wanted to know.

"Well, you have to look a little bit like her. We've got the same body styles and the same color of hair." Callie shrugged.

"How'd you get the job?" Enola wondered.

"I was in the right place at the right time. I did an audition for a commercial, and Jesse Tobin was there, and we got to talking. He said I looked similar enough to Avis, and they needed a stand-in. Mr. Tobin hired me."

"So you live in California?" Kate asked.

"Yes."

"It looks like a pretty easy job," Enola observed. "Do you like it?"

"It's not bad, but I think I already told you, it's not what I want to do."

"You mentioned you were interested in real estate," Kate said.

"I've been taking courses at UCLA. Once I get my degree, I'll get my real estate license, and my sister and I are going to start an agency. You can make a good living selling homes in LA."

Kate listened and the thought crossed her mind, *This is the only perfectly normal person I've met in this whole movie-making business.*

● ● ●

The late afternoon was flooding the earth with shadows, and the sea oats were standing still with no breeze to stir them. Far over to the north, cumulus clouds were gathering, shifting like curtains. The waves had left an arabesque pattern on the sand, and the sun put long fingers of light on the beach, touching the earth with a strange gentleness. It had been a long day for Kate, Bev, Jake, and Enola, who'd done nothing much but stand around and observe. Jeremy was fascinated with every single detail.

Now Bjorn approached them. "It's time to get some shots of the cats."

Enola gave a sigh of relief. "Finally."

"How in the world do you make cats do anything?" Callie asked.

"You don't really," Enola said, "but they're creatures of habit, and you can get them to do a few things by giving them their favorite food, tuna or something like that."

Bjorn was looking at the cats, then he stood up, surveying the coast. "We can start with some shots of them walking along the beach, chasing birds or whatever they do. Is there enough light, Dontelle?"

"Sure. We can get an afternoon shot, and then if you want to stay long enough, we can get some shots of them at night."

"Can we take them down the beach away from the crowd?" Kate asked. "That might make them behave more naturally."

"Sure. Let's go," Bjorn said.

Most of the spectators had left. Jake picked up the carrier that housed Jacques, and Dontelle got Cleo. They started down the beach.

"They'll probably feel better if I'm close," Kate said, "especially Jacques."

"You have to watch out for this one, Dontelle," Jake grinned. "He's a man-eater."

"Just turn them loose, and I'll get the best shots I can. We'll work them in somehow."

The carriers were opened, and Jacques shot out and headed straight for Bjorn. Kate was prepared for this and got between them. "No, Jacques, leave him alone."

Jacques stared up at her and then sat down and began to lick his paws. He waited until Cleo joined him.

This is pretty neat. Cleo was happy with the situation.

Not bad, I guess. We're movie stars. Jacques was working hard to maintain his dignity.

I don't know how to be a movie star, Jacques.

Just act normal.

Cautiously Enola and Kate retreated, and the two cats began to explore the beach.

Have you ever been this far down the beach, Cleo?

No, I usually stay closer to the house.

Well, just stick with me. I come down here all the time.

When, Jacques? I never see you.

I'm always out at night, remember? C'mon.

The two cats explored, stopping to sniff here and there, making sure to avoid the water.

Cleo, here's our chance!

What is it?

Birds. Come on, let's go get 'em.

"Make sure to get a shot of them trying to run those sandpipers down," Bjorn said.

The two cats went into a frenzy, but they were unable to catch any of the sandpipers, who not only ran fast, but had the advantage of flight when their enemies got too close. The cats chased the sandpipers until they were out of breath, and then Cleo caught sight of something else.

What's that, Jacques? Looks like the biggest bird I've ever seen.

Actually it was a tall blue heron that was walking along the beach, taking slow, stately steps.

I'm going to whack him, Jacques said. *I wonder if he's good to eat?*

That's all you think about, something good to eat.

I think about other things, Cleo, whether you know it or not.

I know what you think about—that awful yellow female cat that lives across the highway.

Jacques seemed to grin. *What else is there besides food and female companionship?*

The two ran after the heron, which easily avoided them, then they continued along exploring the beach. Aaron Tobin had come down to watch the filming, and now he said, "You think you got enough, boy?" He spoke with a devious pleasure in knowing it annoyed Dontelle to be called *boy*.

"Enough in this light, I guess."

Enola and Kate got out some tuna to lure the cats back.

"Cleo...Jacques...c'mon..." Kate called as she tapped a spoon on the tuna can. The cats came running and began to eat the food that was held out for them.

Tobin advanced and said, "Those are some cats." He reached down to stroke Jacques and immediately let out a cry and jerked his hand back.

"I warned you, Mr. Tobin," Enola said.

Kate was almost frightened of what was going to happen. Tobin had such a hot temper she fully expected him to blow up. Instead, he laughed and took out his handkerchief. "Just a little slice. It won't hurt me."

"I've got some antiseptic in my vehicle," Enola said. "I'll treat it for you if you want."

Tobin shook his head. "It's okay. We've got first-aid on the set." But he was looking at the cat with something like admiration. "He reminds me of someone." He thought for a minute and then said thoughtfully, "He reminds me of me."

Jacques started walking toward the producer, his eyes snapping.

I'm not like you, you fat slob.

Leave him alone, Jacques, Cleo said.

I'd like to slice him up and feed him to the fish.

The two were captured and put back into their carriers, and Kate said, "I think we've had enough movie-making for one day."

They collected Bev, who was talking to Lexi Colby, the dark-haired actress. She was smiling up at the tall Englishman, and they heard her say, "You've got my number, Beverly. Give me a call."

"Without a doubt," he said cheerfully.

● ● ●

Bev drove his own car while Enola drove Jake, Kate, and Jeremy. They went back to the house, and while Kate unloaded the cats, the rest of them stood there discussing the events of the day.

"I noticed you seemed to make a conquest of that young actress," Enola said to Bev.

"She's a nice young woman, Lexi Colby. She invited me to visit her."

"You must get a lot of invitations like that, Bev," Enola said.

"Oh, it's all purely platonic I assure you."

"Right," said Jake. "We're on to you, Limey."

Kate rejoined the group. "Is anybody else hungry?"

Jeremy jumped in. "I'm starved to death. I want a hamburger."

"That's sounds like a good idea. Could everybody else eat a hamburger?" Jake asked. He saw them all nod and said, "Let me drive. I know a good place."

Enola surrendered the keys. They all loaded up, and Jake gunned the engine as he headed onto the highway. Jeremy said, "Were you scared this morning when that guy came at you, Jake?"

"Scared spitless."

"No, you weren't," Enola said.

"Nah, the guy's a pansy. Couldn't hurt a fly."

They drove west on the Beach Highway, and when they were approaching a row of restaurants, Jake said, "Here's where we can get a good burger."

He pulled into a parking lot filled with cars, and when they got out Kate said, "This is Hooters! We can't eat here."

Jake was in a good mood, and he said jovially, "What're you talking about? They have good food. Come on."

They all filed in and were soon seated at a table. The servers were curvaceous young women wearing the tightest of all possible outfits that proclaimed their femininity.

"This place is so sexist." Kate said. She looked straight at Jeremy. "Avert your eyes."

"Aw, leave the boy alone. It's not so bad," Beverly said.

Jeremy's eyes were large. "Why are the waitresses dressed like that?"

"They do it so guys like Mr. Devon-Hunt will come in and ogle them," Jake said.

"What about you?" Kate said primly. "Your eyes are out on stems."

"I pay no attention to the servers. It's not right to objectify women, you know." Jake turned to Jeremy. "That's the reason I'm so tough, kid. My strength is the strength of ten men because my heart is pure. That's a literary quotation."

Enola laughed. "You would pick this place, Jake. You remind me of Peter Pan."

"Peter Pan? That pipsqueak?"

"Why Peter Pan, Dr. Stern?" Jeremy asked.

"You remember the story. Peter Pan was a little boy who wouldn't grow up. That's the way it is with most men," she proclaimed. "They're kids until they're at least forty."

The waitress took their order, and they chatted until they got their hamburgers. As soon as they were served, Jake, with mischief in his voice, said, "We can't eat yet. You've got to ask the blessing. And don't forget to pray for the servers, Mary Katherine."

"I'm not praying in this place." She took a big bite of the hamburger and Jeremy exclaimed, "Mom, that's the first time I ever saw you eat without asking a blessing!"

"I'm afraid I'd call down fire on the place if I started to pray," Kate said.

They ate their hamburgers and French fries, and Jeremy waded through one burger and then ate half of his mother's. "I'd like to be an actor," he said between bites. "Looks like fun."

"Are you kidding? It'd be worse then being a minor league baseball player," Jake said.

Bev stared at him. "I read the other day about a man who got a hundred million dollars just for signing an agreement to play ball. What's wrong with that?"

"Nothing, but there's only one of him. And he's in the major leagues. Players in the minors hardly make anything." Jake threw his napkin on the table. "Everybody finished? That young woman in the tight uniform has been making eyes at me. I'm afraid she's going to attack me if we stay any longer. Pick up the check, Limey."

Beverly paid the check, and they all walked outside. "Well, I've got to get home and feed the animals," Kate said. "Interesting day, huh?"

"Do we get to go back to the set again, Mom?" Jeremy asked. "I like hanging out with movie stars."

"Not sure. We'll see."

Enola laughed. "Jeremy's got the bug. Well, it'll do him good to see how it really works."

"I guess they're not all a bad influence. Dontelle seems like a good guy. And Bjorn is nice."

"He's all right," Jake said, "but Bo, he's my ideal."

Nine

"I brought you some fish."

Kate smiled at Rhiannon, who had appeared at her front door, and said, "Well, that sounds great—thank you. Come in, Rhiannon."

"No, I've got to get home. I'm worried about Grandpa."

"Is he having a hard time—with his health, I mean?"

Rhiannon had put the bucket of fish down, and now she laced her fingers together and put them over her head as if keeping her head from flying off. She was wearing a Boston Red Sox cap that was much too large for her and came down over her ears. Her eyes were troubled, and Kate leaned over and said, "What's the matter?"

"The mayor came by to see us."

"Mr. Palmer?"

"I think that's his name, but he's not a very nice man. Oh, he seems nice, but that's just a façade."

"Why would you say that?"

"Because he fussed with Grandpa and after that Grandpa didn't feel good."

"What were they arguing about?"

Rhiannon chewed her lower lip, removed her hands from her head, and locked them behind her back. She did a little dance, moving her feet in some sort of rhythm that existed only in her own head. "The mayor said we're going to have to get out of our house."

Kate was taken aback. She stared at the small girl and saw that her eyes were deeply worried. "Here, come and sit down and tell me about it."

"No, you take the fish. I don't have time to clean them for you. You'll have to get Jeremy to do that. He can't clean them as well as I can, but I guess he'll do all right."

"Well, tell me about the argument."

"I didn't understand all of it, but Grandpa was extremely angry. He told the mayor to get out of the house, and after the mayor left I asked him what it all meant. He said they were going to do something down at City Hall that would make us have to leave our house, and the mayor told Grandpa that if he wanted to stay in the house, he ought to sell his book to that movie man."

"Mr. Tobin?"

"That's his name. Grandpa doesn't usually get mad, but he did this time. I've got to go home. I'll pick the bucket up next time I come."

"Can't you can stay and have something to eat?"

"No, I'm not hungry." Rhiannon turned and went down the steps, taking them two at a time. Her weather-beaten dog, Lucky, was waiting for her, and Kate watched as they turned and headed west down the beach. There was something inherently sweet about Rhiannon. She was so vulnerable, and all of her intelligence couldn't protect her from some of the things the world was handing her.

Kate stepped back inside to where Jake was making omelets. "I'm worried about Rhiannon and her grandfather, Jake."

Jake was slicing onions into the omelets, and he looked up with surprise. "What now?"

"Rhiannon says Devoe Palmer, the mayor, came by. There's some kind of a move to get the Brices out of their house."

"I never did like that mayor. You want me to go by and take care of him?"

"It may come to that," Kate said grimly. "I don't trust him. This has got something to do with Aaron Tobin." She thought for a minute and said, "Devoe said Morgan could sell his book to Tobin and be able to save his place."

"So Aaron Tobin and Devoe Palmer have joined ranks. The scum of the earth always stick together," Jake said. He carefully added some jalapeno peppers and bits of ham. Then he said, "I think the easiest thing is if I just go rough him up. It's kind of like Al Capone said, 'You can get more with a kind word and a gun than you can with a kind word alone.' I found out that pretty well works, especially with politicians."

Kate paced the floor, thinking intently as Jake made the omelets. Soon he set three of them down, and Jeremy was called to join in the feast. "I'm too mad to pray, Jeremy. You pray."

Jeremy was surprised, but he shrugged. "Okay, Mom." He bowed his head, said a quick prayer, and then plunged in. He took a huge bite. "Wow," he said, "that's hot."

"It's a fiesta omelet," Jake said. "I stole the recipe from a Mexican."

Jake and Jeremy ate hungrily, but Kate had lost her appetite. She had a highly developed sense of right and wrong, and something was dreadfully wrong with what was going on. She threw her napkin on the table. "Guys, I need to leave."

"What are you going to do?" Jake said.

"I'm going down to the City Hall and give that mayor something to chew on."

"Well, he's just a little guy," Jake said. "Maybe you ought to rough him up yourself."

"It may come to that. I feel mad enough to bite his stupid head off."

● ● ●

"Well, Mrs. Forrest, it's good—"

Kate didn't give Devoe Palmer time to finish his sentence. She had opened the door to his private office and left it open so that the secretary and those waiting to see the mayor could hear it all. She was in no mood to be amiable. "Devoe," she said, "what kind of crummy thing is this you're doing with the Brices?"

The mayor got up and moved cautiously around Kate. Her eyes were snapping, and he said, "Let me shut the door. We don't have to share this with everybody."

Kate said, "I don't care who I share it with. I'm going to put it on the front page of the newspaper."

"Wait a minute, Mrs. Forrest, you just don't understand."

"I understand that something corrupt is going on here."

"You sure you want a witness to this?"

Kate whirled and found Ray O'Dell, the chief of police, wedged into a chair over in the corner. He was going over some papers, and he grinned up at her. He was a strongly built man, the muscles of his chest swelling the front of his shirt, and now he found something amusing. "You want me to arrest her, Mayor? I can come up with a charge. Speaking disrespectfully to a mayor ought to be against the law."

Kate glared at the police chief and said, "You stay out of this, Chief, unless you're in it, too."

"In what?" Ray O'Dell asked in surprise. "I don't know what you're talking about."

"This sorry excuse for a mayor has got some scheme to move the Brices out of their place. I know he's in cahoots with that movie company, and he's going to put that old man and the little girl out." Her eyes were setting off sparks, and both men watched her cautiously, as if she were a bomb about to go off. Her voice grew louder as she peppered Palmer with threats, and finally she said, "I know what you're doing is illegal, Palmer. I'm going to be watching you. You're not going to hurt the Brices." She whirled and left the office, slamming the door behind her.

"Well," O'Dell said, "maybe I *should* have arrested her."

"Look, here's the situation," the mayor said. "Aaron Tobin wants to buy the movie rights to a book the old man wrote years ago. I don't know anything about it, but it's supposed to be hot stuff."

"Of course you don't know about it, Devoe. The last book you read was—what?—third grade?"

"Look, Ray, Tobin says if we put the pressure on Brice, he can guarantee they'll be shooting more movies here."

"Which means ongoing revenue for White Sands. Sweet deal, but pretty tough on the old man and the little girl."

"No, it won't be tough. They'll be paid. They'll have more than enough to buy a much better house. Tobin's willing to pay just about any price for the book. All Brice has to do is agree to sell him the rights. He's got to, otherwise he's going to be forced out."

"How you going to force him out?"

"We declare the house a health hazard. What have we got lawyers for—if not to help us in times like this?"

"What, indeed?" O'Dell said dryly. "That's what lawyers are for, ain't it?"

● ● ●

Another conversation was going on concerning the Brices. Jesse Tobin was listening as his father spoke over the phone to Devoe Palmer. He heard his father say, "I don't know what you can do, but I want the old man pressured. Condemn that shack he lives in. Use eminent domain. Get some crooked lawyers—or is that redundant? I'm going to get the rights to that book one way or another, and if you scratch my back, I'll scratch yours. I'm going to expect you to jump on this thing, Mayor."

"Dad," Jesse said, as soon as his father had slammed the phone down, "This isn't a good idea."

"What are you talking about?"

"Going after Brice. It's pretty crude."

"What do you think this is, a seminary? We're doing business."

"That's what Al Capone said. Always claimed he was just a businessman."

Aaron Tobin glared at his son. "Well, great minds think alike, I guess."

"That wasn't really what I meant—"

"Save it. I'm going to talk to old man Brice. Just like in *The Godfather* movie," he said, grinning to himself. "I'm going to make him an offer he can't refuse."

● ● ●

Rhiannon was reading in the encyclopedia, when she heard the footsteps. She put a marker in the book, laid it down, and said, "Grandpa, somebody's here."

"Who is it, honey?"

"I don't know." Rhiannon opened the door and found three men. She waited for them to speak. "I'm looking for Morgan Brice."

"I'll see if he's available."

"Aren't you going to ask us in?" Aaron Tobin said in a sickly sweet voice.

"No." With this definite word, Rhiannon closed the door again and walked to her grandfather's bedroom.

"Grandpa, there's three men to see you. You want me to run them off?"

Morgan came out. He was wearing a robe, and there was a pale cast to his face. "No, I'll talk to them."

Rhiannon watched the three men step inside, and they seemed to fill the small area. Thad Boland's eyes were moving from point to point, but Jesse's head was down. She wondered if he had something to hide, or if he was simply embarrassed.

"I thought we had our last conversation, Tobin." Morgan's voice was strong.

Aaron shrugged. "I came to talk some sense into you, Brice. I'm going to make you an offer like you've never dreamed."

"I told you before that I'm not selling the rights to *Honor in the Dust*."

"Don't be foolish!" Tobin snapped back. His face grew flushed, and he looked almost like a shark to Rhiannon. He composed himself and spoke very low. "I'll give you one million dollars for the rights to the book."

Rhiannon gasped.

"I've been offered that half a dozen times, and I've always turned it down." Morgan spoke matter-of-factly, but Rhiannon stared at him unbelieving.

Tobin wasn't giving up. "All right, *you* name the price. You can buy a better place to live. You can still afford to live on the beach. How much do you want?"

"I'm not selling the rights to the book. It's not about the money."

Boland stepped forward. There was a sinister look about him, and he glanced down at Rhiannon. "Look, this ain't no place to raise a kid. Take the dough, man." He put his big hand on Rhiannon's shoulder, and when the girl tried to pull away, he held her. "Talk to your grandpa, little girl."

"Let her go," Brice said.

"You never know. Something could happen to a kid in a place like this. It's dangerous."

Morgan shook his head at Thad Boland and then moved over to a table on which sat Rhiannon's rucksack. He reached in and casually pulled out the sawed-off shotgun. He turned and pointed the gun directly at Boland, speaking slowly and clearly. "Get out of here, all three of you. I'll shoot anybody who tries to harm my granddaughter."

"Wait a minute!" Tobin started, but immediately the shotgun was in his face. "All right—all right," he said, "but you're going to be sorry about this, Brice."

The three men left, and as they walked back toward the car, Rhiannon watched them through the window. She heard Tobin laugh. "Well, time for plan B," he told the others.

"You'll win, Aaron," Boland grinned. "It's just a matter of time."

Rhiannon strained to hear what was next, and she thought she heard Tobin say something about the mayor to Jesse.

Jesse's answer carried clearly on the breeze. "I'll tell him," he said, "but I don't think it's the right thing to do."

● ● ●

Jake had been working on his book and for once had been able to knock out three pages of what felt like half-decent writing. He was pleased with himself, and as always when he worked, he shut out the whole world. It was as if all that existed was his computer, his head, and his fingers.

But an unusual sound interrupted his reverie. Impatiently he turned, thinking that maybe Trouble had come upstairs, but when he saw Big Bertha, the Burmese python, slithering across the floor toward him, he scrambled to his feet and jumped on the bed. He yelled in a guttural voice as loud as he could manage, "Mary Katherine...Mary Katherine... get in here!" keeping his eyes fixed on the snake.

Kate appeared at the door. "What's wrong?"

"It's that blasted snake. Get her out of here."

Kate suddenly began to laugh. "Jake, you look ridiculous. She can't hurt you. She's not poisonous."

"I don't care. I don't want that snake up here. Get her out."

Kate reached down and picked up the snake, who immediately began to curl around her arm. "You see. She's no harm at all."

"I'm not arguing about this. Out with the serpent."

Kate stared at him. "You're worse than Trouble. He'd tackle a wild boar, I think, but he's afraid of a little two-pound ferret that couldn't harm him. Now get off that bed."

Jake waited until she was out of the room and then got down. He followed her and said nothing until she had put Big Bertha back in the glass cage and locked it. Heaving a sigh of relief, he said, "I'm going to nail the top of that box down."

"No, you're not. Just be quiet. I want to tell you what's happening."

Jake kept his eye on Big Bertha and listened as Kate explained what Tobin was doing. "He's using the mayor, but he's determined to get Mr. Brice to sell the rights to that book."

"What are you going to do about it?"

"There's a city council meeting in an hour. I'm going out there and I'm going to tell them exactly what I think about it."

Jake shook his head. "I've never known a city council to change their mind when money is a stake. I remember someone asked Will Rogers once if he prayed for Congress, and he said, 'No, I take a look at Congress and I pray for the country.' So watch yourself there. They could condemn this place, too."

"I'd like to see them try it!"

Jake laughed. "I've never seen you this mad before. You ought to stay mad. It improves your complexion."

Kate tossed her head and left. She got into the old Taurus, and once again, waited until it finally started, then followed the road through the sand to the Beach Highway. She was vaguely aware that a vehicle was coming from her left. She turned to her right to see if it was clear, but then suddenly she saw that the ancient van on her left wasn't stopping and was headed straight for her. There was no room to maneuver so she braced herself as the old van rammed straight into her left front fender.

It jolted her but she wasn't hurt. She got out of the car and stood there shaken. The vehicle was like nothing she had ever seen. It was white, apparently, but the paint was faded and scratched and had bumps all over it. The right front was now caved in, and she could see no driver.

Hearing sounds behind her, she turned to see Jake running for her, followed by Trouble. "What happened?"

"I was just waiting to get on the highway, and he swerved off and hit me."

"Well, is there a driver? I don't see anybody."

They started for the car, but at that moment a White Sands police car pulled up. They waited until Oralee Prather got out. Oralee was a short, stocky woman, hard as a rock, and with the reputation of being tougher on criminals than any police officer in the county. "What's happened here?" she said.

Kate's voice wasn't steady. "He ran right into me, Deputy. I was just waiting to pull out and he swerved."

"I don't see anybody," Oralee said. She went around to the driver's side and said, "I know this vehicle. Looks like the driver's been hurt," Oralee said. The window was down, and she reached in. Jake and Kate came to the other side and saw the driver hunched down over the steering wheel.

"It's an old man," Kate said.

Indeed, the driver was elderly and had a wild shock of white hair. His skin was cooked to the texture of leather and he had a huge bump already beginning to swell over his left eyebrow.

"I think he's hurt," Kate said. "We better send for an ambulance."

"Oh, it's just Ocie Plank," Oralee said in disgust.

"You know him?" Jake said.

"Every cop in Baldwin County knows him. Mobile and Pensacola, too. He's a chronic drunk. Now I've got to haul this old wreck of a van in and bring Ocie up before the judge."

She had pulled out her radio, when Jake said, "Wait a minute, Deputy."

"Wait for what?"

"The old man looks like he's in bad shape."

"Stick your head in that window. It smells like a distillery," Oralee said grimly.

Kate didn't understand Jake's concern. He usually kept out of such things.

"Look, the car's not hurt bad, and ours isn't either. The old man's got a bump. Don't arrest him. We'll take care of him."

Oralee Prather sniffed. "You think you're AA? You ain't gonna help him. Might as well get him into the jail. They'll dry him out there."

"I don't think that'd help him much if he's an alcoholic," Jake said. "But if you'll let me handle it, I'll stand for him."

"Suits me," Oralee said. "I ain't got time to be messing with trash like this, but you call me and give me a report as soon as he sobers up."

"I'll do that," Jake said quickly. The officer wrote up her report, then got into her car and drove away.

"Why'd you do that, Jake?"

"Look at his shoulder."

Kate leaned in and indeed the odor was almost unbearable. It was a mixture of sweat, unwashed clothes, and alcohol. She said, "It's a tattoo. Looks like a diamond."

"You see the word in the middle? It's almost faded out." Inside of the diamond was blue but in pale orange letters was the word Rangers.

"What's that, Jake?"

"It's a copy of the shoulder patch the Rangers wore."

"You mean the forest rangers?"

"No, not the forest rangers. He was in the second battalion of the Rangers that landed on Normandy. They had to scale a sheer cliff under heavy fire to get at some guns that were killing our guys coming in from the ships. Always admired the Rangers, especially the second battalion."

"Well, what are you going to do with him?"

"Take him in, sober him up, feed him." He opened the door. The man was wearing a pair of filthy khaki pants ragged at the cuff and no shoes. His grimy T-shirt had the sleeves cut off, and his head lolled as Jake pulled him out. Jake put him into a fireman's carry and looked at Kate as he walked. "You know, I've always wondered if I'd have been as tough as those guys who went up that cliff." He started walking toward the house.

"What'll we do about the cars?" Kate called after him.

"I'll take care of it later. They're fine where they are."

Kate rushed ahead to open the door, and Jake carried the old man easily into the house. "Where are you going to put him?"

"I'll put him up in my room until he comes to. You won't have to take care of him," he said.

Kate felt like she was looking at a Jake Novak that she hadn't seen before—and hadn't known existed.

Ten

Jake squeezed the orange but was keeping his eye on Jacques who, along with Cleo, was watching him. Jacques sat up straight at attention while Cleo lay down in a boneless manner.

"You're the most relaxed cat I ever saw, Cleo," Jake said. "The world would be a better place if human beings were relaxed like you are." He tossed the skin of the orange into a pile on the island and cut another orange in two. He put pressure on it, and at the same time kept his eyes locked with those of Jacques. He had a habit of speaking out loud even when there was no one around. It could be an unhealthy practice at times, but it didn't seem to him that he was in much danger from two cats.

"Well, Jacques, you'd like to get at me, wouldn't you?"

You bet I would, and I'm going to do it if you turn your back on me.

A crooked smile twisted Jake's lips, and he spoke defiantly, "One of these days you're going to buck into someone who's going to peel your potato."

Well, it won't be you, Intruder! Jacques's golden eyes were gleaming and steadily fixed on the man. He didn't turn to Cleo, but his whole body language spoke of his readiness to do battle.

I don't know why he had to come and live with us, Cleo. We had a pretty good thing going in Memphis before he intruded.

Cleo yawned, stretched luxuriously, and half shut her eyes. *Why do you insist on hating him? He's not so bad. He feeds you, doesn't he?*

Human beings are pitiful creatures. You have to teach them respect, especially this one. He thinks he's tough, but he's not.

He's a pretty tough person, I think, Jacques.

He's a softie, Cleo. He took that old bum in and let him sleep in his bed while he slept on the couch. What kind of a tough guy would do a thing like that?

He felt sorry for him. So do I. That old man's in bad shape.

You don't get anywhere in this world helping people. Look out for number one, that's my motto.

Jake knew that some unheard message was passing between the two cats, and as he tossed the orange peel on the growing stack, he shook his head woefully. "You know, you remind me of myself, Jacques. Looking out for number one. Always have to be the toughest one in the crowd. Let me tell you, old boy, it doesn't get you anywhere."

"Are you talking to yourself?"

Jake turned to see Kate who had come from her bedroom.

"No, I was talking to the cats."

Kate smiled. "Had a one-sided conversation, did you?"

"I get more sense in a conversation with them than with a lot of the people I come across. What do you want for breakfast?"

"I'd love to have some French toast."

Jake nodded and scooped the orange peels into a plastic bag, twisted the top, and dropped them into the garbage. Going to the refrigerator, he began pulling things together. He didn't speak for a time, and finally Kate said, "I better go get Jeremy." She went to his room and to her surprise he was already up and dressed. "Breakfast ready?" he asked.

"Jake's fixing French toast."

The two of them went to the kitchen, and Jeremy walked over to where Jake was dropping slices of soaked bread onto a grill. "Why do they call it French toast?"

Jake grunted. "Why don't you go ask Rhiannon? She seems to know everything."

Jake finished making the French toast, and the three of them sat down at the dining table. As always, Kate asked the blessing. When his mother finished the prayer, Jeremy plunged in, cutting his slice of toast into six large portions. He sloshed the pure maple syrup over it until they were floating. He forked a piece and crammed it into his mouth. "Why didn't you let the police take that old man away?"

Jake looked at Jeremy as the boy stuffed another massive mouthful of French toast into his mouth. "I hope when I'm old and washed up, Slick, maybe somebody will help me out."

Kate nodded. "It was a good thing for you to do, Jake. Maybe we can get him into a rehabilitation program."

"Maybe he doesn't want rehab," Jake said. He sliced his toast up into geometrically perfect squares and began to eat them carefully. For a big man with a big appetite, he ate in a manner that was almost dainty.

"Well, we can't keep him here permanently, can we?" Kate said.

Jake chewed his food thoughtfully. "I don't know what we can do. I'll start by taking him some orange juice. With the hangover he's bound to have, his mouth must be as dry as the Sahara Desert."

Taking the freshly squeezed juice in the large pitcher, he went upstairs.

Jeremy was puzzled. "I don't understand Jake. He's inconsistent."

"I don't understand him either."

Jeremy suddenly looked at his mother. "Mom, do you think you'll ever marry again?"

Taken aback by the question, Kate stared at Jeremy. "Why are you asking that?"

"I just wondered."

"It's a strange thing for you to wonder."

"No, it's not. It's natural. You're young enough to get married and have more babies."

"I haven't been thinking about things like that."

"You think Jake would make a good husband?"

"He'd make a terrible husband!"

"I don't think so. He's a good housekeeper and he can cook."

"Then he should get a job as a maid or open a restaurant." Kate was disturbed by Jeremy's question. "Finish up now. Let's get to church."

● ● ●

The computer seemed to stare back at Jake with a malevolent air. He took his glance from it and looked down at Trouble, who was as close as he could get, sitting beside his chair. The big pit bull was panting slightly, his tongue lolling out like a red necktie.

"Why don't you go watch somebody else make a mess?" Jake admonished him.

"Wuff!"

"Wuff, that's all you ever say." Jake turned back, put his hands on the keys, and waited for something to come. He was still waiting when a squeaky voice, rather hoarse, spoke up. "What time is it?"

Jake quickly turned and got up out of his chair. He walked over to the bed and looked down at Ocie Plank, who was rousing from his sleep. "It's about ten o'clock," Jake said.

"Who are you?"

"I'm Jake Novak."

Ocie looked around and seemed to be disoriented. He reached up and touched his head where the huge bump had shrunken somewhat. "Was it you that hit me?"

"No, you had a car accident. Don't you remember?"

"It's starting to come back to me. Got anything to drink?"

"Right here." Jake poured a glass full of the orange juice and handed it to the old man. Ocie lifted his head and glared at it. "What's that?"

"Fresh squeezed orange juice. Good for a hangover."

"When I say you got anything to drink, I don't mean OJ."

"The deputy said your name is Ocie Plank."

"What deputy?"

"The one that was going to take you to jail until I talked her out of it."

The old man struggled to get to a sitting position. He reached out and took the glass and stared at the orange juice as if it were some exotic concoction. He looked old and worn out, but there was still strength in his large hands. Jake noticed that they were a working man's hands, callused and strong, but the rest of Ocie Plank was lean and thin. Jake assumed it was because he drank too much and neglected eating.

"What about my van?"

"I moved it beside the house. Has some damage to the front end."

The old man stared at Jake. He had a hawklike visage and light blue eyes with plenty of red in the whites.

He drank the orange juice, shuddered, and said, "Terrible stuff." He looked up at Jake and tried to focus. "I'm seeing double. Are there two of you?"

"You got a concussion. Tell you what. How about you get cleaned up?"

"Who made you my keeper?"

"It was me or a jail cell. I'm going to make you something light to eat. You think you can take a shower?"

"I can do anything I need to," Plank said aggressively.

"You need to phone anybody?"

"A liquor store. Have a fifth of vodka sent out."

"I'm talking about family."

"Got no family. What'd you say your name was?"

"Jake Novak."

"Well, Novak, that vehicle is my home, and I'd appreciate it if you would go get me some clean clothes out of it. Of course, there ain't no clean clothes in it." The old man suddenly threw the sheet back and swung his feet over the bed. He tried to stand up and swayed so that Jake caught him.

"Maybe you'd better hold off on the shower," Jake said. "I'll bring you something to eat."

"Rather have something to drink."

"Can't help you there unless you want more orange juice."

Jake went downstairs and made some scrambled eggs and toast. He picked up a jar of fresh apple jelly he had bought at a fruit stand and went back. To his surprise he found that the old man was clean and wearing some of his clothes. Plank grinned at him. "You're a big fella. You got some safety pins to pin these clothes of yours on with?"

"I can find some. Here, eat this."

Jake put the tray down and watched as Ocie Plank devoured the meal noisily. *There's nothing wrong with his appetite.* Finally the old man leaned back and looked at Jake steadily. "I guess I'll be moving on."

"You can't do that until we do some work on your van. The fender's pushed in against the front tire, and I think it knocked the front end out of alignment. Get some rest. We'll see about fixing it."

Ocie stared at Jake and then nodded. He made his way back to the bed, plopped down on it with a sigh. He closed his eyes, and Jake thought he was passed out, but then the old man opened them again. "You the local do-gooder or what, Novak? You make a living taking care of drunks?"

Jake looked down at Plank. "You were in the Rangers?"

"How'd you know that—oh, my tattoo. Yeah, that was sure a while back. Why you asking?"

"I don't guess you were in that bunch that climbed the hill at Omaha?"

"Yeah, I went up that hill. You read about that?"

"I don't know if I could have done that, Plank."

Plank stared at Jake. He seemed puzzled. His face was ravaged by drink, his cheeks sunk in and hollowed, but there was still some hint of the strength that must have been his as a young man. "Why you asking about that time?"

Jake hesitated and then said, "My dad was in the second Rangers battalion."

"That so?" Plank was surprised. "What was his name?"

"Tomik Novak."

"Tom Novak?"

"That's what people called him. You know him?"

Disbelief washed across Ocie Plank's face. "Sure, I did. We went up that cliff together. Most of us didn't make it. Is Tom still alive?"

"No, he died when I was about ten."

"He was a good soldier, Novak."

"I'd like to hear more about that time. He would never talk about it."

A crafty look came over Plank's face. "Tell you what. You get me some vodka, and I'll tell you about it."

"You don't need to be drinking with a concussion."

Ocie Plank grinned broadly. "If the enemy couldn't kill me with all they threw at us going up that mountain, a little vodka won't." Ocie studied Jake's face. "You look like your old man."

"You still remember him, Ocie, after all this time?"

A strange expression lit the old man's eyes. "I wish I could forget it all, but I never will. Now go get that booze for me!"

● ● ●

Whenever the weather was right, the membership of the Seaside Chapel met in the large pavilion right on the beach. A great many of the visitors who came down to the coast for the swimming and fishing made their way there for the Sunday morning services. As Kate pulled up into the parking area, Jeremy said, "Looks like they've finished filming here. All the trucks and stuff are gone."

"They've moved over to the Blue House, I heard," Kate said.

"Hey, there's that Englishman's Rolls Royce," Jeremy pointed.

Kate parked the Taurus and got out, surprised to see Beverly there at all. He was apparently waiting for her, and he got out of the big car and came over to greet her with a smile. He was, as usual, dressed in impeccable fashion. He wore a pair of light gray trousers, a soft royal blue cashmere sport coat, and a light blue shirt set off with a pearl gray silk tie.

"I'm surprised to see you, Bev," Kate greeted him.

"Good morning," Beverly said cheerfully. He was freshly shaved and his cheeks glowed with health. "How are you today, Jeremy?"

"Okay." Jeremy was staring at the Englishman with wide open eyes. "Do you go to church every Sunday?"

"As a matter of fact I did back in England, but since I've come to this country your wild ways have made a heathen out of me. Truthfully, this is the first time I've been to church in a very long time."

"Well, what made you come?" Jeremy asked bluntly.

"Just a wild notion, I guess." Beverly turned and looked at the people gathered in the pavilion with a puzzled look on his face. "This is a strange church."

"We meet in the chapel when the weather's bad or the pavilion's not available, but most people prefer to be out by the beach."

"Well, I could certainly use a good sermon," Bev said.

They were walking toward the crowd, and Kate asked, "Are you a Christian, Bev?"

Beverly suddenly laughed aloud. "That's coming right out with it. But, to tell you the truth, Kate, I haven't the foggiest. All I can tell you is that I'm in good standing with the Church of England."

"What does that mean?" Kate questioned.

"It means I was baptized when I was a tiny chap, and I've made duty appearances and contributed hunks of money to the church." He studied her for a moment and shook his head. "But sometimes I think there's more to being a Christian then having a few drops of water spilled on your face when you're a week old."

"You're right about that," Kate agreed. "Come on, I want you to meet the pastor." She led him inside the pavilion and over to Elvis Bates, who was shaking hands with visitors.

Kate said, "Pastor Bates, I'd like you to meet Beverly Devon-Hunt."

"Glad to know you, Mr. Devon-Hunt." Bates was wearing a pair of blue jeans, as usual, and a blue-and-white striped polo shirt, which made his bright blue eyes stand out even more. "Are you visiting?" the pastor asked.

"I'm just a floater, I guess, Pastor."

"Come along, Bev. They'll be starting soon." Kate led him and Jeremy to a seat.

Kate noticed that many of the younger women in the congregation, and some not so young, had their eyes fixed on the tall, attractive Englishman. She shot a quick glance at Bev but saw that he was paying no attention. His gaze was taking everything in. "It's quite informal."

"Yes, it is."

"Very different from the churches I've been to. Everyone had to wear a certain type of clothing and behave in a certain way."

"We've never been to a church like that," Jeremy remarked.

The three chatted for a moment and then she found herself telling Beverly about Ocie Plank. "...so Jake insisted on giving him his bed. I'm going to try and get him some professional help."

"I would never have expected Jake Novak to be so concerned about derelicts, but you know him better than I."

"Yeah, just like I was saying, Mom," Jeremy put in, "Jake's unpredictable."

"He puzzles me, actually," Kate admitted. "He's got a tender side, but he's scared to death that someone will find out about it."

At that point the service began, and for the next several minutes they sang choruses, which were printed on a small sheet of paper. Beverly had a good, clear tenor voice, but he didn't know any of the songs. Once he leaned to the side and whispered, "The churches I've attended always had a trained choir and professional musicians."

"Do you like it here?"

"If I knew the words I might."

Finally Elvis Bates got up to preach, and he held a Bible in his right hand and greeted all the visitors. He gave a rousing sermon from the twelfth chapter of Mark. Elvis finished his message by inviting people to come to the front, where they had put up a tall cross, and spend as much time as they wanted. "Maybe there are some of you who don't know the Lord Jesus as Savior. Now this day, this moment, is a good time to meet Him."

The congregation began to sing, and people began to stream up to the front. Soon the whole area was covered with people kneeling at the foot of the cross. Some were weeping, some seemed to be filled with joy. For a while Kate stole glances at Beverly. He seemed to be totally amazed at what he was seeing.

Kate nodded, and the three of them left the pavilion. Beverly looked back. "How long will they stay there?"

"Some of them stay for an hour sometimes," Kate told him.

"I've never seen anything like it." Beverly shook his head.

"Churches in England don't do that?" Jeremy asked.

"No...it's much more...formal, I suppose you would say. These people don't seem to be afraid to admit they actually need religion."

"They don't need religion, Bev. They need Jesus. They know they can't meet all of their own needs themselves. Haven't you ever felt that way?"

Beverly Devon-Hunt was silent for a moment. They had reached her car, and Jeremy had gotten in. The two stood alone outside the car.

Beverly chewed his lower lip. Usually he was full of wit and laughter, but now he seemed serious. "I guess I've always had the means to pay for what I wanted. Never really needed anything that I couldn't get."

"But what if you needed something that money couldn't buy?"

"You mean like if I were sick?"

"Of course. But money can't buy friendship either—not true friendship, anyway. Money can't make you a better person, and it can't make you happy. Haven't you ever thought about that?"

"A person in my position doesn't have much reason to think those things, Kate. Money has indeed seemed to buy everything I needed."

"But, Bev, the one thing you can't buy is salvation. You know, you remind me of the rich young ruler."

"Who's that?"

"It's found in the Gospels." She opened her Bible and read to him about the rich young ruler who came to Jesus.

"Jesus commanded him to sell all that he had and follow Him. And he failed the test, Bev. The Bible says he went away sad, because he had great possessions. That's when Jesus made an astonishing statement. He said it would be difficult, almost impossible, for rich people to get to heaven."

Beverly shook his head. "I'm confused, Kate. You think it's sinful to have money?"

"No, but it's sinful to love your money above all else. When you trust your money to take care of everything, you naturally don't think you need God. Your God is money. You can take care of all your needs by writing a check." Kate shook her head. "You can't write a check and buy your way into heaven."

Beverly shook his shoulders in a strange, dissatisfied manner as if shrugging a weight off him.

"I guess I'll have to think about this." He gave a brief wave and opened his car door. "I'll see you later."

Kate watched him go and then got into the car, where Jeremy was also watching Bev leave. "What's the matter with Mr. Devon-Hunt?"

Kate started the engine of the old Taurus. It belched and gave an unhealthy cough and hit on five of the six cylinders. "I guess," she said slowly, "he's uncomfortable with the idea that there are some things money won't buy."

"Sheesh, Mom," Jeremy said. "Even I knew that."

Eleven

Kate heard banging coming from outside and walked over to look out the window. She could see Jake's legs sticking out from under the Volkswagen van, and she shook her head, puzzled over Jake's interest in Ocie Plank. She had seen Jake at what she thought was his worst, and his barely hidden violence had flared out. She had seen hints of gentleness, especially toward Jeremy, but this was somehow different. Of all the unlovely human beings she had ever seen, Ocie Plank would have to lead the pack.

She waited for the clanging to stop, but it had turned into a cadence, and she sensed that Jake wouldn't be finished anytime soon. She finally decided to take some fruit up to the old man and see if she could get to know him a little better. She piled apples, oranges, and bananas in a bowl and made her way up the stairs. When she entered Jake's domain, she saw Plank sitting in a chair staring out the window at the Gulf while Cleo and Jacques sat on the floor eying him.

"That's a pretty view, isn't it?"

The old man turned and studied her for a moment. He was tall, at least six feet, and straight as an arrow. He had a beak of a nose and badly fitting false teeth. His hands were in his lap, and she noticed that they seemed like the hands of a much younger man and looked very strong.

"How are you feeling, Mr. Plank?"

"Just call me Ocie." He turned to look at her, then his eyes fell on Cleo and Jacques. "Is that two cats or four?"

"Just two. Guess you're still seeing double, huh?" She managed a brief chuckle. "I brought you some fruit."

She put the fruit on the table next to him, and he picked up an orange. It looked small in his huge hand. "You need anything else?" she asked.

"A fifth of vodka."

"Sorry, Ocie, I can't give you that."

Plank looked at the two cats steadily. "That black one, he's a bad one, isn't he?"

"He can be pretty mean sometimes. We call him Jacques the Ripper."

Ocie grinned and studied the cat more closely. "He sounds like my kind of cat."

"Isn't there someone we need to write or call to let them know you're all right?"

"Nope."

"Don't you have any family?"

"They gave up on me a long time ago."

"Well, it's never too late to mend your fences."

"Yes, it is."

Taking a deep breath, Kate said as firmly as she could, "God can change things. He can give you a new life."

"Sure, He can," Plank nodded vigorously. "I believe that."

"Are you a Christian then?"

"Nope, not yet, but I'm going to be in God's good time."

The answer puzzled Kate. "What do you mean, 'in God's good time'?"

"Well, God's got a time for everything. He's got a time for me to get converted, I reckon."

"The time is when you repent and call on Jesus."

"Not for us hyper-Calvinists."

This sounded like the height of folly to Kate. "So you're a Calvinist but not a Christian?"

"Well, I'll tell you one thing, missy, I ain't a Christian yet, but there are some things I just won't do. I got my standards."

"Like what?"

"Well, like I'll steal from Wal-Mart but not from a mom-and-pop store."

"How do you justify that? Stealing's stealing."

"No, it ain't. You take that Wal-Mart. What's a loaf of bread to them? Nothing. But you take a small store. Every penny counts. I wouldn't hurt someone like that."

Kate rolled her eyes and changed the subject. "I understand you were in the army back in World War II."

"The Rangers."

"You must be very proud of that."

"It was a hard life, but I've had a hard life since." Kate was intrigued by the man, but she couldn't think of anything to say to him. He looked at her with what appeared surprisingly like genuine interest. "What about you? You got a family?"

"Just my son—you met him. Jeremy."

"Good-looking kid. What about your husband?"

"He died a few years ago."

"You brought up here on the Gulf Coast?"

"No, we were living in Memphis, and then we inherited this house." She went on quickly to explain how they had to live in the house, and she saw he was grinning lewdly at her. "You got somethin' goin' with the big guy?"

"No, I don't." Her face flushed.

"I bet he's tried though."

"No, he hasn't. I don't want to talk about it."

"I knew his old man—Tom Novak. He was a good soldier. Maybe you better latch onto him. He looks like a guy a woman could tie to."

The conversation had gotten too personal for Kate. She rose and gestured to the cats as she went to the door.

"Well, enjoy the fruit." Without looking again at the old man, she went back down the stairs and the cats followed her. She went outside, and Jake came out from beneath the car.

"It's time for me to go to the set, Jake. They're going to film inside the Blue House, and Bjorn needs the cats to be there."

Novak straightened up and studied her. He had stripped down to a pair of faded shorts and was covered with dirt and grease. "Aren't you getting tired of that movie nonsense?"

"Yes, I suppose I am. Some people would love to get to hang out on a movie set all day, but I'm finding it pretty boring." She walked over to the old Volkswagen van and studied it. "This thing is a mess. Are you going to be able to fix it?"

"I guess I can get it to running."

"Ocie's in bad shape. He wanted me to give him some vodka."

"I bet you ran right out and bought some, didn't you?"

"Of course I did. Got some for myself, too," she said with a straight face, then added, "Jake, he's going to kill himself drinking."

"Well, we all die of something. Here, I want to show you something." He stepped into the Volkswagen and came out with a small, thin box. "Look at this," he said.

Kate took the box and opened it. She stared down at the gold medal with a ribbon attached to it. "What is this?"

"That's the Medal of Honor, the highest decoration a person can get." He reached down and touched the medal gently with his forefinger. "Ocie was quite a man."

Kate was fascinated. "You admire him, don't you, even though he's in such bad shape?"

"Sure do."

"Well, maybe we can help him, Jake. You have any ideas?"

Jake seemed to brighten up. "I thought about fixing up that room we've been using down here for storage."

"You mean keep him on a permanent basis?"

"Don't know. All we can do is try."

"All right. I'll help you fix it up. You tell me what we'll need, and I'll pick it up when I'm in town."

Jake gave her a surprised look. "I didn't think you'd take to the idea of having a drunk living with us."

"He doesn't have to stay a drunk. I think he's got a family somewhere who's given up on him. Oh, how I'd love to see a miracle and see that family take him back in."

Jake studied her as if she were an alien from another planet even. "You really believe that, don't you?"

"Believe what?"

"In miracles. That things can turn out all right."

"Yes, I do."

He pulled a handkerchief out of his back pocket and wiped his hands on it, not looking at her for a moment. When he did look up, he said, "I'm glad you do, Mary Katherine. I hope you always do."

● ● ●

Kate had taken the two cats down to the Blue House, where the movie was being filmed, and now she stood watching as they prowled around the room sniffing and exploring their new territory. Dontelle was on his hands and knees with a handheld camera and was moving closer to Jacques.

"Be careful, Dontelle," Kate warned.

"Don't worry. I—" Jacques made one swift move, almost too fast for the eye to see, and swiped at Dontelle's hand. He caught the camera instead and nearly knocked it out of the cameraman's hands.

"Boy, look at the reflexes on that cat," Bjorn said. "If I had reflexes like that, I'd get rich in any sport I wanted."

Dontelle stood up and backed away from the big cat. He took a few moments to adjust the camera and resumed filming. Finally Bjorn said, "Cut. We got it. That's good stuff."

Just then a production assistant said to Bjorn, "Erik and Avis are ready for the next scene."

"Send them in five," said Bjorn. "I just wanna fine-tune the lighting."

Kate asked, "Should I put the cats back in their carriers?"

"No," Bjorn said. "Just keep an eye on them, okay? I want them to be comfortable here for the next scene."

Kate watched the crew members scurry around making adjustments to lights, camera positions, and furniture. They worked like a well-oiled machine. She marveled at how many people it took to make a movie.

Erik and Avis appeared in the doorway, and Bjorn called out, "All right, everyone. We're gonna go with this next scene. It's the first one with you two—" he pointed at Avis and Erik—"and the animals."

"I'm not getting close to that black panther," Erik said. "He's already left his mark on me. The mark of the beast."

"You're just a wuss, Erik," Avis said. She walked straight to where Jacques was sitting. She knelt and reached out, and Jacques seemed surprisingly passive. Avis began to stroke him.

"Watch out, Avis," Erik murmured.

Avis sat on the floor. She reached out and drew Jacques into her lap, and when she held him close and stroked his black fur, his eyes closed with pleasure.

What are you doing? Cleo wanted to know.

I'm making friends. That's what you're always trying to get me to do.

You clawed that man and now you're letting that woman pet you?

She's the only one around here who's worth anything. She's not scared of me like the rest of them. Haven't you noticed how they watch me all the time?

They're afraid you're going to claw their eyeballs out!

I like this movie-making business. I may go into it as a steady thing.

Kate watched for a time, shocked that Jacques allowed the woman to touch him. It offended her somewhat, for she hated to admit it, but she was rather proud of the fact that she was the only one who could handle Jacques.

● ● ●

The scene had to be shot several times, and Cleo kept wanting to go to Kate. Bjorn had asked her to leave the room for a while, hoping it would help the cats to cooperate. She'd left and begun to explore the huge house. It had four stories, and each one had long corridors with innumerable bedrooms—more like a hotel, she thought. She found a workout room on the second floor and a bar overlooking the Gulf on the third.

When she got up to the fourth floor, she heard voices. It was clearly Aaron Tobin speaking to a woman. She listened for a moment and thought the woman was Lexi Colby. She could hear anger in Lexi's voice.

"You promised me the lead in this picture, Aaron."

"I know I did, but the backers wanted Avis. You know how they are. They put up the money. They need someone who can guarantee the picture will open."

"You could have talked them into using me."

"Look, Lexi, we had a good time together, but—"

"Admit it, Aaron. You got what you wanted from me, and you're done."

"Baby, that's not the way it is—"

"Don't 'baby' me. I'm not stupid. I know what's going on here."

There was a silence, and Kate turned away, back down the hallway. But she could still hear their voices as she retreated. Tobin began to talk soothingly. "Look, the next picture I make you'll be the star."

"I wanted this one, Aaron. It's not too late. You can replace Avis with me."

"We've already shot too many scenes. The only way I could put you in Avis's role is if she walked away."

"Or if she was dead."

"Hey," Aaron said with a short laugh. "Don't talk like that."

Kate hurried down the stairs and found that the crew was finished shooting the scene with the cats.

"Better take them home," Bjorn said. "I'll let you know if we're going to need them again. It's tough working with cats, isn't it? Can't make them do anything."

"I saw a trained cat once," Dontelle said. "It was in a circus. This cat was on a platform about thirty feet up, and his trainer stood at the bottom with a big pillow. When he gave a signal, the cat jumped right off, sailed down, and hit the pillow. The dangdest thing I ever saw in my life."

You wouldn't catch me doing anything like that, Cleo.

Of course you wouldn't, Jacques. You've got more sense than that. That cat must have been slow in the head.

Kate put the cats in the carriers, and Thad Boland appeared. "Let me help you with that, Kate." He picked up the cage containing Jacques.

"Well, thanks, Bo. They're pretty heavy." She picked up the other carrier. "Cleo's ten pounds lighter, I guess."

The two left the beach house, and as they walked toward her car, he asked, "So, what do you think of the movie business?"

"Well, there's certainly a lot of ego involved."

"You got that right."

"Isn't it unusual for so many members of the cast to hate the producer?"

Bo laughed. "You've been keeping your eyes open. Yeah, it's unusual. People generally get along pretty well in this business. But Tobin—his ego is gigantic, even by Hollywood standards. He likes running over people."

"Why?"

"Who knows? He's not happy unless he's making somebody miserable. If he can't intimidate you, he fires you."

"Even you?"

Bo gave her a surprised look. "No, he wouldn't dare fire me. We've got too much history. And don't tell anybody—" Bo took on a conspiratorial tone, "but I'm one of the few people who could sink him if he got on my bad side."

"I'm surprised that someone hasn't tried to hurt him, or even shoot him," she said.

"They have. That's what he keeps me for." He lifted the side of his shirt slightly, giving her a quick glimpse of a gun. When they reached her car, he helped her load the cats, then stepped back and held the door open for her. "You tight with Novak?" he asked.

"We're friends," Kate answered. "Why?"

"Tell him I'll be ready for him the next time."

"I hope there's not a next time, Bo," Kate said as she got into the car.

He stared at her curiously. "You really are that innocent, aren't you." It wasn't a question. He shut her car door and stepped back.

She started the car, still looking at Bo, but he was already walking back to the house. As she drove away, her mind was full of all she'd seen and heard that day. Her stomach felt unsettled.

● ● ●

Kate set the cats free and opened the front door. Immediately she smelled a rich aroma of spices, and thought, *Jake's fixing a Mexican dinner.*

When she walked inside Jeremy was sitting at the table listening to Ocie Plank. Plank was wearing his own clothing now and looked much better.

Jeremy looked up. "Mom, did you know Ocie was an oil rig firefighter just like John Wayne in that movie?"

"Don't you mean 'Mr. Plank'?" Kate said in her best "mom" tone of voice.

"Aw, let 'im call me by my name," the old man said. "Ocie's fine."

"Is that really your name?" Novak asked.

"As a matter of fact, it isn't. I don't like my real name much."

"What is it, Mr. Plank?" Jeremy asked.

"Oceola Constantine Plank. Ain't that a kick in the head? I don't tell most people what it is. People called me by my initials—O. C.—and then it got to be Ocie."

Jake began putting platters of food in front of them. "All right, everyone, if you don't like Mexican food, you might as well leave." He finished loading down the table, and then sat. "I guess it's your turn to give the blessing, Mary Katherine. It always is."

Kate expressed a quick thanks, and then Ocie pulled a bottle out of his pocket. It was brown and looked like a medicine bottle. He grinned broadly, saying, "I brought some of my special hot sauce."

He took the cap off and sprinkled a dark red fluid over his enchilada.

"Let me try some of that," Jake said.

"No, boy, it takes a real man to use my sauce. You know," he said thoughtfully, "your dad loved my hot sauce. I carried a bottle with me when we went in on D-Day. We put it on our C rations. Killed the taste, sort of."

Jake took the bottle and sprinkled his enchilada. "Can't get a sauce too hot, I always say."

"Well, Novak, don't say I didn't warn you. This sauce should have a skull and crossbones on it. It'll set you on fire." Ocie took a big bite of his enchilada and watched with a grin as Jake cut off a portion and stuffed it in his mouth.

Jake's reaction was instantaneous. His face suddenly turned a fiery red, his eyes began to water, and Ocie yelped gleefully, "Fire in the hole—fire in the hole!"

Jake grabbed a large glass of water and began pouring it down his throat. Finally gasping, he said, "What is that stuff?"

"It's hot sauce for a real man, Novak. Maybe one of these days you'll be tough enough to take it."

Jake was forced to throw his enchilada away and start all over again. He cast baleful looks at Ocie from time to time and drank copiously from his water glass.

A few minutes into the meal, the phone rang and Kate got up to answer it. A moment later, she handed the phone to Jake. "It's Avis."

Jake took the phone and walked into the other room. They could hear him speaking in a low voice but couldn't make out any of the words. Kate tried not to listen as she continued eating her meal.

Ocie ate heartily, and finally he shoved his plate back and said, "Well, I'm going to have to leave pretty soon, I reckon."

"You're welcome to stay," Kate said. "We're fixing up a place here for you."

Ocie turned his glance at her. He looked like a bird of prey with his hooked nose and deep-set piercing eyes. "If I stay, I guess you'll try to convert me."

Kate flushed and looked down at her plate, for that was exactly what she had on her mind. Ocie laughed and said, "You just fly right at it, you hear? Nothing would make me happier. Sooner or later God's going to catch up with me. You can bet on that."

Jake came back into the room and sat down to finish his meal, without saying a word.

Twelve

The task of transforming a storage room into a bedroom turned out to be more work than Kate had anticipated. The room was approximately twelve feet square, but Jake had managed to add a half bath, walling it in and putting up a door. They put in a twin bed that fit along one wall, and desk and chest of drawers completed the furniture.

"This is as good as a Motel 6," Ocie declared as he stood in the doorway. Kate was finishing the cleanup and picking up Jake's tools.

"That air conditioner ought to keep you cool," she said.

"Be plum luxurious. That vehicle of mine was like sleeping in a coffin."

Kate hesitated and then said, "Jeremy's looking forward to that fishing trip with you and Captain Marsh."

"Boy misses his daddy."

"Yes," Kate said, "he does."

"Reckon you miss him, too, don't you, honey?"

Kate shot a quick glance at Ocie. He had a way of worming things out of people that made her suspicious. "I get a little lonely sometimes."

"I was married once to a Mexican woman. I lived down on the border at Brownsville, Texas. Went out on the shrimp boats. We had a pretty good thing going."

"What happened?"

"Oh, she run off with an aluminum siding salesman. Haven't heard of her for years. You know, the Bible says he who finds a wife, finds a good thing." Ocie cackled and shook his head. "I don't reckon the Bible was talkin' bout us."

Novak had put three windows in the small room so Ocie could have plenty of light. Kate got a glimpse of a car pulling up and was surprised to see Avis Marlow get out. She watched silently, aware that Ocie had come up behind her. "Who's that?" he asked.

"She's a movie star. Her name's Avis Marlow."

"She come to see you?"

"I doubt it." For a moment Kate hesitated, and then the words came out in a rather forced fashion. "She and Jake were—" She couldn't think of the word and finally said, "She and Jake were close at one time."

"Close? Is that the way you put it? You mean they was living together?"

"I don't know." She turned and said, "She left him, and it hurt him so bad he's never trusted another woman since."

"Well, that can happen."

They watched as Jake came out of the house with Avis, and the two got in her red sports car.

"I can't believe Jake's going with her. You should have seen him the other day when he first saw her—he was a mess."

"He don't look a mess right now," Ocie observed as the sports car drove away.

"He's making a mistake going out with her."

"Sometimes a man has to learn the hard way, especially about women. The Scripture says, 'For the lips of a strange woman drop as a honeycomb, and her mouth is smoother than oil. But her end is bitter as wormwood, sharp as a two-edged sword. Her feet go down to death; her steps take hold on hell.'" He shrugged and said, "That's from Proverbs, the fifth chapter, verses three through five."

"You know a lot of the Bible, Ocie, for a man who's not a Christian."

"Well, I'm getting ready to become a Christian. I've been studying the Bible a long time, and I know what goes into being a Christian. It just hasn't been my time yet, but it will be one of these days."

"That's dangerous, Ocie. What if you die before you accept Christ?"

"I'm not going to die until I get converted. I had a dream once a long time ago. I dreamed about getting saved, and I believe it's of the Lord."

"Dreams aren't always reliable." Kate was looking out the window thoughtfully. "I wish he'd stay away from that woman. She's going to hurt him again just like she did before."

● ● ●

The club was crowded and filled with smoke. Avis leaned in close to Jake as they sat at the bar with drinks in front of them. Her proximity and her scent brought old memories trooping into his mind. "I don't know why I agreed to come out with you," he said. "Nothing can come of it."

"We're just having a drink, Jake. We need to catch up. I can't believe I'd run into you in this backwater town anyway. How you end up here?"

She listened as Jake gave her a brief sketch of his life.

"So you and Kate have to share the house to get the inheritance."

"Yes, that's right."

"Pretty convenient, isn't it? She's cute. Is she your type?"

"There's nothing like that going on." Jake's voice was flat.

Avis got out a cigarette and put it between her lips, then looked at Jake. Obligingly he picked up the lighter lying on the bar and lit her up. There was something extremely sultry about the way she was looking at him. "I've missed our good times, Jake."

Jake looked away. "Are you saying we need to start up where we left off?"

"Why not?"

"You can't start things like that again."

"We could do it, Jake."

She put her hand on his cheek, and Jake almost flinched. She had smooth hands. Everything about her was smooth. It was her beauty that had attracted him at first, and she was more beautiful now than she had been. "Don't you ever think about the times we had, Jake?"

"No."

Avis laughed. "You're a liar, Jake."

Jake took a drink of his beer and paused for a moment, then said quietly, "I wasn't the one who walked away."

"Maybe I made a mistake," she purred.

"Some mistakes are irreversible." He was determined not to fall prey to her seduction.

Avis put her hand on his. "We could do it. It would be different this time, Jake. I've learned my lesson. I wanted a career and money and success, and when I got it I realized something was missing. I was wrong. You and I are meant to be together."

"Nice to know that now. It comforts me a lot."

"Jake, don't be bitter. It's not like you. I've got all I want now," she said sadly, "except a good man."

Jake felt himself being drawn to her exactly as he had been years before. She had something in her that pulled on a man, and that thing, whatever it was, came across on the screen. That was the success of her movies. He had seen them all, although he hadn't told her about that. He looked at her now, saw her flawless face, the shape of her shoulders, and the shine of her hair, and he remembered the great wave of warmth that had come from her lips, surrounding him with comfort and sweetness. It mingled with the heartbreak and discontent of the last few years.

Avis was watching him. Her expression grew smooth and tight, and a sudden, sharp breath lifted her breast. "Jake, we only get one trip around, as the old saying goes. Just give me a chance. We can have something again just like we did before."

Jake's lips curled with disdain. He was disgusted with himself for wanting her, but he couldn't deny what was in him. His contempt for himself came through in his words. "I suppose you're offering me a job as your gofer. I could go get drinks and open doors for you."

"Don't be cynical, Jake."

Jake Novak suddenly felt himself sinking, his defenses eroding away, his desires wanting to take over. He shook his head, slapped a twenty on the bar, and stood. "I've had enough of this."

She followed him outside. "All right, Jake. Have it your way. I'll take you home."

They went to her car and got in. She put the key in the ignition but didn't turn it.

She turned to him and whispered, "Jake, we had something special. We can have it again."

Jake didn't answer. He had the sensation of a man who was desperately hanging on to something and yet felt it slipping from his grasp. Ever since he and Avis had separated he had had an emptiness that nothing could fill, and now here it was right before him. He knew he was a fool for even thinking about it, but as she moved closer to him, the aroma of her perfume and the touch of her smooth body pressing against him seemed to sweep everything out except the knowledge of her presence.

She put her hand on his cheek and pulled his head around. Jake saw the heaviness of her lips and the pleading in her eyes, and something broke within him. He put his arms around her and drew her close. He knew it was what she wanted, and he kissed her hard and rough. He felt the luxury of it, and knew she did too, but he knew it couldn't continue. It took every bit of strength he had to let go of her and pull back. "You'd better drive me home, Avis."

Avis smiled. He could see that subtle predatory look about her, and he knew she was thinking she'd gotten to him. He silently cursed himself for his weakness.

"I missed you, Jake," she said as she started the car. She waited but he didn't answer. He stared straight ahead, fists clenched and jaw set, all the way back to the house.

● ● ●

The day had dawned bright with not a cloud in the sky, but in this room the opaque blinds were drawn, not letting in a speck of light. The only illumination was a small, squat lamp on the dressing table that shed a feeble beam.

The key in the door made a clicking sound, and then the door swung open. A woman came in and for a moment she stood in the center of the room getting her bearings, then turned. Leaving the door to the room open, she moved over to the closet and pulled open the doors. The closet was lined with dresses and coats, and she began to sift through them, leaning forward to see in the dimness of the light.

She didn't hear the footsteps of the figure that entered and came toward her. She was suddenly aware of a dim presence behind her, and her last thought was that someone had entered the room. She started to turn, but before she could make a move, something struck her on the back of the head. The impact of it was a single, blinding flash of light, and she knew nothing more as she fell forward into the garments.

● ● ●

Enola held Cleo in her lap and stroked her fur. "She's all right, Kate. Just a hair-ball problem. I'll leave medication, and that ought to take care of it." She stroked Cleo and got to her feet, putting the cat down. "Better not let her go in for any movie making."

"No, I hadn't planned to. I think they got all the background shots of both cats."

Enola was watching Kate with a peculiar light in her eyes. She was an astute woman, and now as she studied Kate, who somehow looked troubled, a sudden insight came to her. "Are you worried about Jake going out with Avis?"

"No. He's a grown man, Enola."

"Yes—a grown man you care about."

Kate had been thinking about Jake and Avis a great deal. She had grown to have some sort of protective instinct over Jake Novak. The two of them sometimes fought like cats and dogs, and yet Jake had filled a void in her life. He wasn't a husband, but he was there. At times when they sat together alone out on the deck, there had been some sort of closeness that had brought nostalgia to Kate. But she tried not to think about it. "He's going to get hurt, Enola."

"I don't think—" Enola broke off as Jake walked into the room. He looked at the two women and then said, "Hello, Doc."

"Hi, Jake."

"We got sick animals?"

"Not really. I just wanted to check Cleo."

"I wish this movie thing were over," Kate said. She saw that Jake was watching her in a peculiar fashion. "I think it might be a little bit stressful on the cats. Cleo hasn't been feeling well."

Jake was about to respond, but before he could speak the phone rang. Kate went over and picked it up. "Hello," she said. She stood still without a word, and then finally she said in a voice, which both Jake and Enola recognized as being different from her ordinary tone, "Are you *sure?*" she asked. She listened again and then took a deep breath. "I'll tell him," she said and put the phone down.

"Who was that?" Jake demanded.

"It was Bjorn Kristofferson." Kate swallowed hard and then said, "It's—it's bad news." She had to clear her throat, and then her eyes fixed on Jake's face and she said in an unsteady voice, "It's Avis Marlow—"

"What about Avis?" Jake demanded.

"She's been killed."

Jake straightened up as if he had been physically hit by something. He couldn't answer, and it was Enola who said, "Was she in a car wreck?"

"No." Kate's eyes fixed on Novak. "No, she was murdered in her room."

After her words a silence filled the room, and Kate turned away, unable to face Jake Novak at that moment.

Thirteen

Kate kept her eyes on the road for the most part, but once she turned to glance at Jake, who hadn't spoken a word since they had left the house. His face was set in a way that suggested that he wasn't willing to talk. Kate had tried to think of some way to break through the walls he had put up, but she couldn't. Finally she asked, "Why do you think Kristofferson wants us there, anyway? You'd think they would want people to stay away."

Jake looked at her like she was the dumbest person on the planet. "They want all their suspects in one place."

"Suspects—?"

"Don't worry your pretty little head about it. You're not a real suspect, but I guess I am. I've been seen with her lately."

Kate felt his displeasure, and the rebuke stung her, but she became even more worried about the entire situation. It had never occurred to her that she and Jake could be suspected of the crime.

Neither of them spoke further as Kate drove to the blue beach house, and she saw that there were three police cars there plus the paramedic's van. As they got out and walked across the crushed-oyster-shell driveway, there were two policemen waiting, neither of whom looked familiar to Kate. "Sorry, folks, nobody can go in. This is a crime scene."

Jake looked the man up and down, then said, "I'm Jake Novak. I'm sure I'm on your list."

The policeman looked down at the paper in his hand, then reddened and looked up.

"Go on in."

As before, Kate was amazed at the opulence of it all. Whoever had built the house had spared no expense. The floor was genuine Italian marble; the furniture was carefully chosen. She didn't know art, but she suspected that the paintings on the walls were originals.

They were halted when Ray O'Dell, the chief, met them. His tone was somewhat less than hospitable as he said grudgingly, "Well, you didn't take long to get here, Novak."

"Anything for you, Chief."

"Listen, Novak. Got a favor to ask." The chief lowered his voice and leaned in to Jake. "I could use some help here. No telling when the crime scene people from Mobile are going to get here, and I need an experienced eye to help me get a jump on this investigation. The street cops hanging around this place are worthless."

Jake was taken aback. He and the chief had never gotten along, and O'Dell seemed to revel in belittling Jake's history as a detective.

"Let me get this straight," Jake said in a low tone. "You're asking me to play detective on your crime scene?"

"Nothing official, Novak. Just help me out. Whaddaya say?"

"Where is she?"

"She's upstairs, but beware. Not a pretty sight."

Jake didn't answer, and O'Dell shrugged his muscular shoulders, wheeled, and walked down the hallway. He led them up to the second floor and said, "Her room is right here." Nobody said anything to Kate, so she followed along.

"Who found the body?" Jake asked.

"One of the maids. She called in as soon as she found it." O'Dell nodded at the policeman who was stationed at the door, and the three of them passed into the room. The light was dim and the blinds were drawn. "She's over here," O'Dell said and took two steps toward the closet and then turned to watch Novak. "I don't want anything touched."

Jake went forward and saw that the murdered woman was lying face down. Her blonde hair was matted with blood that hadn't yet dried. He leaned forward slightly, his eyes fixed on the woman. Then he stood up and began surveying the room, his eyes taking in every last detail. "Anything about the time of death?"

"The maid said she saw her at three o'clock."

"Why's it so dark in here?"

"Avis was known to keep her shades closed all the time," O'Dell shrugged. "Avoids the paparazzi—you know they take pictures right in people's windows these days."

Novak turned, and his face was drawn tight as if he had frozen all emotions. Kate glanced at the body and then looked away quickly, somewhat queasy at the sight of the murdered woman.

"Any suspects?" Jake asked abruptly.

"A whole house full of them. Had to be an inside job," O'Dell said.

"What makes you so sure?"

"Because it'd be hard for a stranger to come in and make his way up to the second floor here without being noticed."

"It could be done, though."

"Possible, I guess. What's your instinct tell you, Novak?"

Jake shook his head. "I'm not a detective any more, Chief. Just an unsuccessful novelist."

O'Dell studied the big man and said, "Well, the coroner will be here pretty soon. Let's get out of here. I don't want to disturb anything."

● ● ●

People were gathering in a large ballroom, and Kate stood by as Jake and O'Dell quietly discussed the case. Abruptly the crowd parted, and Aaron Tobin strode toward them. His eyes were wide and his face was pale. "What have you found out, O'Dell?"

"We found out that there's a dead woman in this house," O'Dell said evenly.

Tobin stared at him. "I don't need any smart remarks from you. How did she die?"

"It appears she got hit in the head," O'Dell said. "I want to talk to everybody who's staying in this house." He turned to Oralee Prather and said, "Deputy, make sure the entire cast and crew are in this room."

"Right, Chief."

Kate stayed close to Jake, and ten minutes later the large room had filled up. There was the hum of talk and various people were firing questions at O'Dell, who acted as if he had gone suddenly deaf. Finally he cleared his throat and said loudly, "All right, listen up."

A quiet spread out over the room, and Kate's eyes moved from face to face. The actors seemed to have gathered in one group while the technicians, cameramen, grips, soundmen, and the rest of the crew were separate from them. She turned as O'Dell began to speak.

"As you all know, this is a murder scene now. I'm going to need to interview each one of you."

"What do you think, Chief—that one of us did it?" The speaker was Thad Boland. He was wearing a black T-shirt cut off at the shoulders and the muscles of his body stood out prominently. He looked more like Jean Claude van Damme each time Kate saw him, and there was an arrogance in the man beneath the thin veneer of polite manners.

"You're all suspects. Everybody who was in the house," O'Dell snapped. His pale blue eyes were locked with those of Thad Boland, and Boland opened his mouth to speak but thought better of it.

"I don't want any of you leaving the house until I've had a chance to talk with all of you. As of now, production of the movie is officially shut down until further notice. Which room can we use for the interviews, Mr. Tobin?"

"I guess that one right over there," Tobin said sullenly. He felt everyone's eyes on him and said defiantly, "I can't be held up long on this investigation. I've got to find a new lead female and re-shoot the scenes that Avis was in. I'm losing money by the minute, so I hope you guys can work fast."

Kate felt a sudden rush of antagonism toward Aaron Tobin. A woman was lying dead upstairs, and he was worried about production schedules and budgets. She shook her head in disgust, and Jake caught the motion. "He's all heart, isn't he, Mary Katherine?" he murmured.

"All right, everyone wait in this room. I'll take you first, Mr. Tobin," O'Dell said. He turned and moved quickly across the room, and Tobin followed him, a defiant look on his face. The door shut behind them, and a babble of voices broke out. Kate noticed Lexi Colby standing back against the wall, her face pale. She didn't speak, but Erik Lowe went over and said, "You all right, Lexi?"

"Of course not!" she snapped defiantly. "Why'd you ask?"

"You look—well, you're upset, but all of us are," Erik said.

Lexi shook her head, and her eyes were bitter. "I know who the number one suspect will be, but I didn't have anything to do with it."

Erik Lowe stared at her. "Why should you be the number one suspect?"

"Because I had motive, Erik. I wanted the lead role in this picture. I never made a secret about that."

"But just because Avis is dead doesn't mean you'll get the part."

"Don't be dense. The police will be looking at all of us, digging out our nasty little secrets. Yours too, Erik."

Erik rested against the wall and leaned his head toward Lexi. "Do you have an alibi?" he said in a low tone.

Lexi laughed. "Yes, I was alone in my room reading the script. You think they'll believe that? What about you?"

"I was doing the same thing. Studying my lines," Erik said. "But hey—they'll believe us. That's what most people do on weeknights during a shoot. Especially in a backwoods town like this where there's no decent place to go."

Bjorn Kristofferson had been listening to the conversation. The tall Swede was studying the pair and said caustically, "I think we all better get our lies ready."

"Lies? What do you mean?" Erik asked bewildered.

"I'll say you were with me if you'll say I was with you." Bjorn smiled bitterly. "It's going to be dog-eat-dog here."

Kate was standing next to Jake, who had his arms crossed and a bitterness in his eyes. "They're all so...hard, aren't they?" Kate said. "Avis is dead, and all they can think about is making up alibis and getting on with their lives."

"I think," Jake said slowly, "that these people aren't used to dealing with reality."

"What do you mean by that?" Kate questioned.

"Their whole lives are built around something that isn't so. Just look at them. They wake up every day creating some kind of fantasy. Even their 'real' lives aren't real—the lives those Hollywood types live doesn't even resemble a normal person's life. It's all a lie."

Ten minutes later Aaron Tobin came out of the room. His face was red, and he took out a handkerchief and wiped his brow. He took a quick look around and said, "Jesse, he wants to talk to you."

"All right."

Jesse moved toward the interview room. He had only taken a few steps when suddenly there was a commotion and a sound of loud voices, and the tall lean policeman came bursting in. "She's here!" he shouted.

Kate looked up and saw that the officer was bursting with excitement. His eyes were wide, and he turned to look at the woman who came through the door.

Kate couldn't believe her eyes.

"Avis!" The cry burst from the lips of several in the room as Avis Marlow stepped inside. She stopped abruptly and after a quick sweeping glance of the room, stood still. She was wearing a beach cover-up, and her face was pale. Ignoring the others, she went over and stood before Jake but didn't speak.

Jake's voice was unsteady. "Where have you been?" he whispered.

Avis shook her head. "I—I just went down the beach. I wanted to be alone."

Chief O'Dell stepped in, and when he saw Avis something changed in his face. He came over to her. "Where were you?"

"I went for a walk on the beach. I walked all the way down to the Florida line."

"Did anybody see you?" O'Dell questioned.

"Yes, I got something to drink at the FloraBama, but I was wearing dark glasses, and I had on this floppy hat. I didn't want to be pestered for autographs." She swallowed hard and said, "One of the policeman told me there's been a murder."

"We thought it was you," Jake said quietly.

Bjorn spoke up. "That has to be Callie upstairs."

"Callie?" Avis cried. "What do you mean?"

"She was wearing one of your costumes, and she's a dead ringer for you. It has to be her. We haven't looked at her face yet...she was, um..." Bjorn hesitated. "She was facedown."

O'Dell said quickly, "What would she be doing in your room, Miss Marlow?"

"I told her to go up and look through my closet. She wanted to borrow a dress. She's such a sweet girl...I mean," she said in a halting voice, "she was so sweet. Are you sure it's her?"

"We'll soon find out. I don't want to move her, but it has to be, doesn't it?" O'Dell looked around the room. "Anybody else missing from around here?"

Jesse Tobin shook his head. "I noticed she wasn't here, but I didn't figure that was her upstairs."

O'Dell looked hard at Avis, and then his eyes ran around the group. "This doesn't change anything. The investigation will go on just as it was. I'd advise you all to tell the truth."

Jesse Tobin said quietly, "What about notifying her family, Chief?"

"Where are they?"

"They're in California," Jesse said. "You want me to call them?"

O'Dell hesitated. "Let's hold off on that until the coroner has made the identification." He turned to Jake. "All right. Novak, you and Mrs. Forrest come with me. I'll talk to you together."

The three of them went into the room and sat down. O'Dell said, "Something's going on here."

"You mean that the murderer got the wrong woman?" Jake said.

"Yep. Callie Braun didn't have any enemies, but Avis Marlow has several."

Jake shook his head. "You're right, and from what I've seen in this production company, it's going to be hard to fish it out. Lot of motives floating around."

"What about you, Novak? What's your relationship with Avis?"

Jake's eyes lifted and locked with those of the chief. "We had an affair a few years ago."

"What happened?"

"She wanted a career more than she wanted me."

O'Dell was silent but his eyes were intent. "And you didn't like that."

"It happened a long time ago, Chief."

"Where were you all day?"

"I was at home up in my study trying to work for a while. I went for a walk on the beach."

"Anybody see you?"

"I don't know. They may have. You think I killed her, Chief?"

"What would you think if it were your case?"

Kate saw Jake smile somewhat bitterly. "I'd think just what you think, O'Dell, that everybody who's ever had anything to do with Avis is a suspect."

"What about you, Mrs. Forrest?" O'Dell asked.

"You mean, where was I when the murder was committed?"

"That's right."

"Most of the day I was home. I made a couple of trips to town, but I don't know what time it was."

"Well, you're not really a suspect, but I thought you could vouch for Novak here."

Kate desperately wanted to say something that would help Jake, but the truth was obvious. "He stays in his room working, and I don't see him for hours at a time."

"Well, I've got a lot of people to talk to. Don't leave town." Jake got up to leave, and O'Dell stopped him. "Jake." Jake turned. "Let me know if you get any ideas. Any leads. You know."

"I'd get round-the-clock security on Avis if I were you," Jake said as he turned back to face the chief. "Whoever killed Callie obviously thought she was Avis. The perp is still out there, and Avis is still a candidate for murder."

O'Dell nodded and Jake walked out of the room without another word.

"Can we go home now?" Kate asked the chief.

"Yes. I might want to talk to you later."

Kate followed Jake out of the house and into the parking area. They got in the car, and before she started the engine, she suddenly paused. Jake turned and said, "What's the matter?"

"Callie had her life all planned out, Jake. She was so excited. She had a dream."

"Not a very exciting dream, is it, Mary Katherine? But if she wanted to be a real-estate agent, I'm sorry she didn't get it." Jake slumped down in the seat and dropped his head until his chin was on his chest. "You know, every murder case I worked gave me an odd feeling. Every one of the victims got up in the morning and had no idea it was their last day on earth."

Kate nodded. "There's a verse in the Bible, Hebrews chapter nine, that says, 'It is appointed unto man once to die.' But we don't know when our appointment is."

Jake pulled his shoulders back and shook his head almost fiercely. He seemed to be deeply troubled, and finally he murmured softly, "Better not to know, I think. The most miserable men I've ever known were on death row. They knew the time of their death, but it didn't help them."

Kate took a deep breath. She turned to face Jake and said quietly, "Jake, I know you don't want to be preached at, but I want you to know that I pray for you every day that you'll find the Lord in your life."

Jake Novak turned and looked at Kate. She was watching him silently now, but a woman's silence could mean many things. He wasn't sure what it meant in her, but it pulled at him like a mystery. She was a woman with a great degree of vitality and imagination, but she often held these things under restraint. The thought occurred to him that she was one of the strongest women he had ever known. She had a temper that could swing to extremes of laughter and softness and anger. There was a tremendous capacity for emotion in her, and she had pride that would sweep her violently at times but a humility that somehow pleased him.

Now as he watched her, he was aware that she had an expressive mouth and that there was spirit hidden behind the cool reserve of her lips. "I'm not a good candidate for finding God," he said. He saw that his words disturbed her, and without thinking he reached out and put his hand on her arm. It was a gesture almost like affection, and strangely, it didn't feel uncomfortable to either of them.

"But if I ever did get religion, Mary Katherine, I'd want the kind you've got."

Fourteen

Jeremy was spreading a thick layer of peanut butter on a piece of white bread when he heard footsteps on the stairs leading from Novak's apartment. He expected Jake to come through the door, but instead Ocie stepped inside the kitchen and watched Jeremy.

"Hello," Jeremy said. "How are you feeling?"

In all truth Ocie Plank looked to be in poor condition. His eyes were sunk back in his head, and the bump on his head had discolored the flesh, making a spectacular purple and green splotch.

"I've felt worse. And I've felt better."

"Well, you'll be fine after a while."

Plank grinned and walked over toward the island, where Jeremy was working. "That's good," he said. "I'd hate to think I'd feel this bad for the rest of my life."

"Can I fix you something to eat, Mr. Plank?"

"Remember, you can call me Ocie. If somebody says Mr. Plank, I always think they're talking to my pa. He's been dead for forty years, and it ain't sensible to talk to dead people as a rule. Although," he added judiciously, "I done it a few times myself. What's that you're eating?"

Jeremy grinned, "It's a peanut-butter-and-jelly sandwich. I use the crunchy, spread it on thick like this." He picked up a jar of grape jelly and scooped out a huge dollop with a spoon and patted it down. "Then I put grape jelly on the top. Can I fix you one?"

"I'd rather have a drink, boy."

"Mom doesn't allow any liquor in our house, if that's what you mean."

"I expect that big fellow whose bed I've been sleeping in will have some upstairs."

"I don't think so. Jake doesn't drink either. Not usually, anyway."

"Well, rats!" Ocie said. "I guess I'd better try to eat something then."

"We got just about everything," Jeremy said. "Eggs and turkey bacon and oatmeal, or maybe I can fix you some pancakes. Jake's taught me how."

Ocie shrugged, saying, "Just about anything'll do if I can't get a drink." He turned and saw a small animal creeping close to him. "What is that thing?" he said, "A rat?"

"No, that's Abigail. She's a ferret."

"A ferret? What's she trying to do to me? She's sneaking up like she's going to attack."

"Oh, that's the way she likes to play," Jeremy grinned. "They used to use those things in England. They'd put them down a rat hole, and the ferret would run the rats out, and then they'd kill them. At least that's what Rhiannon told me."

"Rhiannon? What kind of a name is that?"

"A Welsh name, I think. She's a real brainiac. I wish I was as smart as she is."

Ocie pulled out a chair and plunked himself down in it. "Maybe you could fix me some coffee. I got to have my coffee before I'm fit to do business."

"Sure, we got real coffee beans here. I'll show you how to grind them up. Jake says it makes the best coffee. I don't drink it though. Yuck."

"I don't need to grind no beans. You just do it, if you don't mind. I'd rather fix it myself, but I ain't feeling too fit this morning. Just coffee and a little something to eat will be much appreciated."

"I can make you some French toast. That's easy."

"That'll do me, boy."

Ocie sat there watching the ferret, which would come charging at him in her sideways gait, her back up in the air. Ocie reached down and scooped her up and held her at arm's length. "You ain't no bigger than a mite," he muttered. Abigail struggled to get loose, and Ocie stared at her. "She's right cute. Is this as big as they get?"

"Some of them are a little bigger than that." Jeremy went on to explain the nature of ferrets until he had made the French toast and the coffee. He put it down before Ocie and said, "We've got some real maple syrup come all the way from Vermont. Goes good on that French toast."

Ocie stared at the toast, and putting Abigail down, he picked up a knife and poked at the delicacy. "I ain't never knowed nothing good to come out of France, but maybe this here toast will be all right." Taking the syrup, he saturated the French toast, and then with hands not quite steady he cut it up into smaller pieces.

"Why'd you say that about France? I mean, I heard they have the best food anywhere. What about French fries?" Jeremy asked.

Ocie looked at the boy, a bit surprised. He let out a quick laugh. "You're right, boy, you're absolutely right. Shouldn'ta said nothin' about France. Plum forgot about French fries."

Ocie put a big bite in his mouth, and his eyes opened wide. "Why, this is good, boy. What you say your name is?"

"Jeremy."

"Well, you're a pretty good cook, Jeremy."

"Jake's taught me a little bit. He's a great cook."

"Better than your ma?"

Jeremy shifted nervously. "Well, to tell the truth, yeah. Mom's not much into cooking. We used to eat a lot of pizza and frozen dinners and stuff, but Jake believes in starting everything from scratch."

Ocie broke off a piece of French toast and extended it to Abigail, who sniffed at it suspiciously then nibbled at it. "I guess them weasels like French toast," Ocie grinned.

"The animals around here will eat anything. Look, there's Bandit."

Ocie looked over to see a fat coon come in through the pet door. "You folks must like pets."

"Well, we have to have them. Here, Bandit, you leave Ocie alone. He's trying to eat breakfast."

Bandit came over and propped himself up into a sitting position. He pawed at Ocie's leg until Ocie broke off another chunk of toast and fed it to him. "They look just like crooks, don't they, wearing masks and all?" Ocie observed.

"That's why we call him Bandit. Careful, he'll eat every bit of your breakfast. Just like a bottomless pit."

Ocie ate two of the pieces of French toast and washed it down with black coffee. He leaned back and began feeding the third piece to Bandit, who would have climbed up in his lap except Jeremy forbade it. Jeremy was curious about the old man. "You were a soldier, Jake told me, back in World War II."

"A Ranger. That's what I was."

"Did you kill any Germans or Japanese?"

"Never seen the Japanese, but I killed more of the Germans than they killed of me."

"Jake says you fought at Normandy. I've been watching a series about that on the History Channel. I wish I could have been there."

"Well, it wasn't no tea party, boy." Ocie's eyes shut for a moment, and memories seemed to come flooding back. He sat very still, and finally he shook himself and picked up the coffee cup. "This here is good coffee." He suddenly looked over at Jeremy and said, "What's this I hear about some kind of killing?"

"There was a murder, Ocie. They're making a movie here in White Sands, and one of the actresses got murdered."

"What was it, a robbery gone bad?"

"I don't know much about it. You can ask Jake. He was a policeman in Chicago, a detective."

Ocie sat there nursing his coffee along and then got a refill. Finally he looked over and said, "I've been talking to your ma. She said I could take you out on Captain Marsh's boat."

"Oh yeah, Captain Marsh is cool. Mom's let me go out on his charter a couple times. I was thinking I might be able to make some money working on his boat this summer."

"Well, boy, that's exactly what I do. Captain Marsh lets me go along as a deckhand when I need money. Don't amount to much. Just to see that the fishermen get all baited up and ice the fish down."

"Are we gonna fish, or be deckhands?"

"How 'bout you let me be the deckhand this time. Maybe you can catch some dinner."

"When will we go?"

"Well, we'll go out first thing in the morning. Have to be there early."

Jeremy was excited. "That'll be fun, Ocie."

Ocie was watching the young boy, and there was a strange light in his eyes. "I remember when I was about your age, boy. Everything was fun then."

"You grow up in the city?"

"No, sir. In the hills of Arkansas, up around the foothills of the Ozarks. Yep, everything was fun. We went trotlining in the Buffalo River. The woods was stiff with black bears in them days, and I nearly got et by one. I got him just before he got me. It was this way, boy. We went out hunting for deer..."

● ● ●

Jeremy looked at the boat that was lifting slowly with the waves created by outgoing charter boats. He had gotten up early, but Jake hadn't appeared. His mother had fixed them pancakes for breakfast, and while they had eaten she had questioned Ocie closely, telling him he probably shouldn't go out until he got over the bump on his head. Ocie had merely laughed at her and said, "Why shoot, lady, I've been hurt worse than that many a time. Don't you worry about the boy. I'll take care of him."

"I spoke with Captain Marsh yesterday," Kate had said. "He'll be watching out for Jeremy, too."

Now as they strolled down the dock toward the white boat that had *The Lucy Belle* painted on the back of it, Jeremy said, "Look, the boat's getting ready to leave."

"Don't worry. They won't leave without me." The two came to the dock and a big man with a captain's cap and a white T-shirt said, "You're just about to get left, Ocie."

"Oh, come on, Dan. We got plenty of time," Ocie said.

Captain Marsh had a face sunburned to a rich bronze color and a sweeping mustache. "Well, good morning, Jeremy. Come aboard. Let's go catch some fish."

Jeremy jumped into the boat and saw that there were five other passengers, all of them men. None of them spoke to him, and he and Ocie found seats.

"Where we going to fish today?" Jeremy asked.

"I'll tell you about that when we get underway," Ocie said, nodding his head knowingly.

Jeremy watched as the captain went back to the wheel, and slowly *The Lucy Belle* began to pick up speed. The engine seemed to roar loudly, and the propeller made a bubbling noise as they took off toward open water. Jeremy watched as Ocie went into the cabin, saw him take a bottle out of a cabinet, take a long drink, then he came back. "Now I'm ready to catch some fish."

Jeremy looked out over the Gulf. There were many fishing boats in different positions, all headed for the open water. "How do you know where the fish are?" he asked Ocie.

"Captain Marsh here has got charts. He knows where the reefs are. That's where the fish hang out. There are lots of artificial reefs, boy, did you know that?"

"Artificial reefs? What do you mean?"

"They'll load a big barge up with any kind of old junk, old concrete from a parking lot that's been tore up, anything that won't rust. They sink it to the bottom and form a kind of a reef. The fish can hide there. Course, there's some shipwrecks out there, too." Ocie went back in the galley to refresh himself and brought Jeremy a can of soda.

Jeremy was thrilled with the trip. The wind was in his face, and the smell of the salt was invigorating. More than once they passed a school of dolphins, and from time to time, looking up, he could see pelicans flying by.

Finally Captain Marsh slowed the boat down and jockeyed it into position. He turned around and hollered, "Start catching fish!"

Ocie might have been pretty old, but he was active. He went around the fishermen, showed them how to bait their hooks with pieces of squid, and then when they had all dropped their lines over the side, he said, "Come here, boy." Jeremy went over at once, and Ocie thrust a rod to his hand. "Here, you're going to catch a whale, I'll bet." He watched as Jeremy baited the hook.

"A regular expert," Ocie proclaimed, and he pointed to the heavy weight on the line. "We're bottom fishing here, right? You let go of the release on the reel and wait until it stops going down. Then you reel in about three foot of it. That'll keep the bait up off the bottom."

Jeremy held the rod so tightly that soon his hands began to ache. The others were catching fish, and suddenly he felt a tug. He gave a huge jerk upward, and Ocie, who had been watching, laughed. "Well, you got him hooked that time. Bring him in."

Jeremy was so excited he could barely reel the fish in. When it came aboard, Jeremy saw that it was a red-looking fish.

"Look! I got a red snapper!" Jeremy had been on the Gulf long enough to recognize its most common catch.

"You have to throw him back though," Ocie told him.

"Throw him back! He looks big enough to me."

"But he ain't—sorry, boy. There are strict rules about catching fish. You don't want Captain Marsh here to lose his license. C'mere, I'll help you get the hook out."

"I hate to lose that fish."

"We'll get to the big ones pretty soon."

For the next six hours Jeremy was in heaven. He caught four red snappers big enough to keep, and in the meantime Ocie showed him how to assist the fishermen. Their lines often got tangled, and some of them would have almost lost their rods, but Ocie and Jeremy were able to keep everything straightened out.

Finally Captain Marsh said, "Okay, pull up. We're headed home."

The Lucy Belle bobbed on the surface, and Ocie made sure all the rods were set in their places. Most of the men were drinking beer, and Ocie was drinking something stronger than that. Jeremy wanted to say something about Ocie's drinking, but he knew better. Ocie finally came over and plunked himself down beside Jeremy.

"We're gonna have a good dinner tonight, Ocie."

"I'll bet that fellow Jake knows how to cook the snapper some fancy way." Jeremy was quiet for a long time, and Ocie said, "What's a matter, boy?"

"I was thinking about my dad. He took me fishing once. Not on the ocean but in a river." He was quiet, staring off over the water.

"Your dad's dead, is he?"

"Yeah, he went down in a plane. He was a pilot."

Ocie leaned back and pulled his hat down over his eyes. He didn't speak for a long time, and finally he murmured, "Well, we all miss somebody."

Jeremy leaned back against the bulkhead sitting beside Ocie. "Thanks for bringing me, Ocie," he said.

"My pleasure, boy. My pleasure."

● ● ●

I don't understand why everybody's so upset, Jacques. Cleo had been giving herself one of her innumerable baths. She loved to bathe, which was the main reason for the occasional hair balls that gave her trouble.

Jacques, who had jumped up on the counter and managed to open a cabinet door, pulled out a plastic package. *Mmm,* he said, *feline goodies. Why don't they just say cat food?*

He held the package down with one paw and ripped it with the other, sending the pellets rolling. He picked up one and chewed it. *This isn't bad, Cleo. Come and help yourself. There's plenty more.*

Cleo stopped taking her bath and came over to sample the food. *This is real good, but our Person will be mad at you.*

I'll plant the evidence next to Bandit. She'll think he did it.

Don't you feel bad, Jacques, getting him in trouble?

Nah! He deserves it. Look out for Numero Uno; that's my policy.

The two devoured the contents of the packet, and Jacques got another one, although he didn't really want it. He took a bite and shoved it toward Abigail. The ferret sampled it, spit it out, and then ran away.

Jacques lay down on the tile and addressed Cleo as she daintily ate the feline delights. *Somebody got killed over at that place we go get our pictures made. Have you been listening to them talk?*

I don't pay much attention to that. Cleo continued nibbling.

Well, the Intruder was all upset. I got a pretty good kick out of it.

Why don't you like Jake?

Because he said I was like him. I don't want to be like him.

Both cats looked up as their Person entered. Cleo backed away, fearful of what would happen, but Jacques merely looked up and said, "Meow!"

"I'll meow you! What do you think you're doing, getting into that food? I'm going to have to put locks on all the doors." Kate snatched up the packages and dumped them in the garbage. "I'm ashamed of you, Jacques. You know better than that."

Jacques shut his eyes and stretched, sticking his claws out. *How about some tuna?* he wanted to know. Cleo looked at him and shook her head. *You've got some nerve, Jacques!*

Kate was cleaning up the mess, when Jake came into the room. "Where's Jeremy?"

"Ocie took him out on Captain Dan's charter boat."

Jake didn't answer but walked over to the coffeepot. He poured himself a cup and walked to the sliding door, staring out at the Gulf.

Kate hesitated then moved over to stand beside him. "I know you were relieved to find out it wasn't Avis that was killed."

"Yeah. But Callie sure got a raw deal..."

"She was a sweet girl. I really liked her."

Jake stared down into the depth of his cup and muttered, "I need to know what the autopsy says."

"Do the police have any idea who killed her?" Kate asked.

"It could have been anyone."

"But they didn't all have motive."

"You're right. But it's tricky," Jake said. "Sometimes it's the least likely suspect."

"I imagine Avis is pretty upset."

Jake shrugged his shoulders. "Scared, too. Who knows if the killer might try again?"

Kate studied Jake, then asked tentatively, "Did you and Avis ever talk about getting married back when you were, back when you were—ah, dating?"

"That's a nice way to put it." Jake uttered a short humorless laugh. "Dating makes us sound like a couple of high school sophomores."

Kate reddened slightly. "I don't know how else to say it."

"We were living in sin together." His tone was flat. "Yes, we talked about getting married, at least I did."

"She didn't want that?"

"At first she did. But she changed her mind—she wanted a career instead. I guess having a cop for a husband wouldn't have been good press for a rising diva." He turned to face Kate, and he said, "She called about thirty minutes ago. She wants me to come over."

"Are you going?"

"She's scared and needs somebody to talk to. I doubt if she's got any friends in that movie bunch."

"I think you need to be careful about her."

Jake turned to face her. "What do you mean?"

Kate shook her head. "Jake, you know exactly what I mean. She hurt you badly once. She could do it again. You're letting yourself get sucked back in, and you're going to regret it."

"Don't worry about it, Mary Katherine. I'm a big boy."

Cleo and Jacques were listening carefully to this conversation. Cleo nudged Jacques with her shoulder. *She's trying to tell him he needs to stay away from that woman.*

He won't, though.

How do you know that?

Because men and male cats are alike in one way at least. Once they set their sights on a female, it's hard to let her go.

Kate didn't catch the unspoken conversation between the two cats, but she had exactly the same feeling. She wanted to say, *Wake up, Jake, don't be a fool!* But she knew this wasn't the time or the place to say it.

Finally she left without speaking again, and Jake resumed his survey of the Gulf. The cats watched him for a while, and then both went out on the deck, lay down, and went to sleep.

● ● ●

"Let's go take the Brices some of these fish, Ocie." Jeremy was busy wrapping the fish in plastic.

"Who are they?" Ocie asked.

"You know the Brices. I told you about them. Rhiannon Brice and her grandfather. They live right down the beach there. I expect they'd appreciate some fresh fish, although Rhiannon catches lots of fish herself."

"Okay, boy, hope it ain't too far. My legs ain't what they used to be."

Jeremy picked out four of the fillets they had cut from the red snappers and stuck them in a paper sack. As they walked down the beach, Ocie seemed to be depressed, and finally Jeremy said, "What's the matter? Don't you feel good?"

"No, drunks don't never feel good."

It was the first reference Ocie had made to his condition, and Jeremy took the opportunity to ask, "Why don't you quit?"

"Don't want to."

Jeremy was a little puzzled by this. "I've heard people say that alcoholism is a disease."

"That's foolish talk."

"You don't think it's a disease?"

"No, I think it's a sin."

The two were plodding along in the sand, warm beneath their feet. The cry of seagulls made a background to their talk and, from time to time, they would pass visitors from the north who had tried to get their tans in one day and were boiled like lobsters.

Jeremy said, "I don't understand. Everybody says alcoholism is a sickness, not a sin. I've seen some programs about it at school."

"You know the Bible, boy?"

"Well, Mom does."

"The Bible says adultery is a sin, but it don't say that the flu is a sin, does it? You ever hear of anybody asking for forgiveness because they got the flu or because they got pneumonia? No, you never did because that ain't a sin."

"I don't understand you, Ocie."

"But the Bible's pretty strict on drunks, so getting drunk is a sin. It ain't a disease, something you can catch from somebody else."

"You think you'll ever quit?"

"Sure I will, boy, as soon as I get converted." Ocie turned to look at him and grinned. "That surprise you?"

"Well, I didn't think you were a Christian, but what do you mean you're going to be?"

"God's in charge of all this stuff. When He's ready to save me, He'll save me. It just ain't my time yet. But it will be one day. You know," he said, shrugging his sinewy shoulders, "I'm kind of looking forward to becoming a Christian. I'm tired of this rotten life I've been leading."

"Why don't you just become a Christian now?"

"It ain't my time, boy, but it's going to be one of these days. You wait and see."

● ● ●

Rhiannon opened the door and Jeremy extended the sack. "Fresh snapper. I caught it myself."

Rhiannon took the bag but looked up into Ocie's face. "Who are you?" she asked straightforwardly.

"This is Ocie Plank. He's staying with us for a while."

Rhiannon said, "You can come in, I guess, but both of you are a little malodorous."

Jeremy stared at her with distaste. "You've been learning new words again. What does *malodorous* mean?"

"It means you smell bad."

Ocie grinned broadly. "Honey, why don't you just say we stink instead of that big, two-bit word?"

"Don't pay attention to her, Ocie," Jeremy interjected. "Rhiannon uses those kinds of words all the time."

"Indubitably," Rhiannon said with a grin. "Come on in."

As the two entered, Morgan Brice looked up from the table, where he was sitting. He appeared rather frail and tired, and Jeremy introduced the visitor. "This is Ocie Plank. He's staying with us, Mr. Brice. This is Morgan Brice, Rhiannon's grandfather."

Ocie advanced and looked down at the old man. "You the fellow that writes books?"

"I used to."

"I read one of your books a long time ago. *Honor in the Dust*."

"How'd you like it?"

"I don't read many books, but I remember thinking it was good."

"Well, I'm glad you liked it. You fellows sit. Make up some tea, Rhiannon."

Rhiannon made tea, and they were just starting on a lopsided cake that Rhiannon had baked when a knock came at the door.

"Who could that be? We're getting to be popular," Morgan said. "Get it, Granddaughter, will you?"

Rhiannon went to the door and opened it. A man stood there who smiled and took off his baseball cap. "Hello, missy, I'm looking for Mr. Brice."

Rhiannon turned toward Morgan. "There's a man that wants to see you, Grandpa. You want me to run him off?"

"Just let him in, honey."

The man advanced and said, "I'm Jesse Tobin, sir. I think you've met my father, Aaron Tobin."

"Yes, I have," Morgan said. He studied the young man who had a rather mild, thin face, but he saw traces of Aaron Tobin in him. "Let me guess why you're here."

Jesse smiled winsomely. "I think your guess would be right. My father told me it was useless, but I thought I'd give it a try."

"Well, go ahead, young man," Morgan said. "But first let's make the introductions. Ocie Plank, Jeremy Forrest, and my granddaughter, Rhiannon."

Jesse Tobin greeted them with a smile and a nod. "I'm glad to meet you all."

"You see, *he's* not malodorous," Rhiannon said.

"That means you don't stink," Jeremy explained.

"Yes, I know what it means," Jesse smiled. "That's a mighty big word. As for myself, I'm a sesquipedalian."

Instantly Rhiannon straightened up. Her eyes grew bright. "You are, too? That's awesome! I've never met anyone else like me."

"You've done it now. She'll be your best friend for life," Jeremy moaned.

Jesse laughed. "Well, there are worse habits than using long words." He turned to Morgan and cleared his throat. "My father tells me he's tried to buy the movie rights to your book and that you've refused him."

"That's right, Mr. Tobin."

Jesse Tobin looked embarrassed. "I hate to speak against my father, but you may have heard he's a pretty stubborn guy and can get rather—" He broke as if he couldn't find the words.

"He's used to having his own way, and I understand he's ruined a couple people that got in his way. Is that what you mean about your father?"

"It sounds harsh to put it that way, but if I were you, I'd sell him the book rights. Once he makes up his mind, my dad will get what he goes after."

A silence filled the small room, and Morgan Brice studied the younger man. "You seem like a different sort than your father."

Jesse Tobin looked uncomfortable. "We disagree on a few things."

"Well, I'll have to tell you the same thing I told him. I don't like the way that Hollywood treats novels. I think the book is always better than the movie. I wish you could get this across to your father."

Jesse Tobin's shoulders sagged. "Listen, Mr. Brice, I completely understand your reasoning. In fact, I agree with you. I wanted to make a couple of suggestions."

Morgan raised his eyebrows. "Go on."

"You see, there are ways you can negotiate a deal so that if you're not happy with the screenplay, you can get the rights back, and the movie won't be made. You can even negotiate it so that you yourself are allowed to be on the set, monitoring the making of the film. That way, you don't have to be concerned about your book being ruined."

Morgan was intrigued. "Hmm. Interesting, young man. But tell me, would you be able to guarantee this?"

"Well..." Jesse paused. "Well, I couldn't guarantee it. You'd have to hire a lawyer to negotiate your contract so that these stipulations are guaranteed."

"Lawyers, right. And Mr. Tobin, wouldn't this be a lot of extra work for me? Reading screenplays and attending movie shoots and such?"

"Possibly, but you could always hire someone you trust to do it for you." Jesse's voice was hopeful.

Morgan was quiet for a moment and seemed to be processing this new information. Rhiannon watched his face and wondered what he would decide. Finally Morgan spoke.

"Sorry, boy. I'm not in the best of health, and I just can't be dealing with all these lawyers and contracts and screenplays and whatever else goes into it. I'm going to have to say no."

Jesse's head hung low. "Yes, I was afraid you would say that, but I had to try. My father can be a hard man. I really wanted to help you work this out."

"My apologies, Mr. Tobin. You seem like a nice kid. But a man's gotta stand for his principles."

Jesse Tobin seemed suddenly to feel that he was out of place. "I'll leave you now, but let me encourage you to think about it a little more, Mr. Brice. Please don't hesitate to contact me if you change your mind." He headed for the door. "Good to meet you folks."

After Tobin had left the house, Jeremy spoke up. "He seems like a nice man."

"He does seem quite different from his father," Morgan said, "but sit down. Let's drink this tea and forget about all that."

Ocie sat down, and as he drank the tea, he studied the face of Morgan Brice. He had liked the book more than he had said. It was one of the few that he had read repeatedly. The book had a view of goodness and honor and dignity that he liked, and he could see these same qualities in the sick old man that sat across from him. *I hope that boy's daddy don't try to hurt this man*, he thought.

Fifteen

Enola Stern had taken advantage of Kate's offer to use their beach anytime she could get away. She had left her office in charge of her assistant, and now she lay out soaking up the sun. Beside her, sitting in a beach chair under the shade of an umbrella, Beverly Devon-Hunt was layering his face with sunscreen. Enola said with amusement, "It seems a little bit odd."

"What seems odd, Enola?"

"You come down to the beach and then get under an umbrella so that the sun can't touch you."

"I learned my lesson," Bev grinned, "when I first came out to get a tan. Instead of that I got second-degree burns. I thought I was going to die."

Enola was wearing a black bikini that left little to the imagination. She was lying now on her back, her eyes shaded by dark glasses, and she peered at the Englishman and then added, "Do you ever think about going back to England?"

"Oh, I think about it. Perhaps when the time is right, but I'm enjoying myself here in this country, don't you see. Eventually I'll probably divide my time between America and my humble abode across the pond."

"Do you think you'd ever take out citizenship papers over here?"

"Oh, I doubt that." Putting the top on the sunscreen, Beverly put the bottle down and turned to where he could take in the golden-tanned woman who lay on the white beach towel. "I need to get married. After all, I think it's about time I start the process toward producing an heir."

"An heir? What do you mean?"

"Well, I'm the last male in my line. I need a son to pass the title along to. And the money, of course."

Enola sat up and said, "Let me have that sunscreen." When he gave it to her, she began to rub it on her neck and upper chest and then leaning over, began to anoint her legs. "That shouldn't have been any trouble. Women in England must have been lining up for you. Why didn't you marry a woman from your own country?"

"Oh, American women are much more exciting." He gave Enola a look and raised his eyebrows several times. "Don't you think?"

Enola laughed. "I wouldn't know, not having dated any English-women lately." She set the bottle down on the towel and then stood up and looked out over the Gulf. She turned suddenly and said, "I wonder if you have designs on the widow Forrest."

"Why do you say that, Enola?"

"I'm quite an expert in picking out latent romances. I notice you seem drawn to Kate."

"I admire her. She's a strong woman."

"Men don't usually choose strong women. Don't they look for women who are weak?"

"A bit of a stereotype, don't you think, Dr. Stern?" Bev said with a grin. "Women don't usually become veterinarians, either."

"Touché, Mr. Devon-Hunt. Well, if you like strong women...I'm pretty strong. At least I think of myself that way."

Bev was amused. "Are you declaring yourself a candidate?"

"That's always possible."

"You think you'd be up to leading a boring life in England?"

"I suppose I could stand it for a few months a year." Enola suddenly thought of something. "Of course, something a lot more exciting is happening right here. You've heard about the scandal on the movie set?"

"I don't know much about it."

"One of the actresses was murdered. I guess the killer actually intended to kill Avis Marlow."

Bev shook his head. "There's no shortage of intrigue amongst these Hollywood types, is there?"

"Jake's pretty concerned. He used to go out with Avis, you know. Apparently they were almost engaged."

"Is that right?"

"I guess they've been seeing each other again," Enola said. "Too bad. I like Jake—I hope he doesn't let that woman get her hooks in him again."

"Well, he's a grown man. I'm sure the old boy can handle himself."

Enola changed the subject. "Hey, you want to go in for a swim?"

"No, thanks. I always have to go take a shower immediately afterward. Get that salt off, you know, and the last time I got into a bunch of jellyfish. Stung like the very devil."

"Okay, then. Watch my things, will you?"

Bev watched as Enola ran lightly down the beach and plunged into the surf. He watched her as she swam far out and shook his head. "By jove, she's a forward sort! I suppose that's the modern American woman. I'd better get used to it."

● ● ●

Production on the movie was still stalled, but Bjorn had asked Kate to come over to discuss future scenes with the cats. When she arrived, she was surprised to see Enola's Hummer in the parking area. Kate looked up and saw Enola walking out of the house with Erik Lowe. The two passed her and waved, then got into Enola's vehicle and drove away.

Kate was still sitting there stunned when Jesse came out to meet her. She got out of the car.

"Jesse, I just saw Erik with Enola. You know anything about that?"

"Not really, but I've seen them go out a few times. Enola's become kind of a fixture around here."

Jesse walked her in toward where Bjorn had set up his production office. He shook his head. "Dad's chomping at the bit to get back to filming, but the cops won't let us. I think people are too upset over Callie's death, anyway."

Aaron, who had come in just in time to hear this statement, said, "Jesse, you're too soft. You can't stop living when bad things happen."

Jesse turned to face his father and his face reddened. Kate had noticed that although Aaron Tobin usually ruled any situation, Jesse was one of the few who would speak out against him. "I'm so sorry that I think more about people than about making money."

Aaron laughed harshly and put his eyes on his son. "You sound like your mother."

"Good," Jesse said, and faced his father as if he were about to square off. "She had gentleness. Something you lack."

Aaron's voice lowered. "I gave her everything she wanted."

"No, you didn't. She wanted you, Dad, and you never gave yourself."

Aaron ignored his son's statement and walked away.

Jesse watched his father and then turned to find Kate watching him. He laughed shortly without humor. "You must think I have the backbone of a limp piece of spaghetti."

"He's a hard man to live up to, isn't he?"

"I guess all ineffective sons with highly successful fathers go through this. I don't think I'll ever get used to it."

"What would you rather be doing?"

"I wanted to be a poet, but Dad looks on that as an effeminate profession. I guess it's true you can't make much of a living that way. We had quite a battle over it. Of course, I caved in. I'm not a very good director—Bjorn is a lot better than I am. He ought to be directing this picture, not me."

"Surely your dad must know that."

"Doesn't seem to matter, Kate. He's determined to make me in his own image." Jesse was silent for a moment. Then his voice lowered. "He's not going to do it, though. I won't let him."

● ● ●

Kate had her meeting with Bjorn, and when they were finished, he said, "I need to stretch my legs. Walk out to the deck with me?"

"Sure."

They stood looking out over the beach, each absorbed in their own thoughts for a time. "Pretty grim situation, isn't it, Kate?" Bjorn turned to look at her. "I can't get over the fact that Callie's gone."

"She seemed like a different kind of person from—"

Bjorn laughed. "From the rest of us? Well, she was. She was just biding her time here, saving up some money for her business."

"I wonder—" Kate stopped, unsure whether she could say something like this to Bjorn.

"You wonder what?" he prodded.

"I wonder if she was a Christian?"

"Yes, she was. She went to church every Sunday. She told me she was converted when she was thirteen years old. She even talked to me about my sins."

"I'm glad to hear that. Not about your sins but that she was a believer." She hesitated and then said, "So you don't know the Lord?"

"No, I suppose I don't. Guess you're not surprised, huh? Not too many Holy Rollers in Hollywood."

Kate was silent, mulling over being called a "Holy Roller." Finally she asked, "So, any leads on who the murderer is?"

Bjorn gnawed his lower lip and shifted his shoulders nervously. "Obviously they're looking at who might have wanted to kill Avis, even though she wasn't the victim. Avis has a lot of enemies. She trampled on people to get to the top. Erik Lowe is one who hates her. They're having trouble with the love scenes."

"Why does he hate her?"

"Because she tried to make Aaron get another male lead, and Erik knows it. I told him to forget it, but he can't seem to do it."

"He seems like a nice man," Kate commented.

"Erik? He is. But you can't be nice in this business. At least he's not the only one who has a grudge against Avis."

"So he won't be the biggest suspect."

"Right. Lexi Colby hates her, too. It's no secret. Aaron promised her a chance at this role and then gave it to Avis."

"What about you?"

"Me? Oh, I don't have anything against Avis. She's a typical Hollywood star. Egotistical, wanting her own way, hard to get along with."

"You don't hate her?"

"I don't hate her, and I don't like her. But that's not enough reason to kill somebody. It could have been Dontelle, or even Thad Boland."

"Why would Thad hate Avis?"

"Oh, the usual reason. He came on to her, and she made fun of him. Thad's a pretty violent guy. Far as I'm concerned, he's the one person who's capable of such a brutal thing."

"You think he did it?"

"I don't know."

"Well, I've talked to Dontelle Byrd. He doesn't seem to have anything against Avis."

"Oh, Dontelle hates Aaron well enough, but not Avis. And he couldn't kill anybody." Bjorn laughed. "That's enough suspects, isn't it? Listen to us—talking as if we're gonna solve this crime."

"There's no harm in speculating, though. Can't believe we're in the middle of a real murder mystery." Kate shuddered.

"Anyway," Bjorn continued, "the police are checking us all out. They've got detectives here from Mobile and Pensacola now. They're looking for motive and opportunity—and, of course, alibis."

"Do you have one?"

Bjorn grinned crookedly. "Not one that would hold up in court. I was in my room working on the production schedule and camera angles for the next day. Of course, no one saw me there. So you'd better be careful around me—I might be a cold-blooded killer."

Kate looked at him. He was a handsome man and seemed down-to-earth, not at all what she expected out of Hollywood. "I don't think you could kill anybody."

He stared at her for a moment and shook his head. "Anybody can kill. We don't ever know what we're up against until we get squeezed."

● ● ●

When Kate turned the key this time, the old Taurus didn't give even a grunt. "Shoot, that battery must have gone completely dead!"

She picked up her cell phone and tried to get Jake, but he didn't answer. She had Bev's number and called him and said, "Bev, my car won't run. I'm at the Blue House. Are you free?"

"I'll be right there."

Ten minutes later, Bev came wheeling up in his Rolls Royce. He drove her to the house and walked her to the door.

"Come on in," she said. "I can at least give you something to drink."

"That's the best offer I've had all day. I'm parched."

They went inside, and Kate made two tall glasses of sweet iced tea. Bev was looking out the sliding glass door over the Gulf.

"Can't get used to the view here. Jolly good."

"Well, let's go out and sit on the sand," Kate said.

"Sun's going down—I guess it'll be all right now. I was out there earlier with Enola and got a little cooked. I have to watch this fair skin of mine."

They walked out to the beach and sat down, and for a while they didn't speak. Kate finally said, "I can't quit thinking about Callie. Did you talk to her much?"

"I just met her briefly. She seemed like a nice young woman."

"She reminded me a little of myself. Maybe that's why it's so hard to wrap my mind around the fact that she's dead. I'm sad because she had a plan, a dream, and she missed out on it."

Bev gave her an oddly solemn look. "Most of us do," he said thoughtfully. "What about you? You must have a dream."

For some reason Kate began speaking of things she usually avoided even thinking about. "My dream was always marriage, a home, and children. That was all I wanted, Bev."

"Well, you got it, didn't you? You had a husband, and you have a son."

"It wasn't the marriage I dreamed about."

"Was he abusive?"

"Not physically, but he—" She tried to speak but found herself growing almost bitter. "He never paid any attention to me. I always felt starved and lonely. He never told me he loved me. He was interested in flying, and that was all he would talk about."

"Well, I know a lot of men aren't very good at giving women what they need. I'm sorry you had to go through that. But you'll have your dream, Kate."

He leaned over and pulled her close, and she felt a sense of comfort and security. "You're a good listener, Bev—even if you do have a hyphen in your name."

Bev laughed and placed a finger on her chin, turning her face toward him. "Enola asked me what I was doing here. I told her, in effect, I was looking for someone to breed with."

Kate's eyes flew open. "Someone to breed with! Are you on to that topic again?"

"Well, let me say it differently. I'm here to find a woman with whom I will fall in love completely and totally, and then we will get married and have two point six children and a dog, and we'll have a two-story house and two cars." He smiled, and he made an attractive picture as he did. "I think I've asked you before...are you a candidate to become Lady Mary Katherine?"

"I don't think so, Bev. I don't even know which fork to use if there's more than one—I could never fit into your world. I wouldn't know how to be lady anything. Besides..." she looked away from him. "Besides, neither of us wants to marry unless we're in love."

"I've thought a lot about love," Bev said.

"Oh, and what conclusions have you reached?"

"Well, to tell you the truth, love sounds a little bit violent."

She was very much aware of his arm around her and beginning to be very comfortable with it. "What do you mean, violent?"

"Well, just look at the language. People talk about falling in love. Falling's a rather violent thing, don't you think? And look at the symptoms of love. Have you ever read a Harlequin romance?"

"Yes, have you?"

"I read one once. Very enlightening. When a chap falls in love his breathing gets short, he feels weak in the knees, he gets light-headed, he can't eat very much. It sounds very much like a case of Asian flu."

This definition was spoken in the blandest tones, but she saw the humor in Bev's eyes. "You're a fool," she said. "Love's not like that."

"Well, what do you think falling in love is?" Bev asked.

Kate was still for a moment. "Growing old together," she said finally. "Knowing each other and still loving when there's some things that irritate you about the other person. Sharing things." She was quiet for a while. Finally she added, "C. S. Lewis said after he lost his wife that one of the things that hurt him most was the little jokes they had, things that no one else would understand. That was gone forever."

Bev tightened his grasp on her shoulders. "I think I'd rather like that sort of love. Is it available?"

"Not for most people. Most people are looking for something like the Asian flu. You know the best description of love is in a poem by Robert Burns."

"I like Burns. A little hard to read in Scottish dialect. What's the poem?"

"It's just a little poem called *John Anderson, My Jo*."

"Can you say it for me?"

"I memorized it a long time ago," Kate said. "It's about a woman and a man who've been in love a long time, and now are old. I changed some of the old Scottish words to modern English, and it goes like this:

> John Anderson, my jo, John,
> When we were first in love,
> Your locks were like the raven,
> Your bonnie brow was smooth;
> But now your brow is bald, John,
> Your locks are like the snow,
> But blessings on your frosty head,
> John Anderson, my jo.
> John Anderson, my jo, John,
> We've climbed the hill togither,
> And mony a wonderous day, John
> We've had with one another;
> Now we must totter down, John,
> But hand in hand we'll go,
> And sleep togather at the foot,
> John Anderson, my jo.

As Kate's voice faltered at the end, Bev saw there were tears in her eyes. "I say," he whispered, "that's very fine, very fine indeed." He stroked her hand, and said, "I hope we both find that kind of love, Kate."

Sixteen

Cleo, who had been sitting on the back steps of the deck cleaning
her hair, looked up to see Jacques trotting across the sand. He had a
wicked gleam in his eyes, and she noticed that there was a long scratch
on the crown of his head that had left a bloody furrow. *What have you
been doing, Jacques?*

Jacques moved to the watering dish that was kept outside for the
animals, drank deeply, and then he stretched, extending his claws and
raking them across the wood of the deck.

I've been romancing that good-looking Siamese that lives down the road.

How'd you get that cut on your head? Cleo couldn't help but be concerned.

*There was a big tabby there that thought he had the inside track with
Melissa. He tried to move into my territory.*

Trouble came trotting up to the water dish. He began lapping noisily,
and Jacques, moving faster than a speeding bullet, made a leap at him
and raked the dog's side. Trouble yelped and backed off. He gave Jacques
a reproachful look and then went off whining.

*I don't understand that dog, Jacques. He could break your back with one
bite.*

I've got him where I want him. Jacques stretched out and asked, *Has
anybody put any fresh tuna out?*

No, not yet.

Things are going to have to pick up around here. Our Persons haven't quite got it in their heads that we're the important inhabitants of this house. He looked out over the white sand and the green waters and saw Jake sitting close to the surf. *What's the matter with him?*

He's fishing, can't you see?

He's acting nutty lately. Something's wrong with him.

You're not very perceptive, Jacques.

I'm perceptive enough. Jacques examined his razor-sharp talons with satisfaction. *I sure gave it to that big tom! He won't be coming around any more.*

Cleo looked at Jacques. *Is that all you can think about? Look out there at the Intruder. He's not doing so well.*

I know what's the matter with him. He's got woman trouble. That female movie star, she's got him going. As always, Jacques wore an air of superiority.

I'm afraid you're right. Cleo stood up and arched her back in a luxurious stretch. *You know, I think he likes our Person.*

These two-legged creatures sure have funny ideas about romance and love and such.

What are you talking about?

Well, they got the idea that a male and a female are tied together somehow. Neither one of them can have a romance with another human. Why, you take us tomcats. Jacques seemed to find pleasure in instructing Cleo on such matters. *We can have a dozen of what the humans call "romances" all at the same time. Nobody gets hurt as long as the other toms stay away from my territory.*

Well, I think some humans do that, too, Jacques—have more than one love, I mean.

Yeah, but they feel guilty about it. I don't get it, Cleo. Jacques looked into the house and said, *I've got to have some tuna. This romancing is hard on a cat.* He started up the steps and paused at the top to look at Jake. *I feel sorry for the Intruder. He needs to take a few lessons from us tomcats.*

● ● ●

Jake was staring out at the waterline, watching four sandpipers as they performed their rather acrobatic little dance. When a wave came in they would stay just far enough ahead of it to keep from getting baptized, and then as the wave receded, they followed it, picking up invisible tiny morsels of food. "I wonder how they do that?" Jake muttered. He shrugged and picked up his surf-casting rod, reeled it in, and saw that the bait was gone. With a lackluster gesture he put more bait on and threw it out. He jammed the butt of the rod into a PVC pipe he had driven into the sand, then sat back down cross-legged and stared moodily. The wind made a whistling noise, and he didn't hear Kate come up behind him.

"Hello, Jake."

He turned and saw that she was wearing a pair of old shorts that once were blue but now were completely faded. Her trim figure was outlined beneath the man's white shirt that she wore. He watched as she sat down beside him and thought, not for the first time, that there was a grace in her movements that he found pleasing. He wasn't in a mood, however, to be pleased and said in a gruff voice, "What's going on, Mary Katherine?"

"The reporters are swarming into White Sands. Most of them are from the tabloids."

"That figures."

"Some detectives have come over from Mobile to help in the investigation." Jake didn't answer, and Kate asked, "Are you catching any fish?"

"No."

Jake's reply was abrupt, and Kate felt as if there were a real stone wall between them. Kicking off her flip-flops, she dug her toes into the sand and leaned back on her hands. She was thinking that there were very few people that she had ever known who could endure a silence as well as Jake Novak. Most people felt every spare moment needed to be filled with talk, but Jake wasn't one of these people—and neither was she, Kate realized.

A movement caught her eye, and she saw a solemn blue heron come sailing in from the east. He hugged the beach line and, letting down his long spindly legs, came in for a rather awkward landing.

"He comes in every day about this time," Jake said abruptly. "That bird is punctual."

For a time the heron stared at them, then lumbered off flapping his wings until he was airborne again. "You know what he looks like?" Jake said. "He looks like a merchant prince that's just surveyed his tawdry surroundings, lifted his wings, and sailed away."

"I never think of things like that. To me he was just a blue heron."

"I guess it's a writer thing," Jake said and managed a smile.

The two sat there for a time, and then finally Kate broke the silence. "How's the new book coming?"

"Well, I'm getting better at getting some words down every day."

"That must feel good."

"Yeah, but I still...I just don't know if they're any good."

"Doesn't that come in time?" Kate asked.

"Maybe. I hope so."

Kate reached down and picked up a handful of the sand, white and fine. *It's like a sugar beach,* she thought. She let it sift through her fingers, and then finally she tossed the sand aside, dusted her hands, and turned to face Jake. His jaws were strongly defined and shelved squarely at the chin. His coarse black hair was moving with the heavy breeze, and his hazel eyes were half hidden by his lids as if he were trying to shut out the world. At this moment it seemed to Kate that something had painted shadows in his eyes and laid silence on his tongue and touched his solid face with a brand of loneliness. The depression she saw in him was so great that his eyes, for a moment, seemed like empty windows looking out at nothing.

She found herself admiring him. All his features were solid, and his shape was that of a man turned hard by time and effort. "Jake," she said quietly, her voice scarcely louder than the breeze that drove the sand across the beach like small bits of sugar, "you've got a dream and dreams are important."

Her words caught at him. He turned and studied her, and somehow she felt he was looking beneath what he saw with his eyes and saw instead the very spirit and soul. He had that ability and it troubled her sometimes. "Maybe it was the wrong dream." He suddenly twisted around to face her fully. "Are you happy, Mary Katherine?"

Taken off-guard, Kate stared at him. "Well, I'm so much better off,

Jake, than I was back in Memphis. That was a tough life. I was working two minimum-wage jobs and not making it. We lived in a project, and I was afraid all the time that Jeremy was going to get into trouble. But look what we have now. A fine house right on the beach, money coming in every month. I can spend time with Jeremy and be the mom he really needs."

Jake ran his hands through his coarse black hair. "Well, what's your dream aside from having a nice place to live, I mean?"

Kate found it hard to answer Jake's question. She realized what he was asking. *Was it only things she required?* She knew life was more than a fine house and money coming in regularly, but how to explain it to him? She sat there struggling to find words.

"When Vic and I were first married everything was wonderful. It was like—" She stopped and flushed slightly and shook her head with a small meaningless laugh. "It was like something out of a movie where everything was sweet and good. I couldn't wait for Vic to get home when he was gone for a while." She looked at Jake, and there was a sadness in her eyes as she continued. "It didn't last, but I've always thought that it could, with the right person. I dream about it."

Jake had listened closely, and when he saw that she was finished he said, "I've never had anything like that."

Quickly Kate spoke the question that had been on her mind for a long time. "What about you and Avis?"

"We didn't have anything like that," Jake said slowly. "It was—physical. I was hooked on her just like a junkie gets hooked on drugs, but the thing you had—I didn't even know existed."

Suddenly he seemed embarrassed. He came to his feet in a smooth, easy motion, grabbed his pole, and reeled in.

"I've been thinking," he said abruptly, making it clear he was changing the subject. "You've got to get rid of that old Taurus."

"I know," Kate said. "I've been watching the classifieds in the paper and there's a Honda Accord for sale, one owner. I think I'll go take a look at it. They're good on gas and well-made cars."

"Okay, then," Jake replied. "Let me know if you need any help."

Kate watched as he removed the bait, picked up the bait bucket, and said, "I'll see you later."

Without thinking, she blurted out, "Are you going to see Avis?"

Jake stopped as if he had run into a wall. He turned to face her and the expression on his face was unreadable. "I guess I will." He waited for her to speak and when she didn't, he moved away. Kate watched him go and shook her head sadly.

● ● ●

Jake shut off the Harley and had just dismounted, when Avis came out of the blue beach house. Lexi Colby was with her, and they both walked toward Jake.

"Hello, Avis," he said. "Lexi."

Lexi stared at him and then blinked as if to focus her eyes. She didn't answer but turned and glared at Avis. "I'll get him for that. Somehow I will." She turned and got into a sky blue Porsche. The engine caught with a rumble, and she tore out, throwing sand and gravel from underneath the spinning wheels.

"What's the matter with her?" Jake asked.

"She's not a happy camper. Complicated," Avis said. "So what are you doing here?"

"I wanted to see if you were all right. Things have been tough around here."

"Yeah." She was wearing a pair of yellow shorts and a lime green top with flip-flops. Pulling her dark glasses down from her head, she put them on and said, "Let's get away from here, Jake."

"All right. You can't ride the motorcycle."

"We can take my car." She reached into her pocket and handed him the keys. Jake noticed a plainclothes cop who'd been lingering in the shadows, and just then Avis turned toward the man.

"Be back later. I'm with Novak—I'll be fine."

The man nodded, and the two walked over to the Jaguar and got in, and Jake started the engine.

"That's your rent-a-cop?"

"Yep. Woo-hoo, he makes me feel so safe." Her words dripped sarcasm.

He pulled out of the parking area. "Nice ride," he commented. "This rented?"

"Yes, they provide us rentals when we're on location. Some of the cast members drove out from LA in their own cars. But I'm not much for road trips."

He turned down Highway 182 and had gone only a couple of miles when Avis said, "Pull over. Let's get something to drink."

Jake nodded and pulled the Jaguar into a parking lot in front of a place called The Living End. "They make pretty good food here," he said.

"I just want a drink," Avis said. She put on her floppy hat.

They went inside and found a window table over in a corner where they could look out at the Gulf. A young woman came and took their order for drinks, and as soon as she had left, Avis said, "Jake, I'm scared stiff. Whoever killed Callie was after me."

"I know."

"I haven't had a good night's sleep since it all happened."

The young woman came back with the drinks, and Avis tossed hers off at once. "Bring me another," she said.

Jake had ordered beer and sipped at it. "What do you wanna do?"

"I'd like to walk away from this picture, just leave it," Avis blurted. There was fright etched on her face, something that Jake had never seen before.

"So...why don't you?"

"I don't walk away from things, Jake."

"You walked away from me, Avis."

Avis looked up and removed her glasses so that he could see her eyes. "Don't you think," she said quietly, "that I've regretted that a thousand times?"

"Somehow I've never felt overwhelmed by apologies." He sipped the beer.

"Don't—don't hate me, Jake."

"Why shouldn't I, and what difference does it make?"

Avis reached over and took his hand in hers. "Don't."

The touch of her hand brought back old memories, things that had happened long ago, but now they were just as clear and sharp and real as anything that had ever come into his mind. He had told Kate that all he had had with Avis was a physical relationship, but he knew it wasn't true. He remembered how there was an emptiness in him when she wasn't there, just as Kate had spoken about what she felt for her husband. He had told Kate he'd never had anything like that, but he'd lied.

"I'm sorry I treated you so badly, Jake. I was wrong."

Jake was very much aware of the smoothness and the strength of her hands. He admitted to himself at that instant that he'd never forgotten her, although he'd tried hard enough. He looked around at the patrons scattered in the saloon.

"Place is pretty popular with tourists," he said casually, and watched her face fall as she realized he wasn't going to get involved in the conversation she wanted.

They chatted superficially about the beach, and the town, and the locals. They didn't speak of anything important, but they both felt the need to fill the silence up with words.

Avis tossed back another drink. "Where are you going when you leave this bar, Jake?"

"I'm going home."

"To Kate," Avis said. "I'm jealous of her."

Jake suddenly smiled. "You don't have to be. We've done very little but fight ever since we met."

"She's an attractive woman."

"I guess so."

"You guess so," Avis said mockingly. "Come on, Jake, I know you better than that."

Jake hesitated and then said, "I'm cooking supper for the Brices tonight. You want to come?"

"That's the man who wrote the book that Aaron's trying to get the rights to?"

"Yes."

"What will Kate say if you come in dragging your old flame?"

"Nothing to do with her."

A smile played around the corners of Avis' lips. The fragrance of her clothes came powerfully to Jake Novak, and he felt it slide through the armor of his self-sufficiency. He looked at her and felt the strange sensation of his heart settling in his stomach—the kind of thing a man feels when he looks upon beauty and knows it will never be for him.

"Let's go. You can help me fix supper."

"You know I can't even boil water."

"You can watch me. Come along."

● ● ●

Jake set out to fix a Creole supper. He started with seafood gumbo then made up some crawfish bisque. He whipped up a fresh strawberry salad and carefully built his favorite *coeur de filet provençale*. For vegetables he had fixed stuffed eggplant and fried green tomatoes.

Avis Marlow had been prepared for a poor reception from Mary Katherine Forrest, but she'd been disappointed. Kate was gracious and friendly. Avis had sat in the kitchen while Jake did the cooking, and Jeremy joined them. Avis hadn't been around young people much, and she was fascinated by the boy, and when the Brices arrived, she was immediately taken with Rhiannon. The way the girl dressed amused her, and she commented on Rhiannon's innate sense of style—"shabby chic," she called it. The guests had gotten into a game of Scrabble as Jake made the supper, and Rhiannon had beaten them all.

"I've never met anyone as smart as you," Avis said to the girl.

"Yes, I'm very bright," Rhiannon said calmly. She put both hands on her head and stared across the table at Avis. "I saw you in a movie once. I didn't like it."

Avis was amused. "I don't like many of them, either. What was the name of it?"

"Murder at Midnight."

"That was a stinker," Avis agreed.

"Yes, it was. It was absolutely malodorous." Rhiannon, as usual, kept a completely straight face.

"You better watch out, Miss Marlow," Jeremy put in. "She's a sesquipedalian."

"And what does that mean?"

"Somebody that likes to use big words," Jeremy said. He changed the subject abruptly. "Did you ever meet the Terminator?"

"Yes, I have. As a matter of fact, he's been the governor of California for quite some time now."

"Did you like him?"

"He's actually a pretty good guy—for an actor turned politician."

Morgan Brice had been rather silent. He laughed now. "That's speaking right out. You don't sound too positive about your own profession."

"Most movie actors are all ego," Avis admitted. "I haven't escaped the trap—I don't like myself too well sometimes."

Kate saw that Jeremy was fascinated by talking to a real live movie star. She herself was weighing Avis Marlow's attraction for Jake. The woman didn't even try to hide it. More than once she went over and stood beside Jake as he was cooking. She smiled up at him in a way that a million American men would have died for.

Finally, when the meal was ready they sat down, and just as they did Ocie Plank came in. His face was red, and there was a liquid shine to his eyes.

"Sit down, Ocie," Jake said. "We have an honored guest tonight, Miss Avis Marlow. She's been in White Sands for the movie they're shooting."

Ocie sat down and said, "I don't like movies, not most of them anyway. I like John Wayne, though."

"I suppose everybody liked John Wayne." Avis smiled politely.

Ocie looked right at her. "I guess you're wondering what I'm doing here, and I guess you probably think I've been drinking, too."

"I didn't think anything about it," Avis said tactfully.

"Hey, that's my kind of girl," Ocie said with a flirtatious wink. "Well, I may be the slightest bit inebriated, but I'm going to dig in to this here meal." He looked over at Rhiannon. "How are you, missy?"

"Very well. You shouldn't drink. It's bad for your liver."

Ocie laughed. "I think you're right about that."

"Let's have the blessing so we can eat," Jeremy said. "It smells good."

There was a moment's awkwardness, and then Kate said, "Why don't you ask the blessing, Jeremy."

Jeremy gave her a startled look, but then he bowed his head and said, "Lord, we thank you for this food. Amen."

Jake laughed. "That's the kind of praying I like to hear. Short and to the point."

Avis insisted on helping Kate serve the food, and for the next hour the dining room was filled with laughter. Ocie may have had a bit too much to drink, but it didn't disturb his wit. He told several humorous stories about his life in the Rangers and on oceangoing ships.

Kate was somewhat surprised to see that Avis fit right in. She saw that the men seemed to be fascinated by her, even Morgan Brice. As a result, Kate grew quieter and felt a bit left out.

Finally, after the meal was over, Kate said, "Jeremy and I will do the dishes."

"No, I'll do the dishes," Ocie said. "I've washed many a dish to pay for my booze. You all just clear out."

"Well then, I suppose I'd better take you home, Avis," Jake said. "It's getting late."

"I think so. It's been a lovely evening. Thank you for having me." She turned to Kate and said, "I shouldn't have barged in like this without an invitation."

"It was good to have you," Kate said warmly.

Rhiannon was watching Avis, and she said, "I read that most movie stars are amoral. Is that true?"

A silence fell over the room for a moment. Morgan's voice boomed out, "You shouldn't ask questions like that, Rhiannon!"

"Well, how am I going to learn if I don't ask?"

Avis wasn't embarrassed. "I expect the article was right. Most of us don't have very high morals. But *amoral* is better than *immoral*, don't you think?"

Rhiannon's eyes darkened. "I suppose, but neither is really very good."

"You know what, Rhiannon?" Avis told her, "I think you're right. I need to develop better morals."

"I've got a tract here that tells you how to get saved." Rhiannon fished in her pocket and brought out a limp yellow sheet of paper. "I wrote it myself."

Avis took the paper and smiled, "Thank you, Rhiannon." She looked at the heading, and her lips turned upward in a smile. "I like the title."

"What is it, Avis?" Jake asked.

"This tract is called 'Turn or Burn.'" She straightened her face and said, "I'll read every word of it, I promise you, Rhiannon."

"You'll be a good woman after you get saved," Rhiannon said. She locked her hands behind her back and studied the movie actress. "You're pretty, though."

"Thank you, sweetie." Avis said her good-byes to everyone, and Jake led her outside to the car. As Jake started the car, Avis slumped against the passenger seat with a huge breath.

"Wow, Jake. What a group," she said. "That's the most enjoyment I've had in a long time. I love that girl Rhiannon."

"She's pretty blunt."

"Yes she is. Maybe that's why I like her."

Jake pulled up in front of the house, and the two got out. "Good night, Avis."

Avis hesitated then came over. Without preamble she put her arms behind Jake's neck, pulled his head to her, and kissed him. She felt the shock that ran through him, and she held him even tighter.

Finally she stepped back. "Memories, Jake?"

Jake shook his head. "Memories I'm trying to forget." He turned, straddled the Harley, kicked the engine on, and roared away. Avis watched him go. There was a small smile on her lips. She stood there watching him until the Harley disappeared, then turned and went slowly into the house.

Seventeen

Jake couldn't help but notice that Kate was cool toward him for
two days after he had brought Avis home for supper. She was pleasant
enough, but there was a resistance in her that he hadn't sensed before.
One of the things he had always liked about Kate was her cheerful spirit,
and now he was aware that he had crossed some sort of line that had
displeased her. It was after he had fixed his special po'boy sandwiches for
lunch that she had turned her back on him and walked away to feed the
pets. He looked down at Trouble, who was watching him with his head
cocked to one side. "Well, where's your doghouse, boy?" Jake whispered.
"I guess I'll go find it and crawl in."

"Wuff!" Trouble said and came to sit on Jake's feet.

"I never saw a dog that had such a foot fetish." He turned and went
outside and found Ocie replacing some deck boards. "Let me give you
a hand, Ocie."

"Don't need any more help. Me and Jeremy here, we got this thing
sewed up."

Jeremy's face was alight with interest. He was handing screws to
Ocie, who drove them in with a power screwdriver, and he said, "Is Miss
Avis going to come back and see us again, Jake?"

"I doubt it."

Jeremy's face fell. "Why not? I like her."

Ocie cackled and wiped the sweat from his brow. "You and about fifty
million other males. Don't get tangled up with a woman like that, boy."

Jeremy looked quizzically at Ocie and cocked his head. "She was real nice, Ocie."

"I imagine rattlesnakes are real nice when they're not biting somebody. The trouble is you never know when you can trust the varmints."

"You oughtn't talk about her like that," Jeremy cautioned.

"I wouldn't expect her to come back, Jeremy," Jake remarked. He looked out over the Gulf, resting his eyes on the far-off horizon. The water was so blue it was hard to tell where it met the blue of the sky.

"Was she your girlfriend?" Jeremy asked.

"We were close at one time."

"Gosh, why didn't you marry her, Jake? If you had, you'd be a millionaire. All movie stars are millionaires, and she's the prettiest woman I've ever seen—except for Mom, of course."

"That's right, boy. Always stick with your folks." Ocie grinned. He looked up and said, "By the way, Jake, why *didn't* you marry her?"

"Just didn't work out," Jake remarked. The conversation displeased him, and he turned to leave, but Ocie's voice followed him. "Well, I had a few women who didn't work out."

Jeremy turned to face the old man. "Were you ever married?"

"Only three times."

"You were married three times?"

"Well, I took them one at a time, Slick." Ocie had picked up Jake's nickname for Jeremy. "It'd be illegal and impolite to have three wives at the same time unless you was one of them foreigners."

"What foreigners?" Jeremy asked.

"Them Arabs or whatever you call 'em. They can have four wives according to their bible."

"They got their own bible?"

"Of course they have, boy. The call it the Koran."

"Did you ever read it?"

"Sure did. Read it all the way from first to last. Wish I hadn't. Wasn't worth the effort. Those fellows have got a funny idea about heaven. They think every man that pleases God is going to have a whole herd of young women to wait on him and take care of him."

"What do the women get?"

Ocie winked lewdly, "I reckon they get to wait on the men."

Bandit had mounted the steps and come over. He propped himself up into a sitting position and waved his paws in the air. Jeremy grinned. "I know what you want." He walked over to a small garbage can, reached in, and scooped out some dog food. He put it down, and Bandit at once came over and began picking the nuggets out.

"Look how he uses them paws of his," Ocie said with admiration. "Almost like little hands, ain't they?"

Suddenly Jacques appeared from nowhere, a black streak, and Bandit fell to all fours and scurried off.

Jeremy reached out and picked up Jacques, which was quite a task. "Why do you have to be so mean, Jacques?"

"Reminds me of my brother-in-law," Ocie said, "the mean one, that is. He ain't mean no more, though."

"Why not, Ocie?"

"Because he got to sit in Old Sparky in the pen at Huntsville, Texas."

"What's Old Sparky?"

"That's what they call the electric chair, Slick."

"He was executed?"

"Plum dead. Well, look there," Ocie said. "There comes that little girl-friend of yours."

"She's not my girlfriend, Ocie. She's only ten years old."

"And you're twelve. That means by the time you're forty she'll only be thirty-eight. That ain't much difference."

Ocie put his tools down and walked over to the edge of the steps and waited until Rhiannon reached them. He watched her expectantly because he had learned that she always said something entertaining. He had told Jeremy privately, "That's the smartest young 'un I ever saw. She's going to be president of the United States, or maybe something *really* important."

Rhiannon looked up at Ocie and put her hands behind her back. She gave him a cold stare and said distinctly, "Are you drunk, Ocie?"

"Not completely."

Rhiannon shook her head and said, "Oh, God! That men should put an enemy in their mouths to steal away their brain."

"What in the world kind of talk is that?" Ocie said.

"That's from a play called *Othello*. Shakespeare wrote it."

"Why are you reading that?" Jeremy said. "Shakespeare's for grown-ups."

"Grandpa's reading the story to me. I don't like it much, but he says I need to read stuff I don't like."

"Well, if doing something you don't like is a requirement for your grandpa, tell him you know the world's champion," Ocie offered. "I've spent my life doing stuff I didn't like. What are you doing here?"

"Grandpa's supposed to go to the doctor, and the car won't start. I came to ask somebody to take him."

"Shore, I'll take him," Ocie said.

"No, you're drunk." She turned to Jake, who had paused to hear the conversation.

"Sure, I'll be glad to, Rhiannon." Jake said.

"Not on your motorcycle. I don't think he could hang on."

"No, I'll use Mary Katherine's car. I charged the battery. I guess it'll make it that far."

● ● ●

The sky was darkening as Ocie and Jeremy walked along the beach. They weren't fishing, but they had made a habit of taking long walks together just about twilight. It was a little earlier than that, and Ocie was telling Jeremy a story about his youth.

"There was bears where I grew up. One of them almost got me once. I come on her, and she had two cubs, and I didn't have any better sense than to get between her and the cubs. Why, she piled out after me, and she looked like a freight train with big teeth. I took off running, but those things can outrun a horse for a short ways."

"What happened?"

Ocie reached over and tumbled Jeremy's hair. "She killed me, boy."

"No, she didn't. What really happened?"

"A woman shot him."

"What woman?"

"Her name was Patience. Patience Satterfield was her name. The Satterfields were bootleggers in our part of the world, and all of them was good shots. Patience was the best shot of them all, I reckon. She threw that rifle up and drilled that mama bear right between the eyes. Stopped her dead where she was."

"What happened then?"

"Well, we skinned that bear, but the big thing that happened was I felt so grateful, I married her. Patience Satterfield, wife number two."

"What happened to number one wife?"

"She run off with a John Deere salesman. I sure was grateful to that salesman. She was a pain."

"And what happened to the one that killed the bear?"

"Well, shooting that bear was the best thing she ever done for me. She was sweet enough when we was courting, but she was the most jealous woman I ever saw. Why, would you believe she shot *me* one time?"

Jeremy looked up with astonishment. "She shot *you?*"

"Oh, just in the leg. I was talking with a little redhead outside the Palace Drugstore, and Patience didn't like it much, so she shot me in the leg. She told me, 'That ought to fix you so you won't chase any more redheaded women.'"

Jeremy was trudging along. "Is that really true?"

"Shore is, Slick. I don't never lie—unless it's absolutely necessary. But I'll tell you one thing I—" Suddenly he broke off and lifted his head. "Look there. The Brice house, smoke's coming out the window. Come on, boy!"

The two started at a dead run. As old as Ocie was, he outran Jeremy. The two burst through the front door, and Ocie yelled, "Go hook up that hose, boy! I think we can get it stopped." It was a small fire at the front of the house and hadn't spread yet. Ocie ran into the bedroom, yanked a blanket off the bed, and began beating the fire back. Jeremy ran outside and turned on a hose. He dragged the hose inside and sprayed the flames while Ocie beat at them with his blanket.

They fought it hard, and just as they were getting the last of it, Jake and Morgan Brice came bursting through the door, followed by Rhiannon.

"What happened?" Morgan cried.

"The house caught on fire."

Rhiannon said, "There was a conflagration?"

"Yeah, and a fire, too," Ocie said. He looked down at his hands.

"You got a burn there," Jake said. "Let's get you to a doctor."

"No, I got some stuff that'll take the sting out of it."

Jake began looking around, and when he came back to stand before Morgan Brice, his face was stern. "It was arson, Morgan. Somebody set the fire."

Morgan Brice was sapped by disease, but suddenly a fire burned in his dark eyes. "I've got a pretty good idea who's behind it."

"Yeah, me too."

"He wouldn't do it himself, but he can hire someone."

Jake hesitated and then said, "I believe the fire knocked out the wiring, but we can rig something up. I've got a five-hundred-watt generator. I'll go get it, and you can run off that until we can get the wiring put back."

"Thanks, Jake." Morgan was clearly grateful.

"Now, you two want to come and stay at our house for the night?" Jake asked.

"No, we'll just stay here."

"All right. I'll go get the generator then."

● ● ●

Ray O'Dell had made the trip after Jake had called the police. He looked around the house and said, "Definitely arson. They weren't very careful, were they?"

"No. Looks amateur."

"Don't have enough to make an arrest. I'll ask around though. This house is so isolated probably nobody saw anything."

O'Dell had something else on his mind, and Jake asked, "What is it?"

"Don't guess you heard about this. The Marlow woman had an expensive diamond bracelet. It was missing, and we did a search."

Jake looked hard at the chief. "Did you find it?"

"Sure did. It was in Thad Boland's room."

"The bodyguard?"

"That's the one," O'Dell confirmed.

"What'd Boland say?"

"He said he found it and didn't know it was hers. He was going to ask around to see who lost it. Said he didn't know it was real diamonds. Thought it was costume jewelry."

"You believe that?"

"I don't believe anything the first time I hear it, but I don't have enough to arrest him on. Can't prove anything, but I'm keeping my eye on him."

● ● ●

Jake had spent two hard days getting the Brice house repaired. The inspector had come out and given them a hard time, and Jake was pretty sure that the fine hand of Aaron Tobin was there somewhere. He had glared at the inspector and said, "How come you're being so tough on the Brices?"

"I'm tough on everybody."

"Not this tough. You're not getting paid extra to be hard on these folks, are you?"

"You accusing me of something? I can be tougher if you want."

Jake took a step forward, and the man suddenly held up his hand and his eyes widened. "Wait a minute! I didn't mean anything by that."

"You better go over that list of things you say have to be done to the house and narrow it down a little bit. Otherwise I'm liable to get upset. When I get upset, it's a sight to behold."

"Sure...sure—I'll go over it, Mr. Novak. Maybe I was a little bit strict."

Jake needed to get away and went night fishing under the bridge that spanned the inlet to the harbor. He had caught several nice sheepshead and was getting ready to quit, when his cell phone rang. He picked it up. "Hello."

"This you, Jake?"

"Yeah, it's me. Who's this?"

"Al Jennings."

Al Jennings owned a small restaurant and bar where Jake had eaten several times. "What's going on, Al?"

"One of them movie stars is in the bar here. She's drunker than Cooter Brown, and she's gonna get in trouble."

"What's her name?"

"Lexi something, I think. If she tries to drive that car of hers home, she's liable to kill half a dozen people."

"Why you calling me, Al?"

"Novak, gimme a break here. I don't know no one on that movie crew. I thought you might help me out, get this chick home where she can't be a danger to herself or anyone."

Jake shook his head and sighed. "I'll come and get her, Al."

Jake threw the fish back and walked to his Harley. Ten minutes later he was pulling up in front of the Open Season, the name of Al Jenning's place. As soon as he walked in, he heard Lexi yelling at the top of her voice. Al Jennings, a short, rotund individual, came over and said, "Get her out of here, will you, Jake? She's bad for business."

"I'll take care of it. Thanks for calling."

Jake walked over to where Lexi Colby was sitting at the bar. Her hair looked like it had been combed with an egg beater, and her eyes were glassy. "Hello, Lexi."

"Who's that?"

"Me. Jake Novak."

A drunken smile came to Lexi's lips. "Well, good ol' Jake. Le's have a drink."

"I think maybe you've had enough."

"Who says so?"

Jake began talking softly, and Lexi quieted down. Finally he said, "Let's go outside and get some air."

"Okay. Suits me. I'm tired of this dump anyhow." She yelled a ribald statement, and Jake said, "How much does she owe, Al?"

"About fifty bucks."

Jake took Lexi's purse, pulled out some bills, paid, and then took her by the arm. As soon as they were outside, he pulled her car keys out of her purse and pushed the alarm button. A Porsche in the parking lot immediately lit up, horn blaring, and he guided her to it.

"I gotta have a drink," Lexi slurred.

"Sure, babe. I'll get right on that."

Jake had to lift her up and put her in the car, and when he started the engine, she immediately lolled over bonelessly against him. He drove back to the Blue House and saw that most of the lights were out.

"Which is your room?"

"Second floor."

He had started to get her up the back steps, when she collapsed. He picked her up, carried her upstairs, and said, "Which room?"

"That one there on the end."

The door wasn't locked, so Jake pushed it open and walked over toward the bed. She said, "I'm going to be sick."

He took her to the bathroom and sure enough, she was spectacularly ill.

He washed her face off, put her on the bed, and removed her shoes. She opened her eyes and tried to focus. She could only speak in a rough whisper after all her screaming. "It ain't fair! Nothing's fair."

"No, it's not. If life was fair," Jake said quietly, "we'd all be born with rich daddies."

"He lied to me—an' I'll get him for that. I'll get him! You wait and see if I don't."

Lexi drifted off, but periodically came awake cursing. She finally seemed to be going to sleep, but began muttering. "I know...I know... who killed Callie."

Instantly Jake leaned forward. "Who was it, Lexi?"

But there was no answer. Lexi had gone to sleep. "Wake up, Lexi. Who was it? Who killed her?"

"Can't tell. I'd get killed, too. Leave me alone." She passed out as if someone had struck her a blow. Jake stood up and waited indecisively.

It came to his mind that he ought to call the chief of police and tell him what he'd heard, but actually he hadn't heard anything meaningful.

I'll come back in the morning, he thought, *and get it out of her then.* He turned and left the room and drove back to the house, thinking how strange it was that the people who made movies led such sordid lives.

● ● ●

"Hello, Chief. What are you doing here this morning?" Jake had opened the door and found Chief O'Dell standing there.

"Got to talk to you, Jake."

"Sure. Come on in."

"No, you come with me."

Instantly Jake was alert. "Is this a bust?"

"No, come on out on the porch. Just tell the folks you'll be back soon."

"They're not even up yet." He stepped outside, and O'Dell walked to the squad car. Jake got in beside him and said, "What's the big secret?"

"You saw that movie actress Lexi Colby last night?"

"Yeah, Al Jennings called me from his place. She was drunk, and he was afraid she would kill somebody coming home."

"What time was that?"

"Must have been about one or a little later."

"Did you stop anywhere along the way? Did anybody see you?"

"No, I was driving her car. It was late so I just drove her car home— see, it's sitting right there. My Harley's still out at Al's place. What's all this about?"

"She's dead, Jake."

A shock ran over Jake. "She's dead? What happened?"

"You were the last person to see her alive, I guess."

"Spill it, Chief. What happened to her?"

"Well, it looks like suicide. She was in a bathtub full of water, and she slit her wrists."

"I don't believe that. She was too drunk."

"I don't either, but maybe that's what somebody wanted us to think."

"She leave a note?"

"Yeah, on the computer."

"A computer suicide note? Doesn't sound likely for Lexi. She's more the scrawl-on-the-bar-napkin type."

"Well, you were with her last night, so once again you're officially a suspect. But listen," O'Dell said with an air of confidentiality. "I just want your eye on this. Capiche?"

They arrived at the Blue House, and it was like déjà vu. There were people stirring, and the yellow tape lines were out. Jake followed O'Dell upstairs and into the bathroom. Lexi was fully dressed, and her eyes were wide open, staring at the ceiling. The water was crimson and, as always, Jake had a queasy moment.

"What do you think, Jake?"

"I don't think it was suicide. She wasn't making much sense last night, but the last thing she said before she passed out was that she knew who'd killed Callie Braun."

"You're kidding me. Why didn't you tell me sooner? Who'd she say was the killer?"

"She passed out before she could tell me. I was on my way over here this morning to get it out of her."

O'Dell shook his head. "Looks like somebody beat you to it."

"You don't buy the suicide?"

"The coroner has already said she was suffocated. Never heard of anybody killing themselves by suffocation and then getting into the bathtub and slitting their wrists. Somebody did this."

"Can I see the note?"

"It's on the screen over there."

Jake went over and stared at the screen. "Life doesn't mean anything anymore. I can't go on like this. I'm sorry I made such a mess for somebody to clean up." Jake looked up. "That doesn't sound like her."

"All right. Let's go downstairs. You were the last person to see her alive except the killer. So I want to know everything she said and everything you two did."

They got situated in yet another makeshift office. Jake started out by saying dully, "I was fishing under the bridge when I got a call from Al Jennings..."

Eighteen

Jeremy and Jake were working in the front yard, when Ocie came from around the house. He headed for his old Volkswagen van, which he and Jake had patched back together.

"Where you going, Ocie?" Jeremy called out.

Ocie turned around to look at the pair. "I'm going to get drunk," he said defiantly and then scratched his head. "And do I dread it!"

Jeremy wanted to laugh but knew better. "If you dread it, why are you doing it?"

"If I knew why I was doing it, I wouldn't do it, would I?"

Jeremy shook his head sadly as Ocie started to get into the old van, but Jake crossed the yard quickly and held out his hand to Ocie, palm up.

Ocie just stared at Jake, puzzled.

"Keys," Jake said.

"Well, no, I...can't you see I'm leaving?" Ocie stammered.

"Keys, NOW." Jake's voice was frightening. Ocie slowly got back out of the driver's seat, then slammed the door of the van. He stood in front of Jake, who still held out his hand.

Ocie dropped the keys in Jake's hand, shaking his head.

"Don't know what's got into people these days. All this fuss 'bout drinkin' and drivin'. Why, I been doing that for half a century and look at me. I'm fine." Ocie stared defiantly at Jake.

Jake gave him a stern look. "Yeah, Ocie. You're fine. But who knows how you'll be half an hour from now, when you're drunk? Maybe not so fine then."

Ocie shook his head, turned around, and started walking down the driveway toward the highway.

"What're you doing, Ocie?" Jake called after him.

"Still goin' to get drunk, just like I said," Ocie said. He turned onto the highway, and Jake and Jeremy watched him until he disappeared.

"I wish he wouldn't do that, Jake. I like Ocie."

"I like him, too."

"You know what he says. He says he's going to be a Christian some day."

"I hope he is."

"Well, why doesn't he do it now?"

"Don't ask me theological questions, Slick. I'm having enough trouble with my own life."

● ● ●

"That'll be fourteen dollars and twenty-six cents."

Ocie reached into his pocket and pulled out some bills. He took the bottle of vodka that had been put into a bag, and when he got his change back, he said, "Well, that ain't hardly enough to go on a vacation to Hawaii, is it, Earl? A man can't do much on that."

"Sure you can. You can buy a lottery ticket. You're just a quarter short. I'll set you up for that."

Ocie glared at him. "I ain't never won nothing in my life, Earl."

"Maybe you'll win this. It's up to twenty-two million dollars now."

Ocie laughed roughly and threw the money down. "Give me the blasted ticket. Maybe it'll be the Lord's will for me to win."

"You're a funny one to be talking about the Lord's will."

"Don't you believe in the Lord, Earl?"

Earl Simmons was from the hills of North Carolina and was known as a rough character. He stared at Ocie now and grunted, "What do you care whether I do or not?"

"You ought to be a Christian. I'm going to get you a Bible and bring it by here. It may be your time to get saved."

"You're preaching at me?"

"Yeah, I'm preaching at you."

"Well, you're a fine one, Ocie. You're nothing but a drunk."

"Why, that's true, come to think of it. But that don't matter—I ain't the one that's going to save you. Jesus is going to do that."

Earl found this funny. "Well, you get your own life straightened up and then you can come and preach at me."

"It ain't my time yet, but one of these days I'm going to get saved. It may be your time, Earl. You nearly died last year with that heart problem. Maybe God was knocking at your door, leaving you a little warning."

Simmons shifted back and forth on his feet. "Get out of here, Ocie. I don't want to listen to your preaching."

"I'll bring that Bible by. I like to give King James Bibles away. Don't like these new versions. They don't sound right." Ocie started toward the door.

"Crazy nut," Earl muttered, shaking his head. Ocie looked over his shoulder, and Earl said, "I must be losing it, listening to drunks telling me how to get saved. You won't even remember to bring that Bible— you'll drink that bottle up and forget you ever said anything."

Ocie made his way down to the beach and sat where the water was lapping at his feet. He took off his shoes, stuck his toes into the sand, removed the cap of the vodka, and started in on it. "Go on body, get drunk." He gasped for breath and then said, "Lord, I wish it was my time to get saved. I'm sure tired of living like this."

He sat there waiting for the liquor to hit him, and old memories came trooping before his eyes. The tide was coming in, and he let it cover his legs. The water was warm, and the vodka was warm as he swallowed it as quickly as he could keep it down.

● ● ●

"You going to pay his fine, Novak?"

"Sure am, officer. How much is it?"

"Fifty dollars. Won't do any good. He'll be back the next time he gets enough money for a bottle."

"Probably will, but I'll take care of him this time." Jake forked over the money and waited. He looked around him at the small police station, amazed that cops could function in such a tiny place. He waited there until Ocie shambled out, his hands unsteady and his eyes bloodshot.

"Come on, Ocie, let's go home. You'll feel better tomorrow."

"That's good. I sure don't want to feel this bad."

Jake got him into the Taurus and asked, "So did getting drunk accomplish all your goals?"

"Sure did, Novak." Ocie paused. "Wise guy."

Jake had noticed that Ocie's drinking followed a pattern. He would go for a while without drinking and then drink himself into insensibility. Then he would go calm and be good for another dry spell.

Jake knew better than to try to talk to a drunk about giving up the bottle, so he was quiet. But as he passed the Blue House, he was surpised to see it surrounded by police cars and a crowd of people.

"What now?" he wondered.

"Looks like a convention," Ocie muttered.

"I thought they'd permanently shut down production by now. The crew was just waiting for the okay to get out of here." Jake pulled the car up. "I'm going to go find out what's going on. You stay in the car."

Getting out, Jake walked over toward the group of people that had gathered outside. "What's going on, Dontelle?"

Dontelle shook his head. "Somebody tried to kill Jesse Tobin."

"When did this happen?"

"About an hour ago. Of course, the police have been here asking questions, but this one they can't pin on me. I was with Avis talking about the next film we might do together."

"Did somebody take a shot at Jesse?"

"No, looks like he was attacked with a knife of some kind."

"Hey, Novak!" Jake turned to see Bjorn Kristofferson coming toward him. "I'm glad to see you. I was going to call. Aaron wants to see you."

"What about?"

"Who knows. He's at the hospital with Jesse."

"Is Jesse hurt bad?"

"Not too bad, I don't think. He got some bad cuts, but he's not going to die."

"Well, who did it?"

"Don't know."

Jake was dumbfounded. "How could somebody be attacked at close range with a knife and not know who did it?"

"Don't know, Jake, but whoever it is, they're probably the same person that killed Callie and Lexi. They're still on the loose."

Jake drove Ocie home, put him in bed, and then found Kate feeding the fish. "Never a dull moment in White Sands," he said. "Looks like there's been an attempt at another murder."

Kate turned to stare at him. "Another one? Who was it?"

"Jesse Tobin. I don't know much more about it. Somebody tried to knife him. Got a few whacks at him, but I hear he's okay."

"I'm glad to hear that."

"Aaron Tobin wants to see me."

Kate wrinkled her brow. "About what?"

"I don't know. I'll tell you when I get home. All right if I take your car again?"

"Sure, of course."

He turned to go, and then turned back. "Oh, by the way, I got a line on a great car to replace the Taurus. It's a Lexus. It's in great shape."

Kate's eyes grew wide. "I'd love a Lexus. When can I see it?"

"Later," he said. "Remind me when I get back."

Jake left and drove to the South Baldwin Hospital located on Highway 59 just north of Foley. He went to the emergency room and was told that Jesse Tobin had been put in a private room.

"What's the room number?"

"Two sixteen."

Jake went to the second floor and when he got to room two sixteen, knocked on the door. "Come in," a voice said, and he went inside to find Jesse lying in a bed with Aaron standing beside him. Aaron's face was cloudy, and he said, "You get my message?"

"Yeah, I did. What's going on? I heard someone tried to kill Jesse."

"They did. We don't know who it was, though," Aaron said.

Jake turned to Jesse. "What did he look like?"

"The room was dark. I couldn't see him. I woke up, and there was this figure coming at me. I let out a holler, but he got me with a knife. I grabbed him, and he sliced at me. I started fighting and yelling at the top of my lungs, and he seemed to get scared. He ran out."

"You didn't get a look at his face at all?" Jake pressed.

"He was wearing a ski mask or something like that," Jesse said. His face was pale, and he shook his head. "If I had been asleep when he came in there, he'd have stuck that knife all the way through me."

Jake looked hard at Jesse, not bothering to hide the skepticism in his expression. Finally he asked, "How bad is it?"

"Not as bad as it might have been." Aaron Tobin's face was pale. He was standing beside Jesse, and then he did a strange thing. He reached over and put his hand on his son's shoulder. It was an awkward gesture, and they all seemed to notice it. Jesse looked up with astonishment but said nothing. Tobin dropped his hand.

"There's some kind of maniac loose, Novak." His face was stiff. "I want you to find him."

"That's not my job anymore."

"With your history, Novak, this kind of thing is second nature to you. I don't trust these local cops. Somebody's out to get my people, and I want it stopped." A tone of desperation came into Aaron Tobin's voice. It was the first sign of weakness that Jake had seen in the man.

"I don't have any authority, Aaron. The police won't let me do anything or give me any information."

"If you had a PI license they would."

"I don't have one."

"You can get one."

Jake shook his head. "It's not that easy, Aaron. You have to go through a pretty strict procedure."

"Novak, with your training, I'm sure you can bypass all that. Your résumé alone would get you the license, especially a temporary one specifically for your employment with me."

"That's probably true..." Jake paused. "But why should I do it? I don't need a job."

"I've got to have somebody I can trust."

Jake was curious. "Why would you trust me, Aaron? You don't even know me."

"I did some checking on you. You're smart, and you're tough, and that's what I need."

Jake shook his head. "I don't know, Aaron. Your production team is probably heading out of here soon, anyway. They can't keep you here forever."

"O'Dell said that with this latest attempt, the crew could be here another week or more. We're pretty much sequestered and can't even leave the house without permission. They need us in the same place for the investigation. This is killing me financially. Every day here without shooting costs me thousands."

Jesse interjected, "Not to mention it almost cost you your son."

Aaron looked at Jesse. "Right. Right." He turned to Jake. "What do you say? Help me out here?"

"I'll have to think about it."

"Do that. Let's talk later." Aaron seemed to feel that Jake would come along. He was used to having people agree with him.

"What about Bo? Why aren't you asking him?" he said.

"He's tough, but he's not smart. He's still gonna work security for me while we're stuck here. But I need you, too."

Jake Novak had thought many times about going into business as a PI. He didn't like Tobin, but it seemed like a good opportunity to do something he was good at, just for a short time.

"All right, Aaron, I'll do what I can."

● ● ●

Kate listened to at Jake until he had finished and said, "You're going to work for Aaron Tobin?"

"That's right."

"I thought you came here to get away from all that and write novels?"

"I'm taking a break."

Kate paused, then shook her head. "I know why you're doing this."

"Because there's a killer loose who needs to be stopped."

"You're doing this for Avis, aren't you? You're afraid for her."

Jake Novak faced her squarely. "I'm doing what I'm good at, Mary Katherine."

Nineteen

"How would you like to take a group of young people down to Belize on a mission trip, Kate?"

Kate looked up with surprise at Pastor Elvis Bates. The two of them had been working in the church office for over an hour, making plans for the youth group. Elvis had asked her to come down, and now she knew he'd asked her here to put this question to her.

"Belize? I don't even know where that is. Don't they speak Spanish?"

"Yes, but a few speak English. I'm acquainted with a missionary family down there, James Golden and his wife, Merlene. They've been there a long time. He does most of the translating for the visitors who go in. He could travel with you, I think."

"It sounds to me as if you've been thinking about this for quite some time."

Elvis Bates leaned back in his chair, locked his fingers behind his head, and grinned slyly. "Well, you know, I have forty great ideas a day with gusts up to eighty-five or ninety, but this is one I can't seem to get out of my head. I think our church needs to spread its wings a little bit. You know, we're living in a Disney World here in this country."

"What do you mean?"

"I mean if you've ever been to a developing country—"

"I never have."

"Well, I've made several trips to Central America and South America, and the most beautiful sight I've ever seen in my life was the clean, shiny restroom in the airport in New Orleans when I got back."

"The bathroom facilities aren't too good down there, I take it."

"In a lot of places, they're practically nonexistent. I might as well warn you—it gets pretty tough."

"I'll certainly pray about this," Kate said. "Can I have some time?"

"Of course." Bates grinned and reached out to pick up a baseball that he kept on his desk. He held it in his hands in a peculiar way and said, "I used to throw a pretty mean knuckleball when I was pitching. Drove everybody crazy."

"What's a knuckleball?"

"Well, you hold it like this with the end of your fingers dug in and your thumb under it. You try to put no spin at all on the bal,l and the thing is, when you throw a knuckleball, nobody knows where it's going. The pitcher doesn't know, the catcher doesn't know, and if they don't know, the batter can't know. Pretty tricky."

"Was it hard to leave professional baseball to go into the ministry?"

"Not a bit. It was a crazy life, Kate. Traveling all the time. It was exciting at first but not later. It got to be just like going to work at the office."

The two talked for a time, and then Bates frowned. His eyes were piercing, and sometimes Kate thought he could look right through people. He seemed to know what they were thinking.

"Are you close with Enola Stern?" he asked.

"Enola? Yes—we're friends. Why?"

"I'm a little concerned about her. I've seen her around town a couple of times with Erik Lowe. I don't like to see her get involved with people like that."

"Well, to tell the truth, Pastor, she's gone out with worse."

"I guess so, but I worry about her. She's always dating these guys casually and never seems to want to get serious with anyone. I've felt burdened to pray for her, for some reason. I don't think she's a Christian."

"I doubt it," Kate admitted. "She's almost antagonistic when I mention anything about the Lord. I've tried to get her to come to church, but she won't do it. And every time I try to talk to her about Jesus, it's like she slams the door in my face."

"Well, she's half Jewish. That would cause some resistance, I guess," Bates observed. "She's such a fine woman, though. You know she doesn't charge half the poor people who come in there with their animals?"

"I know," Kate replied. "Enola could get rich, being the only veterinarian on the coast here. But she doesn't seem to be interested in that."

"She's sure interested in men, though, isn't she?" Bates asked with a grin.

Kate laughed. "Well, of course she is. What woman isn't?"

"What about you?"

Kate blinked with surprise. "What do you mean?"

"You think you'll ever remarry?"

"If I find a man I love and who loves me and loves my son, and God tells me it's all right, I will. And what about you, Pastor Bates? I bet when you were a baseball star the women lined up to get at you."

"They were lined up, but they weren't trying to get at me. They were after what I did, not who I was."

"I can see how that would happen."

"People who chase after celebrities don't care what's on the inside, they're just after the public part. I nearly married one of those women, but I made my escape. It wasn't me she wanted, it was the celebrity trappings."

"Do you think you'll ever marry?"

"In a flat second—if I could find a woman to love, one who loves me too. I've found women I respect, but I guess I'm fooled by the Hollywood image."

"What's that?"

"Oh, you know, a man's walking along the street. He looks across and sees a beautiful woman, and it's just like he got hit in the head by a baseball bat. He's devoted to her for life." Elvis laughed ruefully and ran his fingers through his hair. "That's not what love is like."

For an instant the two exchanged glances, and something went beneath the glance that Kate couldn't describe. The pastor was good-looking and full of humor—and she found his love for God very attractive. For a brief moment she realized that her feelings for him weren't altogether spiritual. She suddenly laughed, for she sensed that Elvis was feeling the same thing.

"It seems like I've been having a lot of conversations about love lately," Kate said with a smile.

"Really?" Bates asked, a bit surprised. "With who?"

"Oh, never mind," Kate said. "It's not important."

● ● ●

Kate was headed home but remembered one more stop she needed to make. She turned into the library parking lot and went inside. The librarian, Mary Simpson, was waiting for her. The two had become good friends, since Kate was an avid reader and frequent visitor to the library. She never bought books at a bookstore until it was proven she would want to read them again.

"Hello, Mary," she said. "I've got some books to return here."

Mary, a short, well-formed woman with a pair of merry blue eyes, laughed. "You always do."

As she checked the books in, Kate said, "You know, Orange Beach has got a big new library, and there's a new two-story one going up in Foley. When is it going to be our turn?"

Mary shook her head sadly. "When a millionaire drops by and leaves us a bundle."

"Isn't that always the way? Any new books I'd like?"

"Well, we've got half a dozen new novels. Most of them are pretty graphic, though."

"That seems to be the way things are going," Kate lamented. "Either too violent, too much sex, or the liberal use of rotten language."

"Yes. Sometimes I feel like piling a bunch of our books on the street and torching them."

"Last week I was in here and I picked up three new books. On two of them, I didn't get through page five. These authors used offensive language on the very first page!"

"That's what's called *reality*, Kate."

"Yes, well, Hemingway didn't use profanity. He did pretty well."

"Faulkner, too, and come to think of it, every great author prior to the past couple of decades. Well, there's always Jan Karon."

"Yes, there's always her. I wish there were more like her."

Kate walked among the stacks, selected three books she thought had some possibilities, and went back to her car. As she drove home, she noticed the seasonal crowds—the "snowbirds" here for their retirement, and the singles, who came for romance but usually settled for sunburn. Many of them were overweight and wore bathing suits that emphasized this condition. There were some truly beautiful young women, but Kate found the skimpiness of their dress to be distasteful. As she passed the public beach she wondered, *Is that what you have to do nowadays to find a good man? Walk around in public nearly naked, and get so tanned that you're a walking ad for skin cancer?*

● ● ●

The house was full of the sound of shouts and laughter. Kate walked into the kitchen and found Jeremy playing Monopoly with Ocie and Jake.

"Mom, I'm beating them!" Jeremy beamed.

"You haven't beaten me yet," Jake said. His faced looked grim, and Kate put the books down and walked over. She saw that the board was covered mostly with hotels and that Jeremy had a pile of the play money in front of him, while Jake was practically busted.

"Jake just landed on Boardwalk. That makes two thousand dollars he owes me."

"Well, I haven't got it, Slick," Jake said.

"Then you lose," Jeremy crowed, his eyes laughing. At that moment he looked so much like his father that for a moment Kate felt her heart constrict.

"You're beaten, Jake," she said out loud.

"Wait a minute. Give me a chance, will you?" Jake said. Kate knew he hated to lose even at a silly board game like Monopoly. "Look, let me pay what I've got, and I'll owe you the rest."

"Nothing in the rules about that, Jake." Jeremy grinned.

Jake turned to Ocie, who was grinning broadly. "Lend me some money, Ocie."

"Eat dirt, you chump. I ain't lending you zilch."

Jake's eyes flashed. "This is a dumb game."

"You don't say that when you win," Ocie laughed.

"I don't care whether I win or lose." Jake's voice was gruff.

"That's not true. You always get mad when you lose," Jeremy said.

"I'm not mad, and this is a sinful game anyhow."

Kate was amused. "What do you mean sinful? There's nothing sinful about Monopoly."

"It promotes greed!" Jake said. "Everybody's trying to beat everybody else and build hotels and take all the money away to make people go broke. It's a sinful game! It ought to be taken out and burned. Stamps out the generous instincts that we men have."

"What about women?" Kate said, baiting him.

"Women don't have any generous instincts. Every woman reminds me of a praying mantis."

"Praying mantis? Why?" Jeremy said.

"Because a female praying mantis, when she gets married, lets her mate do his job, and then she eats him."

"Is that right, Jake?" Jeremy asked, wide-eyed.

"No, it's not *right*," Jake snapped, "but it's *true!* Women are like that."

"Some of them are," Ocie said. "Some of them ain't. Why, Kate there, she ain't like a praying mantis."

Jake looked at Kate, and for a moment he seemed to be willing to continue the argument, but he got up abruptly and said, "I've got to go to work."

Kate's eyebrows raised. "Go to work? So you decided to take the job with Tobin?"

Jake reached into his pocket and pulled out his billfold. He held it out and flashed a license.

"I'm now a certified, hard-nosed, streetwise private eye. I can carry a gun and shoot anybody who disagrees with me." He pushed his shirt aside, and Kate saw the automatic in a holster on his hip.

"When did all this happen?" Jeremy asked, surprised.

"Aaron Tobin pulled a few strings and got me a temporary license. He wants me to run security for him until we find out who's knocking people off."

"But, Jake, what about your writing?" Kate questioned.

"What about it?"

"Well, you can't give it up."

"It's not like this is a permanent gig. The book can wait."

Kate opened her mouth to argue, but she saw that Jake was looking at her expecting just that. So she only said, "How do you start trying to figure out who's the murderer?"

"I round up the usual suspects and twist their arms until they confess."

"No way, Jake," Jeremy protested. "You've got to find clues."

Jake suddenly laughed. "That's right, Slick. I'm just being silly. And you're right. I don't like to lose at Monopoly."

"Or anything else," Kate said with a grin.

"Everybody loses sometimes," Jake said. "I've got to go."

Kate followed him to the door and stepped outside with him. "I still don't get it. I honestly thought you were through with the detective life."

"Well, maybe I'm just tired of staring at a blank screen on that blasted computer. Give me a break, okay?"

"You're doing it for Avis, aren't you?"

Jake had turned to leave, but now he suddenly whirled. "You said that before. I'm tired of listening to it." There was something almost violent in his reaction.

Kate recoiled. "You don't have to get mad."

"I'm not mad. I'm doing this because it's what I do." He turned and mounted the Harley and roared out of the driveway, slinging gravel and oyster shells.

I stepped over a line that time, she thought. She knew she was right about Avis, but regretted bringing it up to him.

Stepping back into the house, she saw Trouble and remembered it was time to take him in for his shots.

"Jeremy, I'm taking Trouble over to Enola's. You take care of things here for me?"

"Sure, Mom. At least let me finish beating Ocie here, and then I'll feed the animals."

● ● ●

Trouble loved to ride in cars. He would sit straight up in the passenger seat and stick his head out the window. He kept his eyes slitted and evidently loved the wind as it blew on him.

"You're going to get bugs on your teeth, Trouble," Kate warned.

That didn't seem to bother Trouble, who didn't even turn around. He kept his face in the breeze until they got to Enola's clinic. "Come on, Trouble." Trouble was an obedient dog, and Kate didn't even have to put a leash on him. She stepped inside and saw the young veterinarian in training, Caitlyn Purvis, behind the desk. "Is Enola here, Caitlyn?" she asked.

"Yes, she just got back. You'll never guess where she was." Caitlyn was an energetic twenty-three-year-old who was finishing up veterinary school by doing her internship with Enola. She was an attractive girl, and now her blue eyes were literally flashing. "She went out with Erik Lowe. He came right in here and gave me his autograph. Look." She held out her hand, and there, on her palm, was a scrawled signature.

"Well, you're not going to be able to keep it very long," Kate said.

"I'm not going to wash it," Caitlyn giggled.

"That'll be quite a trick. How do you wash one hand?"

"I'll wear a glove over it. Isn't it exciting, Kate?"

"Um...not really."

Caitlyn stared at her with surprise. "Sure it is. Going out with a movie star? Wouldn't you be excited going out with Brad Pitt or Tom Cruise?"

Enola came swishing in from the back. "Who's going out with Tom Cruise?"

Kate laughed. "Nobody. Your assistant here is a little excited about getting Erik's autograph."

"Well, why wouldn't I be?" Caitlyn protested. "He's a movie star."

"Oh, don't be impressed with that," Enola said airily. "He's just like anyone else."

"But he's rich, and he has such a romantic life," Caitlyn said dreamily.

"Not to burst your bubble," Kate put in, "but he's been married three times."

"Well, he can change. I think Enola could change him." Caitlyn turned to her boss. "Right, Enola?"

Enola grinned. "I suppose I could...if I wanted to."

"What—you don't want to get married?" Caitlyn was shocked.

"Maybe she's not looking to marry Erik Lowe," Kate said gently. "They've only been dating for a couple of weeks."

Caitlyn seemed disappointed. "Well, she's got to marry someone."

Kate decided to change the subject, and turning to Enola, she said, "Can you give Trouble his shots today?"

"Sure, let's go on back."

Trouble was an excellent patient and cooperated perfectly. Enola was checking him over when she said in a quiet voice, "You know, Kate, this thing with Erik is nothing serious."

"That's what I assumed," Kate said.

"He's going to be gone in a couple of weeks anyway. I'm just enjoying myself." Enola looked into Kate's face. "Does that bother you?"

Kate looked down at Trouble and absently patted him. "No, Enola... well, yes..." She laughed. "I just worry about you."

Enola got out her syringe and some vaccine. "Here, help me hold Trouble." She gave him a shot, then announced, "You're fine, boy."

Trouble stood up on the table, and Kate hugged him. Enola was watching the two of them.

"Don't worry about me, Kate, okay? I know what I'm doing."

Kate paid the bill and left the office, still feeling unsettled.

Twenty

Jake found Chief O'Dell in his office sitting at his desk, staring up at the ceiling.

"I see you're right at it—catching criminals right and left, Chief."

O'Dell stared at Jake. He got up and without a word went over to one end of the room, picked up a putter, and placed a golf ball on a green strip of carpet. He tapped the ball, and it went toward a plastic contraption that was designed to catch the ball and shoot it back. The ball missed by a full foot, and O'Dell suddenly flung the golf club at the wall, where it knocked a dent in the sheetrock.

"That'll fix it," Jake said cheerfully.

"What do you want, Novak?"

"I've come to give you the benefit of my copious experience."

O'Dell scowled, shook his head and said in his flat Oklahoma drawl, "Just what I need—a big-time Yankee detective fouling up my case."

"Well, it seems to me just recently you were happy to have my help," Jake said.

O'Dell stared at the dent he had made on the wall. "Why'd I do that?" he said.

"I did the same thing when I was working homicide in Chicago, only instead of throwing golf clubs, I threw suspects."

"So what do you want?"

"Aaron Tobin's hired me to run security as long as his company is still holed up in that house. He also wants me to find out who's killing his people before they're all dead. Thought you and I might want to join forces."

"Sit down. You want some coffee?"

"Sure."

Jake sat down, and O'Dell poured coffee out of a Mr. Coffee machine. It seemed to Jake that it poured slowly, like tar. He tasted it and grimaced.

"That ought to take the enamel off of my teeth."

"There's no such thing as a bad cup of coffee," O'Dell said. "Just weak men."

"So what have you got in the way of leads?" Jake asked.

"Tell you the truth, Novak, I've got leads galore." O'Dell seemed depressed. "But I've got three investigations running simultaneously—two murders, one assault—and it's taking awhile to establish motive and opportunity for all of them. Not to mention establishing alibis for the three different times."

"How are the alibis checking out?" Jake wanted to know.

"Most of them are flimsy. You know these Hollywood types. All in each other's beds or out partying, who knows? Hardly anything verifiable."

"What about Thad Boland? He's the most likely one of the bunch, I'd say."

"When Jesse Tobin was attacked, Boland was in his bed but claims he wasn't alone. He picked up a chippie in Mobile."

"What was her name?"

"Mandy."

"Sure it was. Good luck finding her."

"He claims she was gone when he woke up. Said she took every dime he had."

"Well, there's plenty of people without alibis. Oughta make it interesting." Jake thought for a moment. "If we could find that knife, it would be nice."

"Things don't work out nice, Novak. Not like in Chicago, where you solve all the crimes in the first twenty-four hours."

Jake grinned. "Yeah, it was always like that. There was one murder that we solved before it even happened. Boy, we were good."

O'Dell didn't smile. "Maybe CSI will give us something."

"They'd better."

● ● ●

Ocie and Jeremy were at the Brices' working to put the house back together. They were putting up new paneling, and Ocie was telling stories of his three wives when the mayor drove up.

"I don't like that fellow," Ocie said.

Devoe Palmer knocked on the door, and Morgan Brice came out of the bedroom. "Hello, Mayor, what can I do for you?"

"I've got some bad news, Mr. Brice."

"I'll bet you have," Morgan said flatly.

"Well, the building inspector has rejected your application for the permits to restore your house."

"What does that mean?" Morgan inquired.

"It means you're going to have to leave this place."

"Not a chance," Ocie interrupted. "We can fix this place up, Devoe."

Palmer turned to look at Ocie who had come over. "You're out of jail, I see."

"Sure. Sober as a mayor. What's all this about Mr. Brice having to move?"

"You heard what I said." Devoe's voice took on an authoritative tone. "Buildings have to be up to code."

"You mean like that shack you own down past the bridge?" Ocie asked.

"That's different. That's just a place I use for weekends."

"So," Ocie said, "you've got two codes. One for shacks the mayor uses, and one for everybody else. Is that right?"

"I'm not going to discuss this, Ocie." Palmer turned to Morgan Brice. "I'm sorry about this."

"You get your orders directly from Aaron Tobin?"

Palmer drew himself up to his full five feet six inches. "I don't take orders from that Hollywood phony."

"Sure you do," Morgan said. "You take orders from anybody who puts a dollar in your pocket."

"There's no need to talk like that, Mr. Brice. I don't have anything to do with the building code. You'll have to talk to the inspector."

"I wonder," said Morgan, "how quickly the codes might change if I were to agree to sell Tobin the rights to my book."

Palmer sent a steely gaze in Morgan's direction. "You'd better start packing. This place is being condemned."

Devoe Palmer turned and left without another word. Morgan looked at Rhiannon. "Well, that's not good news, honey."

"We're going to have to leave here?"

"Unless a miracle happens, we will."

● ● ●

Kate was watching Miss Boo, the flop-eared rabbit, chew on an extension cord. "If you electrocute yourself again, you're history. Jake's not here to give you CPR," she said, "and I'm not going to do it." Miss Boo raised her head, considered Kate with her pale gray eyes, then went back to chewing on the cord. "You're the dumbest rabbit I've ever seen."

As Kate got up, Bad Louie circled her and landed squawking on her shoulder. He muttered a vile curse word in her ear, and she reached up and swatted at him. "I've told you not to use those words!"

Bad Louie gripped her with his talons and rasped, "Hallelujah! Praise the Lord!"

"That's better, Louie." The doorbell rang, and shooing Louie, she went to answer it. Beverly stood there in all his sartorial splendor.

"The prodigal returns," he said airily. "May I come in?"

"Sure, Bev. Where have you been?"

"I went to Kentucky. One of your Midwestern states, I believe."

"No, it's not Midwestern. It's mid-Southern."

"I was never good at American geography."

"Come on in and have some coffee," Kate invited. "Or I suppose you'll want tea."

"Either will be fine. You know that stereotype of the British drinking tea is outdated. I can drink coffee like any good American."

The two went into the kitchen, and Bev sat down at the island, and when she poured a cup of coffee, he put several spoonfuls of sugar and a dollop of cream in it. "Kills the taste," he said.

"If you don't like the taste, why do you drink it?"

"I told you—I'm trying to act like an American."

"You'll never pass," Kate smiled. "Too much British blood in you. What were you doing in Kentucky?"

"I went out there to look at a horse farm."

"Why would you do that?"

"I raised racehorses back home. I'm thinking I might like to start a breeding farm over here."

"That always seemed like the most boring thing to me."

"What, breeding horses?"

"No, racing them. Horses running around in a circle. Everybody makes such a thing over the Kentucky Derby, and it's over in three minutes or something like that."

"How plebeian you are, Kate! It's the sport of kings."

"Well, I'm not a king. See, I told you I'd have no chance among the royals."

"How have things been going here? Did they ever find out who killed Callie Braun?"

Kate paused. "Oh, Bev, you're behind on things. You wouldn't believe what's been happening."

"Do tell!"

"Well, another actress was killed...it was Lexi Colby." Kate remembered that Lexi had taken a shine to Bev when he'd visited the set.

"Lexi...? Oh my," Bev said shakily. "You can't be serious."

"Yes. Whoever did it tried to make it look like a suicide. I'm sorry, Bev. I know you liked her."

"Well, I didn't really know her...but still." He shuddered. "This comes as quite a shock. Any idea who's behind these murders?"

"Not yet. Jake's working on it, though."

"I thought he was writing novels."

"He's taking a break from that, I guess. Aaron Tobin brought him on to work security for the production company while they're still sequestered out at the house."

"Really! Well, if there's anything I can say about Novak, I'd say he's the man I'd want on the case. Aaron was smart to hire him."

"Oh, and one more thing, too. Somebody attacked Jesse Tobin. So they're working on three crimes now."

"Good night! Didn't White Sands used to be a peaceful, relatively crime-free hideaway?"

Kate shook her head. "It was until the movie people hit town."

They were quiet for a moment, then Bev said, "You know, I think you need a break from all of this. Something to distract you."

"Oh yeah?" She grinned. "What did you have in mind?"

"A date with me, of course."

"A date?!" She said with mock surprise. "With you, of all people?"

"Not only with me, but with half the population of Mobile and Baldwin counties. I've been wanting to see one of your American baseball games. How about we go see the BayBears play?"

Kate thought for a moment. "I'll tell you what. I'll go to the game with you if you'll go to church with me again."

"That's a bargain. The game is tonight. We can go to church tomorrow. You know," he said with a mischievous grin, "I think I just got myself a heck of a deal."

"What do you mean?"

"I asked for one date, but got two. Pretty clever of me, I'll say."

Kate laughed. "All right, we'll go to the ball game, and then you can buy me a foot-long Coney dog at the Sonic."

"Sounds like an abomination, something designed by the Antichrist."

"They're really good. You'll like them."

● ● ●

"I still don't understand that game. It's not much like cricket."

Kate was sitting beside Beverly in his Rolls. They had attended the baseball game and afterward, ordered foot-long hot dogs from the Sonic, which Beverly professed to like very much indeed. Now they were headed back toward White Sands with Beverly breaking every speed limit known on Highway 59.

"Well, I don't understand cricket either."

"When you come to England, I'll explain it to you," Bev said, glancing over at her.

"I'd like to go to England."

"I think you'd like it, Kate, in the summertime, at least. The grass seems greener there, and the flowers are beautiful."

"What about winter?"

"Very unpleasant."

"Really? I always think of England being a nice sunny place."

"Haven't you seen those postcards that say 'Winter in London'? They're just a plain white card—nothing on them. That about sums it up. Foggy and nasty."

"Hmm," Kate said thoughtfully. "I probably wouldn't like it. But I wouldn't mind visiting someday."

"Would you like to fly over and see my ancestral home and meet all the varlets that work for me and my disreputable family?"

"They're not disreputable."

"Yes, they are, pretty much. I'm the only admirable one in the whole crew."

"I'm overwhelmed by your humility, Bev."

"Well, I don't have much to be humble about."

Kate laughed. She enjoyed his quick wit and always had fun with him. "What's so admirable about you?"

"Well, I help old ladies across the street when it's not too much trouble."

"That's admirable," Kate said sarcastically.

"I'm always polite and respectful to the young ladies I take out."

"I'll bet."

"Really, I am. Have I ever been anything less than chivalrous toward you?"

"I've been waiting for you to show the dark side of your character."

"Ah. I thought I could pull the wool over your eyes. You're too sharp for me, Kate. I'm nothing but a dashed lecherous Englishman."

They chatted in this vein until he pulled up in front of her house. She started to get out, and he said, "Wait a minute. Let me ask you this. Have you ever thought of me as a man you might marry?"

"We've been through this, Bev. The answer is no."

Bev's eyes flew open. "What do you mean 'no'? Couldn't you at least be coy and flirtatious, keep my hopes up?"

"I don't think we'd be right together, Bev."

"I'm not *that* hideous, am I?"

"Haven't I told you all this before? I don't want to be 'Lady' Mary Katherine."

"Why not?"

"I'd have to behave myself."

Beverly suddenly laughed. "I can see you don't know much about English nobility. The word 'Lady' is a title. It doesn't have anything to do with behavior. I always liked what Mark Twain said about the royal family—something like, 'The English should have cats instead of a royal family, because felines are smarter and their morals are higher.'"

Kate giggled, but said, "You don't want to marry me, Bev. I don't know why you're even talking like this."

Bev turned to face her, reached over, and took her hand. He held it in both of his and was silent for a moment. "I don't want to go home to England alone," he said. "I'm tired of being lonely, Kate."

"Everybody gets lonely, Bev. It's pretty much part of the human condition. But not a great reason to get married."

He grinned. "I'm sure we could come up with a few more reasons, if we tried."

Kate stared at him. "I can't believe you're serious. We've only known each other a few months, Bev."

"I'm not proposing or anything like that, Kate. Just opening the door. If we see a lot of each other, you never know what might happen."

"Well, I suppose that'll be all right." Kate suddenly giggled. "Enola is running around with a movie star. I guess I can run around with a duke or earl or whatever you are."

She got out of the car, and he walked her up to the door.

"Perhaps we can go out more often," he whispered.

"My, you're forward! And do what?" she asked.

"Hmm. Is there a pool hall here? We could shoot pool and drink beer."

"I'm not into shooting pool."

"You'll drink the beer, though?"

She laughed. "You're crazy!"

"Well, you pick it then."

"Come on over," Kate said. "I'll fix you something to eat, and we'll play Scrabble."

"I'm not sure I can stand the excitement." He smiled and said, "It's good to see you again, Kate. I missed you."

"I missed you, too, Bev. Good night."

She stepped inside and closed the door. "I can't decide whether he's a fool or what. He certainly can't be serious about marriage."

Twenty-one

"Mom, I'm going fishing with Rhiannon," Jeremy said. "We're almost out of fresh fish."

Kate was standing at the sink preparing strawberries, and she turned quickly to say, "Take some berries to the Brices. Here, take these I've already cleaned."

Jeremy watched as Kate put strawberries into a zip bag. He gnawed his lower lip in a worried fashion. She handed him the bag and then looked into his face.

"What's the matter?" she asked.

"Um...I've been afraid that Aaron Tobin's going to do something bad to the Brices."

"Well, he's a powerful man, Jeremy. I'm worried, too. Tobin doesn't like it when he doesn't get what he wants. He has lots of money and that's dangerous."

"It's dangerous to have lots of money?" Jeremy asked.

"It can be. Some rich people are generous and do a lot of good, but others just use the money to gain power. They get what they want, no matter how it affects others. I think Tobin's that way."

Jeremy straightened up and said almost harshly, "Well, why doesn't God give him a heart attack or something?"

"That's up to God, not you or me," Kate said. "He'll be judged. You know, Jeremy, we live in a terrible, messed-up world. Sometimes people do awful things, and they don't seem to get punished for it, but the

Bible says they'll stand before God one day and give account of what they've done."

"It doesn't seem fair, Mom."

"I know it doesn't. You know C. S. Lewis said we're living in enemy-occupied territory. That means we Christians are in a world that has been made bad by sin. The devil's the real force, and we have to fight against him. But one day Jesus is coming back." She patted his shoulder and smiled brightly. "And then He'll make a new heaven and a new earth."

"I like to think about that. Will the new earth be like this one?"

"What do you mean?"

"Well, I mean will there be good things to eat like strawberries, stuff like that?"

"Anything God makes will be good. The only thing I'm sure of about heaven is that it'll be better than anything we can imagine. Now, I've run out of theology. You ask Pastor Bates about the rest."

"Okay, Mom. See ya later."

"Take Trouble with you. He needs some exercise." Suddenly she thought of something. "Oh, Jeremy, I'm going out in a while. Jake and I are going to look at a car."

"All right, Mom. Good luck—you really need a new car. Come on, Trouble." The dog, who had been leaning up against the counter watching the conversation as if he understood every word of it, came to his feet at once. Jeremy left the kitchen, and the dog followed along after him. The two turned westward and walked along the beach. The breeze was warm, and the surf made a low rumbling sound as it came curling up on the beach. Jeremy stopped more than once to watch the waves that came ashore. They started far out as a long rising in the sea, and then when they got close in they got higher until finally, a few yards from the beach, they broke, throwing white drops that caught the reflection of the sun. Jeremy watched for a time, then turned, and broke into a trot. From time to time he would bend over and pick up a sand dollar or another shell and stick it in his pocket. When they were almost at the Brice place, he turned to see that Trouble had found a piece of driftwood bleached white by water and sun. He grabbed it and held it high, carrying it with a purpose as if he intended to build something with it.

"You're a crazy dog, Trouble. Put that thing down."

But Trouble ignored him and carried the large piece of wood until they went up to the door. He kept it as Jeremy knocked on the door. Rhiannon opened it, and Jeremy pointed at the dog.

"Look at Trouble. He brought you a present."

Rhiannon didn't smile. She looked at Trouble and said, "He's always trying to bring stuff in here. Come on in."

"You put that piece of driftwood down if you want to come in, Trouble," Jeremy commanded.

Trouble dropped the wood and followed Jeremy into the house. Lucky, Rhiannon's ragtag dog, was lying on the rug. "Hello, Lucky," Jeremy said. Lucky barked once, and Trouble went over, and the two dogs touched noses.

"Do you want some lemonade?" Rhiannon asked.

"Yeah, I'm kind of thirsty." He sat down in a chair, and as she got the lemonade and poured it out, she said, "My grandpa's not feeling too good today. He's lying down."

"That's too bad." Jeremy drank the lemonade eagerly, and they were quiet. Rhiannon seemed subdued, and rose up suddenly and went over to sit on the couch. She was so quiet that it troubled Jeremy.

"What's the matter, Rhiannon?"

"A man came by and told us we're going to have to leave this house," she said softly.

"Leave? What are you talking about?"

"I guess the house is going to be condemned. We have to move out."

"They can't do that."

"Grandpa says they can. He says there's nothing he can do about it. The house doesn't meet the building code standards." Rhiannon looked around the house and said, "We love this place here."

Rhiannon looked away, but Jeremy saw that tears were in her eyes, and this was so unlike her, he was shocked. He didn't know what to do, so he put his arm around her, and she seemed tiny to him. *She talks so grown up,* he thought, *it's hard to remember she's only ten years old.*

Jeremy did his best to comfort her. "It'll be all right. You'll see."

Rhiannon wiped her eyes on her sleeve and then turned and said, "Are you a Christian, Jeremy?"

"Sure I am. I've been saved since I was a little kid."

"Well, I've been looking in the Bible. Pastor Bates said that the Bible has an answer for everything, so I started looking as soon as the man left, and I found something." She got up, went over to the table, and pulled out the worn black Bible.

"This is Grandpa's Bible. I read the parts he underlined, and this is the book of Matthew in chapter eighteen. Look here."

Jeremy took the Bible that was put together with scotch tape on the inside and duct tape on the outside, and read aloud the verse she indicated: "'Again I say unto you that if two of you shall agree on earth as touching any thing that they shall ask, it shall be done for them of my father which is in heaven.'"

Jeremy looked up and said, "Did you ask your granddad about this verse?"

"No, I just found it before you came. What do you think it means?"

"Mom always says the Bible means what it says."

Rhiannon looked down at the verse and then resolutely turned to face Jeremy. "Will you do what it says with me?"

"What's that?"

"Well, we agree that we don't need to lose this house, and it says this promise is good for anything, so why don't we agree that God will do something to let us keep our house? Will you do that for me and Grandpa, Jeremy?"

Suddenly a warm feeling flooded Jeremy. Rhiannon was a pain in the neck at times, but she was now vulnerable, and he wanted to help.

"Sure I will. God can do it—I know He can. There's nothing too hard for God."

"Okay, we'll agree, and it says anything they shall ask—so we have to ask God. You ask Him, and then I'll ask Him."

"Okay."

The two bowed their heads and Jeremy, rather haltingly, said, "Lord, You can do anything, and this verse says that if we agree, You will give it to us. So we agree that Rhiannon and Mr. Brice need to keep this house—so I ask You to do whatever it takes to let that happen. In Jesus' name. Amen."

Rhiannon hesitated then said, "I agree with what Jeremy says, and I believe You are going to do it, Lord. Let us keep this house. In Jesus' name. Amen."

The two sat there silently, and finally Rhiannon turned and smiled. Tears were brimming in her eyes, and she reached out and patted Jeremy's cheeks, something she had never done.

"Now," she said firmly, "we're copacetic."

"What does that mean?"

"It means we're united, and we're asking this thing as a team. Me and you, Jeremy."

● ● ●

Jeremy told his mother the bad news about the Brices being told they'd have to leave their house, but he didn't say anything about the agreement he had made with Rhiannon. The next day Ocie took him fishing out on Lake Shelby. The two were sitting on the bank casting far out and hoping for speckled trout. Speckled trout was the best-tasting fish in the world to Jeremy, and they had caught three of fair size, but that wasn't enough for dinner.

Suddenly Ocie said, "Look out. You got a bite there, Slick."

As Ocie had taught him, Jeremy jerked the pole upward to set the hook. "Gosh," he whispered, "he must be big. I couldn't even move him." The line was moving rapidly away, and Jeremy pulled up and reeled in at the same time.

"That ain't no speckled trout. They don't act like that," Ocie said. He watched as the boy struggled, and finally something splashed about twenty feet out.

"Well, I bet you never caught one of those before."

"What is it, Ocie?"

"It's a danged old alligator. Come on. Pull him in, boy."

Jeremy's heart was beating fast as he pulled the alligator in.

"He's just a little one. Ain't more than two feet long. Got some sharp teeth, though." Ocie reached down, grabbed the alligator, and put his foot on him while they removed the hook. He picked the gator up then and said, "Kind of reminds me of my third wife."

Jeremy laughed. "She looked like an alligator?"

"No, don't be nutty. She was a Cajun girl from the swamps of Louisiana. She was the best-looking of all my wives, but she had a temper like dynamite." His eyes grew dreamy, and he said, "I smart-mouthed her one time, and she hit me with a stick of stove wood. Knocked me cold as a wedge."

"What'd you do?"

"I had to beg her pardon for talking bad to her. She was some gal. She loved alligator meat. I seen her jump in once, right in the bayou, and wrestle an eight-foot gator. Killed him with a knife. Wasn't scared of nothing."

"Where is she, Ocie?"

"Well, sad to say. She got bit by a big cottonmouth and died. She was a handful, but I miss her. She was the best of my three wives."

The two released the alligator and sent him back out in the lake. They baited up and cast out again. Ocie glanced over at Jeremy and studied him carefully.

"What's the matter, Slick?"

"Nothing's the matter."

"Sure there is. You know, when I was in the Rangers, I was so mean they sent me to see one of them psychiatrist fellows. He asked me a bunch of fool questions, but one thing he said I thought was pretty smart."

"What was that?"

"He said it wasn't good to bottle things up. Kind of ferments and spoils, don't you see? What's eating on you, Slick? Tell Ocie about it."

"Well, I'm worried about the Brices..." He told Ocie about the problem that confronted the old man and the girl, and then after hesitating he told Ocie about the verse in the Bible. "I can't remember where it's at, but it's in the Bible. It says something about two people agreeing."

"That's Matthew 18:19."

"That sounds right. How come you know that?"

"Because I studied the Bible, boy. Why do you think? That's a good verse. So you and that little girl agreed for her and her grandpa to keep her house."

"Yeah, we did." Jeremy turned and looked at Ocie. He had become very fond of the old man and said, "I wish you were a Christian, Ocie. If you were, you could join us. If two is good to agree, then three would be better."

"I'll pray with you, boy," Ocie said.

"But...you're not even a Christian."

"Now looky here, Slick. I've told you before I'm gonna be a Christian one day when God's timing comes around. Now, I'm going to explain this to you very carefully. You see, you and me and every human being is locked into time. It's like we're in a parade. You know in a parade there's a time when that parade starts, and then it makes its way down—and if somebody was standing on a certain block, what would they see?"

"Well, they'd see the first of the parade, then the middle, and then the end."

"That's right—in that order, the beginning, the middle, and the end. But suppose there was a fellow up in one of them blimps looking down. He could see the whole thing at once. He could see the first of the parade, then the middle, and then the end all at the same time."

"That's right, but I don't—"

"Well, listen now, boy. God's not like us. He can see the beginning of everything. He can see the angels that was around before the world was even created, and He can see the end, what it's like when Jesus comes back. And He sees the middle, and He sees it all at the same time. He knows I'm going to be His one day, so I'm just going to do a little bargaining here."

"Ocie, you can't bargain with God!"

"What are you talking about, boy? Didn't you ever read the story of Abraham in the book of Genesis?"

"Which story?"

"Well, God told Abraham he was going to destroy Sodom, and Abraham said, 'Well, Lord, if you found fifty righteous men you wouldn't destroy it, would you?' And the Lord said, 'No, I wouldn't.' So Abraham bargained. 'How about if there was forty-five?' And he kept bargaining with God, and God kept agreeing, and Abraham got Him worked down to ten, and he thought surely he ought to be able to find ten Baptists or Methodists or somebody in the whole town. But he didn't. Anyhow, you see God was listening to him. So I'm going to remind God that I don't see it, but He does, about the time I'm going to get converted. I'm going to get baptized, and I'm going to be one of the best witnesses Jesus has got."

Jeremy stared at the old man in wonder. "Is that so?"

"You just hide and watch me!" Ocie pulled his hat off and bowed his head. "Lord, I need an advance on the time that I'm going to get saved. Jeremy here and that little gal are joined to ask You to save their home-place, and I want to join them. Lord, save their home, and then, Lord, I ask you to please hurry up and save me from the rotten man I am. I'm mighty tired of being what I am, and I'm ready for You to come to my rescue. Amen."

Jeremy was shocked. He wasn't at all sure about Ocie's theology, but he had grown to admire the old soldier, and he said, "Thanks, Ocie. I bet God heard that prayer."

"That's right. Now you can quit worrying about that house of them folks. It's all did, Slick!"

Twenty-two

"Jacques, I wish you'd get away. You're such a pest!"

Kate had set herself to cleaning the Lexus. She had taken Jake's advice to buy the car and was excited about having a reliable vehicle instead of the old Taurus that had long been ready for the junk heap. The problem was that the car had belonged to Lexi Colby. She'd had to think long and hard about whether to buy it. Finally her practical nature had won out—it was, after all, a great car at a great price. Still, the fact that its previous owner had been murdered made her uncomfortable.

As always, whenever she went outside to do any kind of work, she collected a four-legged audience. Trouble, Abigail, Bandit, and Jacques swarmed around the car, and Cleo in her laid-back fashion had put herself on the rail of the deck. She was watching Jacques who, as usual, was sticking his nose into every possible crevice.

Why do you want to aggravate our Person, Jacques?

Jacques looked up at Cleo and wrinkled his nose. *I've told you before, Cleo, our Persons are for our convenience. We're not for theirs.*

What are you looking for in that car?

Sometimes people drop food down on the floor and it gets kicked under the seat. Remember that delicious McNugget I found in our Person's Taurus?

With resignation Kate stepped back and watched as Jacques went over the interior of the Lexus. "Curiosity killed the cat, Jacques. One of these days you're going to get bitten by a spider or something."

Jacques paid absolutely no attention, as was his custom. He had gotten under the steering wheel and now was reaching as far back as he could. He clawed out a candy bar wrapper and grunted with disgust but continued to probe the crevice.

Ah, there's something. He extended his claws and drew out a small brown envelope. *Rats, that's not good to eat.* He gave it a kick, and Kate came over to see what it was.

"What's that you dug out, Jacques?" She picked up the envelope which was approximately two by four inches square with a gummed flap at the top. It was sealed, but there was something inside, something hard and unyielding. Pulling the end loose, she shook it, and a brass key fell out in her open palm.

"Well, a key. I wonder what it fits?" Picking up the key, she examined it, but the only thing that was on it was the number 220.

She shrugged, put the key back in, and then stopped abruptly.

"Oh my gosh. This could be important. A clue about Lexi's death. I've got to tell Jake."

Excitement gripped Kate, and leaving the car she ran around the house. Jacques watched her go.

You're welcome. Sheesh, I get no respect around here.

Kate ran to where Jake was installing a new fork on his Harley.

"Jake, look at this."

Jake was wearing a pair of cutoffs, and his bare upper body was wet with perspiration. "What is it?" he said.

"Look at this key."

Reaching out, Jake took the key and turned it over, then shrugged. "What's it the key to?"

"I don't know. It was under the front seat in Lexi's car."

Jake's eyes lit up with interest. "Lexi's car, eh? I'd like to know what this fits."

"Look, it's got number 220 on it. Could that be a safe deposit box?" Kate asked.

"It could be." Jake nodded.

"Well, how would we know which bank it would be in?"

"The good old police method," Jake said.

"What's that, Jake?"

"We go to the banks and ask if it's their key."

"Let me change clothes," Kate said excitedly. "I'll go with you."

Jake held onto the key and, moving out of the sun, went over and put on his shirt. As he studied the key, Ocie came out of the house weaving uncertainly. Jake looked up and saw that drink had flushed his face and put red in his eyes.

"Ocie, don't you know what vodka does to your body?"

"Of course I do," Ocie said. He leaned up against the side of the house and scratched his stomach. He hadn't changed clothes for two days and was getting rather ripe. "Lots of people have told me."

"You're going to kill yourself drinking that stuff."

"Son, I've been almost killed so many times I don't even want to think about it."

Jake had been meaning to talk to Ocie, and now he said, "I read the citation that won you the Medal of Honor."

"Yeah, I read that one time."

"It says you crossed a field under fire from two enemy machine guns and brought back five of your men who were pinned down and wounded."

"I don't remember, but I guess I done it if that's what it says."

Jake stared at the old man and asked the question that had been burning in him. "Was one of them my dad?"

"The last man I brung in was Tom Novak."

"If you hadn't saved his life, I wouldn't be here."

"I guess that's right, but that means you ought to be a better man."

Jake grinned faintly. "You don't think I'm a good man, Ocie?"

"You're two kinds of a fool, Jake." Ocie scratched his head violently, dragging his fingernails across his scalp and then examined the results. "I'm going to have to wash my hair. It's getting sticky."

"What makes you say I'm two kinds of a fool?"

"You're a fool for messing around with that Marlow woman. You know she's no good for you."

Jake flushed. "You never went after a woman knowing it was wrong, Ocie?"

Ocie cackled, and shaking his head, grinned slyly at Jake. "A heap of times—that's why I see what a blamed fool you are."

"What's the other way I'm a fool?"

"You've tried to cut God out of your life, son. You need to get converted."

This one stung, too. Ever since he had come to live on the coast, he had been face-to-face with living Christianity. He had comforted himself before with the thought that most of the so-called Christians he met were phonies, but watching Mary Katherine Forrest had forced him to reevaluate what a Christian was like. He knew she was the real goods, and now he muttered, "Well, you need to get saved, too, Ocie."

"I'm on the right track, Jake. I'm like some kind of a deer, and there's a big hound on my tracks. I read a poem about that once. Called "The Hound of Heaven." It was about this feller who was running from God, and God was pictured as a big hound, and the feller knew he was going to get caught. I guess that's about like me. God's on my trail, and He's gonna get me."

"When will that be?"

"That's God's business." Ocie pulled out a huge pocketknife, opened the blade, and began to clean his fingernails, which were caked with black dirt. He shook his head. "You know what? Tom Novak was the best man I ever met. He'd be downright ashamed of you for the way you're running around after that woman when you ought to be running after God." He took the bottle of vodka, saw that there was an inch left, turned it up, drank it, and then tossed the bottle in the garbage can. "Besides, the woman who lives right here in this house with you is about the best one you're ever gonna meet."

Jake stared at Ocie, who was staggering off, weaving almost violently back around the corner of the house. He turned as Kate came out. She had put on a lightweight blue dress.

"What's wrong with Ocie?" she asked as she watched him disappear.

"Just drunk again." Jake hesitated, then said, "He saved my dad's life, Mary Katherine. He said my dad was the best man he ever knew."

It was the first time that Kate had ever heard Novak talk about his family. "Were you close to your father?" she asked cautiously.

"No. He tried to make a good man out of me, but I had other ideas."

He looked down at the ground, and then when he lifted his head, his eyes were filled with a sort of grief that Kate hadn't seen. "We had a big blowup before I ran away and joined the army."

"Did you ever make it up to him?"

"No." Jake's voice was bitter. "He died before I got my first leave. I've always hated that."

Kate reached out and put her hand on Jake's arm. He turned to face her, and she said gently, "You'll see him again, Jake."

"Not likely," Jake said brusquely. He held up the key and said, "Well, this sure isn't a car key. And it's not a house key. It's got to be a safe deposit box."

"Wouldn't it be something if she had put something in there that would be a clue?"

"Crimes don't usually get solved that easy. But we'll have to try. There are a lot of banks in this area. Maybe we ought to turn it over to O'Dell."

"No, let's you and I do it, Jake."

Jake shrugged. "Okay. We'll take the Lexus. It's a smooth-running vehicle."

"To tell you the truth, it still creeps me out."

Jake stared at her. "Why?"

"Knowing that it belonged to a dead woman. I'm not sure it's right."

"It's just a car, Mary Katherine. Come on, let's go."

● ● ●

The sand was blowing lightly across the surface of the beach driven by a stiff breeze. Ocie and Jeremy were walking along, and Ocie said, "My head's splitting open."

"Is it a hangover?"

"Can't be nothing else, boy."

Jeremy turned to give Ocie a cautious look. He started to say something about Ocie's drinking but had discovered that such talk did little good. The old man was stubborn as a mule and would do exactly as he pleased.

"I don't see what good it's going to do to work on that house, Ocie," Jeremy remarked.

"Got to be fixed up. It ain't livable like it is."

"Yeah, but—" Jeremy broke off as he saw something out in the Gulf. "Looky there. It's a shark."

Ocie turned to look at the dark shape that was moving slowly parallel to the beach. "That's a big 'un," he said. "He could take your head right off, I reckon."

Jeremy shivered. "Sometimes I'm scared to go in the Gulf."

"If you don't do nothing you're scared of, you'll never get nothing done."

"Aren't you scared of anything?"

"I had all the scare scared out of me, Slick." Ocie turned and gave the boy a tight smile. "Besides, I know I ain't gonna get kilt before I get saved."

"I don't think you know what you're talking about. You can get saved any time you want. Just do it."

"That's what folks say, but I don't believe it. God's got it all written down in a book somewhere. Like it's written down, maybe, that I'll get saved on the next Fourth of July. There ain't much I can do if God's made up His mind about that."

"That would mean we're nothing but puppets!"

"I don't know about that, but I've gotten so I'm just about ready to park my vehicle on a railroad track. If it's gonna happen, it's gonna happen." As the two walked along, Ocie was quiet for a while, and then he said, "I think I got to feeling like that when I was in the Rangers. So many good fellows got killed alongside of me, and I never got touched. I got to thinking that God was taking care of me and nothing could happen until He was ready, so I stopped being scared after that."

Jeremy struggled with this concept but could come up with nothing—although he felt there was something terribly wrong with it. Finally, as they came in sight of the Brice house, he shook his head. "We're just wasting time. They're going to make the Brices leave."

"You done forgot about that verse? I'm plum ashamed of you. Didn't you know the Bible says without faith it's impossible to please God? So don't let me hear any more talk like that. Come on. We're going to work on that house, and God's going to rear back and do a miracle to let them folks keep it!"

● ● ●

The moon was high and casting a brilliant beam on the Gulf as Kate stared absently out the window into the darkness.

"Can I have a piece of that pie that Jake made, Mom?" Jeremy's words startled her out of her reverie.

Kate nodded. "Yes, it's good, isn't it? I wish I could make pie that good."

"You could if you worked at it."

Kate smiled. "I don't know. I think cooking's a gift, like almost every-thing else."

Jeremy went over and opened the refrigerator door. He pulled out a pie plate with a slice of lemon meringue pie in it. Bringing it over, he said, "There's just one big piece left. Can I have it all?"

"Sure."

Jeremy grabbed a spoon and began shoveling the pie into his mouth. Cleo came up and began pawing at him. "Get away, Cleo. You don't like lemon meringue pie."

"She just wants to be petted."

"She sure does love it," Jeremy remarked.

"Well, you do, too."

"Aw, Mom, I don't either."

"I don't notice you pulling away when I'm patting on you." Kate came over and put her arm around Jeremy. "See. You like it just like Cleo does."

Jacques had been taking all this in. He was lying up on the counter looking like a miniature sphinx. Now, he glanced over at Cleo with a look of disgust. *I wish you'd stop that.*

Stop what?

Nuzzling around on our Persons. It's disgusting, is what it is.

It doesn't hurt to show a little affection.

I'd rather have a can of tuna or a nice fat juicy mouse.

Kate glanced over at Jacques. "I guess I'll give Jacques a snack."

"What for? He hasn't done anything to deserve it," Jeremy said.

Kate laughed. "Look, he's disgusted with you." She went over and began to rub Jacques's head. "You're a good cat, Jacques, even if you are a little bit violent sometimes."

Cleo watched this and triumph was in her eyes. *I don't see you pulling away, Jacques.*

Jacques was nonchalant, as usual. *She likes to do it. It doesn't mean anything to me. Now, how about a treat, Person?*

While Kate went over to get a can of tuna out of the cupboard, Jeremy said, "Hey, Mom, any luck at the banks? Did you find a safe deposit to go with that key?"

Kate shook her head dejectedly. "No luck. We need some new ideas."

"Bummer. Where's Jake, anyway?"

"He's on guard tonight. He and Thad Boland are putting an around-the-clock guard on the house."

"He'll be gone all night?" Jeremy asked.

She nodded. "Yep. Oh—that reminds me. I told him I'd bring him a snack."

"I'll go with you."

"No, you get to bed. It's late."

"All right, Mom, if you say so." He got up off the stool and put the plate in the sink. Turning, he said, "You talk to Ocie much, Mom?"

"Some, why?"

"He's always talking about the Bible. And today he got mad at me for not having faith like the Bible says." Jeremy turned his head to one side and asked, "How can he believe the Bible and not be a Christian?"

"Ocie's got a strange mind, Jeremy. I don't know what to think of him."

"He says he's just waiting to get saved and that God's already planned the date."

"Well, don't get your theology from him. As far as I'm concerned, whatever day Ocie decides to accept Christ is the day God's got written down."

"That's what I thought."

"Now I'm going to take Jake something to eat. You get some sleep."

"All right, Mom."

● ● ●

Kate parked the Lexus and grabbed the paper sack and the thermos jug before getting out. Leaving the car, she moved toward the house. It was getting late now, after eleven o'clock, and most of the lights in the house were out. She didn't see Jake and didn't want to call his name. Circling the house, she peered through the darkness but couldn't see anyone.

"What are you doing here?" a voice snapped.

"Jake! You scared me to death!"

"You're lucky I didn't shoot you." Kate's eyes weren't accustomed to the darkness yet, but the moon was bright, and the stars cast their light on the earth. "What are you doing here, Mary Katherine?"

"I brought you something to eat."

"Something you made?"

"No, I went by the Waffle House and got you a hamburger and some coffee."

"Waffle House, eh? Well, that's better than nothing. Let's sit down over here."

He led her to a bench on the deck and sat down. "You brought three of them. You must have thought I was hungry."

"I'll eat one."

Jake handed her one of the hamburgers, unwrapped his own, and took a bite. "It's not bad for take-out. I could do better on my grill."

"Yes, you could, but there's no time for that."

They ate silently and Jake took the lid off the thermos and poured coffee into it. He leaned forward so he could see her face. "This that instant stuff?"

"You underestimate me, Jake. I made a special stop at the Dizzy Bean for some French roast."

"No kidding." He sipped the coffee. "Hits the spot. Thanks."

The two continued to munch on their sandwiches. "Anything interesting going on here at the house?" Kate asked.

"No, pretty much everybody has gone to bed."

Kate looked up and saw that a window on the second floor was illuminated. "Somebody's up," she said.

"That's Aaron's room."

Kate watched and saw a figure walking back and forth. "What's he doing?"

"Pacing the floor. I don't know. Probably worried about his career. Not many producers have two murders committed on their set. Anyway," he added, "I'm pretty sure he's not worried about the two victims."

"You think he's a hard man, don't you?"

"Typical Hollywood mogul. Got the morals of a mink."

They finished the hamburgers, and Jake put the wrappers in the sack and put it down on the bench beside the thermos jug. "I'll have the rest of the coffee later. You better get on home. It's late."

"Oh, I don't know. I'm not sleepy." She looked up at the stars and said, "Could we walk around a little bit?"

"I guess so." Jake got up, and the two began to walk. "Let's stay on the perimeter of the house. I'm guarding this place, after all."

The two of them ambled on the walkway while Jake kept his eyes darting around into all the dark places.

Kate said, "I'm worried about the Brices."

"I've thought about them, too. Aaron Tobin's really messing with them."

"Looks like they're going to have to leave their house. I think this has something to do with Devoe Palmer. I guess I'd better go see him again. See if I can talk some sense into him."

"You? Don't you think—"

When Jake broke off his speech Kate looked up and saw that Jake was peering over toward the left of the house. "Stay here," he said.

"What is it?"

"Somebody moving over there."

Jake began to move forward, and as he did, the figure became visible. He couldn't see any features, but whoever it was had a rifle and was aiming at the window where Aaron Tobin was standing.

Jake whipped out his nine millimeter and shouted, "Hold it right there!" Kate instinctively dove behind a nearby shrub. The figure whirled, and Jake put off a shot, not aiming to kill the man but disable him.

The sound of a rifle cut through the night, and Jake almost felt the bullet whistle as it went by his ear. He threw himself face down, and was aiming with the intent of knocking the shooter down when suddenly another shot from the rifle hit the sand and filled his eyes. He pulled the trigger anyhow but knew he had missed.

Blinking until he could see, he got to his feet and took off in the direction he thought the shooter had run. Searching frantically, he went around the entire house twice, but there was no sign of the rifleman. He was in the parking area darting between cars when he noticed Kate standing up against the house, terrified.

"Go see if Tobin's okay," he whispered to her. "Careful."

Kate ran up the steps and through the back door. She turned to the left and took the stairs two at a time. When she got to the second floor, she turned and went at once to the room on the end that she thought was Aaron's. She banged the door.

"Mr. Tobin, are you all right?"

"Ye—yes." The voice was unsteady, but the door lock clicked, and it opened. Tobin stood there holding his hand on the right side of his neck.

"Somebody shot me," he said as if this were the most incredible thing in all of the world.

"Let me have a look." Kate pulled Aaron's hand away and nodded. "You're okay. It just grazed you."

"Where's Novak?"

"Chasing down the shooter."

Just then Jake came striding down the hall and into Aaron's room.

Aaron glared at him. "You're supposed to stop things like this from happening."

"If somebody wants to assassinate a person, there's no way to stop him if he's willing to pay the price."

"Who did this? Did you get him?" Aaron demanded.

Jake shook his head disgustedly. "He—or she—got away."

At that moment people began rushing into the room. Jesse came in first, his face pale. He was wearing a pair of gray slacks and a dark T-shirt. "What happened, Dad?"

"Somebody took a shot at me."

"Are you okay?" Jesse went over and looked at the blood on Aaron's pajamas. "We'll have to get you to a doctor." He spun around and said, "Who did this, Novak?"

"I couldn't see. I got a shot at him, but he got away. The first thing we do is call the police and don't let anybody leave the house."

"We're going to go through all that again?" Bjorn was wearing what passed for pajamas. His hair was mussed, and he was staring at Tobin. "You're lucky you didn't get killed."

Jesse said roughly, "Come on, Dad, let's get you to the hospital."

"No need for that," Jake said quickly. "It's just a scratch."

Jesse was angry. "It's not your neck, Novak! Dad, you can't risk your life like this anymore. The next time it might be fatal."

Something changed in Aaron Tobin's face, and both Jake and Kate noticed it. Jesse's concern seemed to change the older man's countenance. "It's all right, Jesse," Tobin said. "I'm okay."

"I'll have to take care of you, Dad. Looks like your bodyguards aren't doing much."

Jake saw Tobin's face change again. He reached up and put his hand on Jesse's arm. "Okay, son. Let's cooperate all we can. We need to find out who's killing our people."

Twenty-three

"Well, it looks like the shooter is going to get away with it."

Ray O'Dell had been at the crime scene most of the night, and now the sun was halfway up in the sky. Jake had gone over every inch of the ground outside while O'Dell and Oralee Prather had interviewed the inhabitants of the house.

"What we've got is *nada*," O'Dell said, with faint disgust sweeping across his brown face.

"Well, we've got the bullet that nearly did Tobin in," Jake shrugged.

"Yeah, a lot of good that does us. It's a thirty-thirty. You have any idea how many rednecks in this state have thirty-thirty rifles?"

"Quite a few," Jake guessed.

"Anybody can go in and buy a thirty-thirty. If we could find the gun, we could match the slug to it, but so far nothing."

"We need a break in this case soon." Jake shook his head. "It's really out of hand."

"Too bad you didn't plant one right between the shooter's eyes," O'Dell said. "That would have solved some problems."

• • •

Kate had gone into a cleaning frenzy which she did occasionally. Living in the same house with Jake had at least improved her habits in this area. She had just finished mopping the tile on the kitchen floor, when she heard a strange noise coming from the foyer.

"What in the world is that?" She started for the foyer with Bad Louie flying at her saying, "Praise the Lord!"

"That's a good Louie. No more cussing."

Louie, as if to get equal time, uttered an obscene phrase, and Kate shoved him away. "Get away, you Bad Louie." She went into the foyer and stopped and stared down at Jacques. "Jacques, what have you done?"

Me? I haven't done anything.

"You've torn open the package I had all ready for the mail today."

I thought it had chocolate or something in it, but I can't get at it.

Kate swooped down on the package and picked it up. The tape had held, but the paper itself was shredded and the address was ruined.

"I've got to get this in the mail. You're a bad cat!"

Not my fault. I didn't want it anyhow. I was just playing with it. I think Cleo was the one who thought of it first.

Kate rushed into her bedroom and couldn't find any wrapping paper. "I'll have to go to UPS and have them wrap it for me. It's got to get off today." The package was a gift for her aunt who lived in Washington state. She was late with it, and now she put on clean shorts and a top and headed out the front door, holding the tattered package. She stopped to stare at Jacques, who was looking innocent and licking his front paw.

"Cats have no shame," she murmured.

There was a self-righteous look on Jacques' face—as there usually was.

Kate got into the Lexus and, leaving the house, turned west on 182. When she got to 59 she made a sharp right and drove to the shopping center that contained the pack-and-ship store. Kate went inside, and Sally Bates, who attended the Seaside Chapel, smiled and said, "Hello, Kate. What can I do for you?"

"I've got to get this package off today."

"Where's it going?"

"Washington state."

"No problem."

"We'll have to rebox it. My cat tore it up."

"Cats do that."

Kate handed the package over and then, taking a deep breath, she leaned against the counter. As Sally began to box the package, Kate's eyes suddenly narrowed. Right across from her was a bank of what appeared to be mailboxes. It had never occurred to her that they would have mailboxes at a pack and ship, but her eyes suddenly zeroed in on number 220. Her shoulders went stiff, and she plunged her hand down in her purse and came out with the key. She and Jake had been to every bank in the county with no success. Jake had said that it was probably the key to a box somewhere in California, where Lexi was from, and he had returned it to Kate.

With hands not quite steady, Kate walked over and tried the key.

It worked.

Opening the door carefully, she peered in and carefully removed the contents. There were two large envelopes, and her heart started thumping. Shakily, she threw a twenty-dollar bill on the counter and said, "I'll be back later for my change, Sally."

Kate ran out, got into her car, and roared off.

● ● ●

"Wake up, Jake!"

Jake was in bed flat on his back snoring. He woke up suddenly, sat up, and said, "Wh...what are you doing here?"

"I've got something to show you."

"Couldn't it wait? I was up all night."

"The key in Lexi's car—it fits a mailbox here in White Sands at the pack and ship. Jacques tore my package open, and I had to get Sally to redo it. Total coincidence that I ended up there." She reached in the sack and pulled up the envelopes. "These were inside the mailbox." Jake stared down at what Kate pulled out of the sack.

"Let's go. We've got to take these to O'Dell and let him open them. Don't want to tamper with evidence."

"This could be our break, couldn't it, Jake?"

"Could be. Good for Jacques. He's the best detective on the block after all."

● ● ●

The entire production company had been called once again into the largest room of the Blue House. It was crowded, but O'Dell had insisted that everybody be there. There were complaints and mutterings, and it was Aaron Tobin who spoke up. "You got something, O'Dell?"

O'Dell's eyes were noncommittal. "Listen up, everybody. Novak has something to tell you."

Avis suddenly straightened up. "What is it, Jake?"

Jake ignored her and stood up. He had his back to one wall, where he could face the entire company. His eyes ran around the various members of the cast and crew.

"Finding a murderer is a nasty job. Sometimes you get answers, sometimes you don't. Often you don't like what you find."

"You know who the killer is?" Thad Boland frowned. "Why didn't you tell me? I'm part of security."

Jake ignored him. "All of you are aware that Callie Braun was killed by a blow to the back of the head with a blunt instrument. You're also pretty much aware that there was no motive for anybody to kill her."

A silence had fallen on the room, and Jake saw that Dontelle Byrd was staring at him with intense concentration.

"You also know that the so-called suicide of Lexi Colby wasn't a suicide. She was chloroformed and then put in the bathtub, and her wrists were sliced."

"What's going on?" Jesse said. "If you've got something, tell us."

"Well, we've been looking for some hard evidence. Suspicions are no good for getting convictions. Some of you don't know that I was with Lexi the night she was murdered. She had been drinking, and she told me she knew who the murderer of Callie Braun was."

"Who was it?" Aaron burst out. "Tell us, man, for heaven's sake!"

"She didn't tell me. She passed out before she could talk."

Jesse groaned. "Well, that's a big help. So you don't really know anything, do you?"

"Oh, I wouldn't say that," Jake said, and a small smile turned the corners of his mouth upward. "You know crimes are often solved by accident. In this case the key to the whole thing was given to us by our cat, whom you've all met. Jacques the Ripper. And when I say he gave us a key, I mean it literally." Jake reached into the paper sack he'd brought and came out with a plastic bag. "Jacques found this key under the seat of Lexi Colby's Lexus. The best day's work he ever did."

"What's the key to?" Jesse asked. He leaned forward and peered at it. "What does it open?"

"It opens a mailbox here in White Sands. Lexi mailed two things to herself, and I have them here." He reached down into a sack that had been on the table and pulled out a small red-leather book and a hammer, both of them in plastic bags. "This is the murder weapon that killed Callie Braun."

"Then Lexi killed her!" Jesse exclaimed.

"That's not quite right, Jesse, because her fingerprints aren't the only ones on it." He looked at Jesse, and the silence ran on, and then he said quietly, "*Your* fingerprints are on it, Jesse."

"That can't be!" Aaron Tobin cried out. "It's impossible!"

"We had the prints checked by experts in Mobile and also by the FBI. This is the murder weapon, and your prints are on it, Jesse."

Jesse turned pale. "There's a common tool chest around here. We all use those tools. I could have used them anytime."

"I'm sure that's what your defense lawyer will say, but that's not what Lexi says."

"What are you talking about? She's dead," Jesse cried out.

"She's dead, but she wrote in her journal some very interesting things. Let me read you this item."

Taking the diary out, he began to read. "June the sixteenth. There's only one way for me to get the role and that's if Avis steps aside. She's not going to do that, so I'll have to find another way, and I think I have it."

Jake eyed Jesse Tobin. "The second entry is on the eighteenth. She writes, 'I found a way. I told Jesse what I had to have. We've been together now for six months. Aaron would have a fit if he knew. I think sometimes Jesse loves me only because Aaron doesn't. In any case, he said he'd help me get rid of Avis.'"

Jake looked up and saw that Jesse's face was pale as dough. "The next entry is on the twenty-second. 'So he did it. Jesse killed her with a hammer.' There's more. Lexi found out that Jesse had killed the wrong person. This one's interesting. She wrote it, evidently, the day before she was killed. She said: 'I told Jesse I couldn't live like this. He said I couldn't go to the police because he wasn't going to the gas chamber for me, but I just laughed at him. He's no good and never was. I'm going to tell what I know'."

Jake looked at the crowd, who were all mesmerized. "One more entry. The last one. 'Jesse's gone crazy. He said he's afraid I'll tell, and when I said I wouldn't, he said he didn't believe me. I'm afraid of him now. I'm going out to get something to drink, but I've got to be sure I'm safe, so I'm going to mail this journal to myself. The hammer he used, too. That way I'll have something to hold over his head.'"

Aaron Tobin was staring at his son with disbelief. "What about last night?" he whispered. "Was that you who tried to shoot me?"

Jesse's face was contorted. "You've never cared anything about me. Sure, I took a shot at you. I'd have got you, too, if it hadn't been for Novak."

Novak couldn't help but laugh in Jesse's face. "You know, I never believed that phony story of you being attacked by a mystery man with a knife. Cut yourself up, huh? Nice try."

O'Dell stepped forward, and he began the litany. "You have the right to remain silent..."

Aaron Tobin watched as his son was handcuffed and led away. He called out, "Don't worry, son. I'll get you a lawyer."

Jesse Tobin turned and said, "You stay away from me. I hate you and I always have."

"What will happen to him, Jake?" Kate whispered.

"He'll do some time."

"He won't go to the gas chamber?"

"Not likely. Not for a long time, if ever. Rich guys like that hardly ever get the death penalty."

"He would have gotten away with it, too, if it hadn't been for Jacques." Kate tried to smile and said, "Let's stop and get him some fresh fish. He deserves a reward."

Twenty-four

"Look at this, Jake. You're on the front page of the *Mobile Register*."

Jake had been pounding away at the keyboard of his computer, when Jeremy burst into his room, followed by Kate and the two cats.

Jake took in Jeremy's shining eyes and said, "What is it, Slick?"

"Look at this." Jeremy spread the paper out, holding it up. "See? Right there in the headlines. 'Crimes Solved by Cat.'"

Jake took the paper and began to read. "Two murders were solved in White Sands, Alabama, by a large black cat named Jacques. The animal discovered a missing key leading to evidence that resulted in the arrest of Jesse Tobin, the son of movie producer Aaron Tobin."

Jacques preened himself and jumped up on Jake's desk. *That's me. I'm the detective around here.*

Oh, Jacques, don't be so egotistical! Cleo tried to climb into Jake's lap, but Jake was reading the rest of the story and laughing at Jacques. "This cat's going to be impossible to live with."

I think I need to get a little more respect around here—and furthermore, I've heard about things called "rewards." What do I get out of all this?

Kate came over and stroked Jacques' head. "I always said you were the smartest cat in the world."

Jeremy said, "It goes on about how the governor is going to give Jacques a medal to wear."

A medal? Can you eat those things?

Jake began to read the story aloud, which gave a fairly accurate report of the two murders. "They don't say much about him attempting to shoot his own father," Jake commented.

"I wondered about that," Kate said.

"Well, they'll try to get Jesse off. Somehow Aaron's pulled some strings. We never actually proved it was Jesse who took that shot at his old man."

"But he admitted it."

"Not admissible in court. He hadn't been read his rights." Jake shrugged.

"Well, I think this calls for a celebration," Kate said.

So do I. Jacques jumped to the floor and headed for the door. *Come on. Let's see what's in the icebox.*

"You're a celebrity now, Jake. It says you worked on the case," Jeremy said.

"I got fired, though."

"But the governor said he was going to let you keep your PI license. Aaron Tobin couldn't stop that."

"I don't think there'll be a lot of crimes to solve around here in White Sands. Not much call for a private investigator."

Not as long as I'm on the job. Come on. Let's get some tuna fish on the table. Jacques headed down the steps followed by the rest of them, and was soon stuffing himself with tuna packed in spring water.

Don't eat so fast. You'll choke yourself, Jacques! Cleo said.

You mind your own business, Cleo. Us heroes can eat any way we want to.

They were still sitting around the kitchen talking, when Ocie came in through the back door. "That movie star is here," he said. "Go on, Jake, make a fool out of yourself."

Jake shot a quick glance at Kate, and then without a word, headed out the door.

"What does she want, I wonder?" Jeremy said.

"She wants Jake, boy," Ocie said. "I reckon she's going to get him."

"Gosh, that'd be something, wouldn't it?" Jeremy said. "Jake married to a famous actress!"

● ● ●

As soon as Jake stepped out the front door and saw Avis, something seemed to happen to him. He had been thinking about her almost constantly since they had met after so many years. He had imagined a hundred different scenarios, but somehow none of them seemed like they would work. He couldn't picture being with Avis—but didn't want to imagine being without her, either.

"Hello, Avis," Jake said and walked down to meet her.

"I have to talk to you, Jake."

"Want to walk on the beach?"

"Yes."

Jake turned, and the two of them walked down around the house. The beach was empty except for one old man fishing about a hundred yards to the east. They turned west and started moving slowly along the shoreline. "Did you hear the picture was officially cancelled?"

"No, but I'm not surprised."

"I guess Aaron's throwing himself into getting Jesse off."

"Huh. How's Jesse feel about that?"

"Well, he's bitter, but he knows Aaron is his only chance to get a light sentence. Do you think there's any chance that a jury could find him innocent?"

"Never underestimate what a jury will do. If you have any doubts, look at O.J. Simpson."

"Well, it's all over. I feel like I've been through a wringer. I'm not used to all this violence like you are." She shivered and cast a sideways look at Jake. "I'd be dead if things had been a little bit different."

"Jesse's mistake was your salvation. Better be grateful for it."

The two walked on slowly and eventually stopped and sat on the sand.

"I've been thinking, Jake. I never got over what we had together."

"I never did either."

Avis put her arms around his neck. She pulled him toward her and kissed him, but she felt some resistance. Drawing her head back she looked into his eyes. "I guess you know what I came to say. I want us to get back together."

"The problem is still there." He pulled away from her.

"It wouldn't have to be. I've got money now. We could go anywhere we wanted to. We could live in Mexico."

"And you'd be happy not being the center of attention?"

"I could try, Jake. I know some people think I've got everything, but I don't."

"You can have any man you want. They're running after you by the thousands."

"Any man but you, Jake?" Her eyes flashed.

"Maybe."

Avis Marlow seemed to shrink. She stood and walked over to where the waves were coming in and stared out at the Gulf. Jake didn't follow, but he faced her. Finally she turned around and took a deep breath. "Well, I tried, Jake. You can always remember that. I tried."

"Remember what Humphrey Bogart said to Ingrid Bergman at the end of *Casablanca*?"

"I remember." She smiled and said, "We'll always have Paris. Well, Jake, I guess we'll always have Chicago."

"And White Sands, Alabama. Good-bye, Avis."

"Good-bye, Jake. I wish you well."

Avis gave him one last look. "Don't forget all about me, Jake. You remember the good things."

"I think it's better to put things like that away and put the lid on them. You do the same, okay? Find yourself a good man. I want only the best for you."

She began walking back up the beach toward the house. He sat there gazing out over the Gulf, and stayed for a long time.

● ● ●

Kate, Jeremy, and Ocie stared at Jake as he came through the kitchen door.

"What are you all looking at?"

"We want to see how it all came out, don't we?" Ocie said. "What happened?"

Jake shrugged. "We split the blanket, Ocie."

"Good! Smartest thing you ever done!" Ocie exclaimed. "I'm plum proud to death about you, boy, and your dad would have been proud, too."

"I don't get it. You mean you broke up with Avis?" Jeremy said, confused.

"That's what he means, Jeremy," Kate said gently.

"Gosh, I don't see how you could do that, Jake," Jeremy said.

"I think it was the right thing," Kate said in the silence that followed.

Jake looked at Kate and came up with a tentative smile. "I'll have to get a T-shirt done. It'll say, *I could have married a movie star, but I had more sense.* Well, what do you want me to cook for supper?"

"Let's have Mexican, Jake," Jeremy said, and Kate put her arm around her son and said, "I think that would be wonderful. We're all proud of you, Jake."

"Oh, I'm pretty good at kicking women out. Had lots of experience."

Kate suddenly felt a wave of tenderness. She knew what it had cost this man to say good-bye to the dream of a lifetime. She wanted to go over and put her arm around him, but she didn't think it was the right thing for this moment.

"I'll make the tacos," she said. "It's hard to mess up a taco."

Jake summoned a grin. "You'll find a way," he said.

● ● ●

The furor over the murders had died down, and the long legal process had started for Jesse Tobin, with the tabloids having a field day for days after the arrest. Life went on, and though people in White Sands still tried to get them to talk about the case, at least the fires were dying out.

Kate had invited the Brices over for the afternoon. The status of their house was still in limbo, and everyone was trying to spend as much time with Rhiannon and her grandfather as possible, offering them moral support. The group was on the back deck enjoying some cold drinks.

"Where's Jake today?" Morgan asked.

"Not sure, but he's supposed to be back soon," Kate said. "He's going to grill some steaks for dinner."

Just then they saw a car drive up, followed by Jake on his Harley. Devoe Palmer got out of the car and waited for Jake to park the bike, then the two of them approached the group.

Kate's brow wrinkled. "Is something wrong, Jake?"

"No—in fact, just the opposite." Jake looked straight at Morgan and cleared his throat. "You know that miracle we've all been waiting for?"

"You mean about our house?" Rhiannon said eagerly.

"Exactly," Jake said.

"We got our miracle? What's happened, Jake?" Jeremy couldn't contain his enthusiasm.

"Palmer?" Jake said to the mayor. "Want to tell them?"

"Ahem. Yes. Well..." Devoe Palmer stammered.

"Out with it, man!" Morgan prodded.

"It seems the building inspector has decided to approve the permits on your house, Mr. Brice. It won't be condemned, and nobody will be bothering you about it any further."

They all erupted into cheers and clapping. Morgan was quiet, then he addressed the mayor.

"And what about Mr. Tobin's threats, Mr. Mayor? Does he still want the rights to my book?"

"That's over and done with, Mr. Brice," Devoe replied. "Aaron Tobin has left town, and he's got other things on his mind."

Morgan smiled, and Rhiannon went over to hug him.

"I knew God would come through, Grandpa. We don't have to worry about losing our house anymore."

Morgan held on to Rhiannon, and the others could see a tear in the corner of his eye.

● ● ●

Jake was grilling rib eye steaks on the huge grill. Everyone was in a celebratory mood, laughing and joking together. They had called Bev and Enola to join them as well, and the group was getting ready for supper.

"Aren't the steaks about done, Jake?" Rhiannon asked.

"Depends. If you want it rare, they're okay. I like mine pretty well done."

"Mine, too," Morgan put in.

Kate laughed and said, "Look at Jacques." Everyone turned to look at the big cat. He was wearing a medal around his neck. It had been sent by the governor, and it said "Big Time Detective" on one side and had the governor's signature etched on the other side. Jacques insisted on wearing it.

I think it's egotistical for you to wear that thing around your neck. Cleo had sniffed and turned away from Jacques disdainfully. *It makes you look silly.*

You're just jealous, Cleo.

Jealous of a piece of metal hanging around your neck? Don't be silly.

It means I'm a hero. I've known it a long time, but now everybody knows it.

Ten minutes later, when the steaks were done, they all sat down at the table, and Kate said, "I wish Ocie were here. He loves rib eye steaks."

"Where is he, Mom?" Jeremy asked.

"I don't know. Haven't seen him in a while."

"Well, let's eat. I'll say the blessing," Jeremy said. They bowed their heads, and he said in a hurried tone, "Lord, we thank You for these steaks and this salad and all this food that Jake's cooked up. In Jesus' name."

Rhiannon said, "That's the worst blessing I ever heard in my life."

"What do you mean?" Jeremy said. "You're not supposed to criticize other people's prayers."

Rhiannon was wearing her usual outfit of worn shorts and an even more worn T-shirt. She stared with disgust at Jeremy and said, "When you're talking to God, you ought to be more formal."

"I'm not sure that's altogether true, Rhiannon." Morgan Brice looked somewhat better than he had. There was color in his cheeks, and he was smiling at his granddaughter. "Maybe God likes for us to be more familiar with Him."

Bev looked skeptical. "Well, you wouldn't want to say, 'Hey, how ya doin', God?' would you, Morgan?"

"No, nothing like that, but sometimes I think our prayers get pretty artificial. You know, occasionally I get to where I can't think of how to pray, and I just say, 'Lord, You know what I mean.'"

"I know what I'm going to do," Rhiannon said. "I'm going to write all the things I pray for on a piece of paper, and then I'm going to put it over my bed, and every night when I get in I'm just going to say, 'There are all the things I need, God, thank You very much.'"

Everyone laughed and Jeremy exclaimed, "That is absolutely ridiculous!"

"It is not!" Rhiannon said. "And anyway, God doesn't want to hear your old amorphous prayers."

Everyone turned to look at the girl, and Jeremy said, "*Amorphous?* What does *that* mean?"

Enola jumped in. "Good word, Rhiannon." She turned to Jeremy. "*Amorphous* means shapeless or fuzzy. Maybe vague, unstructured. Something like that."

Rhiannon nodded and swallowed a bite of steak. "That's the way your prayers are, Jeremy. They're not organized."

"Unorganized prayers?" Jeremy yelped. "Oh, and I suppose yours are."

"They certainly are. My prayers aren't amorphous. I organize them so that God doesn't have to sort through them."

"Organize them?" Bev said. "How do you organize your prayers?"

"Well, Roman numeral one is things I want God to do for me. The second major division is people I want God to look out for. Number three is, I thank God for all the things He's done for me."

Rhiannon went on until she got to Roman numeral nine, and Jake threw up his hands. "I never heard of such un-amorphous praying in all my life," he said. "I'm sure God is very grateful for your organizational efforts, Rhiannon."

"Let's just eat," Kate said. She was highly amused at Rhiannon's method of prayer.

They enjoyed the steak dinner, and just as Kate put the dessert on the table, fresh strawberries with whipped cream, they heard the front door slam.

"That must be Ocie. I hope he's not drunk," Kate said.

Ocie came in the door. He did indeed seem to be intoxicated, and yet his eyes were clear and he wasn't swaying.

"Well, hello one and all," Ocie said. "Sorry to interrupt your meal."

"That's all right, Ocie," Kate said. "You're just in time for dessert."

"Well, maybe. But I'm glad you're all sittin' down, because you ain't going to believe what I've got to tell you."

Everyone looked at Ocie, and he came over and put his hands on Rhiannon's shoulders. "Well, honey, the Lord's done come through."

"What do you mean, Ocie?" Rhiannon said, her eyes growing large.

"I mean you're going to get to keep your house."

"Well, we know that, Ocie, the mayor came by to tell us," Rhiannon said.

"But you don't know the whole story." Ocie had a mysterious grin. They all looked at him, questions in their eyes.

"Not only do you get to keep your house, you're gonna get it rebuilt. It's gonna be the grandest house on this beach." Ocie slung himself around and faced everyone at the table. "I ain't never won nothing in my life and never expected to, but a few weeks ago I went in to buy some vodka, and I had just enough money left to buy one thing. Can you guess what it was?" He looked around and nobody spoke. "It was a lottery ticket. Only one I bought in my life. So guess what?"

"You won the lottery!" Rhiannon cried out. "Ocie won the lottery! He's going to rebuild our house."

Morgan Brice had turned slightly pale. "That can't be true, can it, Ocie?"

"It shore can, and if you turn on the TV news tonight, you'll see me right there. It was up to twenty-one million dollars. I expect I'll get ten million after the government gets through taking their part."

"Ten million dollars, Ocie!" Jeremy exclaimed. "I never knew anybody who had that much money."

"You be sure and watch channel 5 tonight. I got interviewed by one of them reporters."

Kate's eyes were wide.

"What a day," Jake said in wonder.

"Well, I expect you'll be richer than me, old chap," Bev put in.

"What are you going to do with all that money?" Enola asked.

"Well, I could throw it away like all the other fools that win it. You read stories all the time about how people win millions of dollars, and then a year later they're dumb flat busted."

"You're not going to do that. It would be unseemly," Rhiannon said.

"That's right, honey, it would be. I don't know what I'm going to do. Except the first thing I gotta do is bring a King James Bible down to Earl over at the liquor store, where I bought that lottery ticket. Then...well, what I think's happening is God is getting ready to save me. And a saved man with ten million dollars can do lots of good." He looked around and said, "I guess you folks will be my committee."

"What committee's that, Ocie?" Jake smiled.

"Why, the committee in charge of me. Keeping me from making a blasted fool out of myself, helping God find me and helping me find good ways to use that money."

Kate came over and hugged Ocie. "I'm so proud for you, Ocie. Does this mean you won't drink anymore?"

"Well, that's up to God. As soon as He saves me, that'll be the last drop I ever touch. Come on now. Let's celebrate. You got anything left there to eat?"

● ● ●

The front page had been devoted to the winning of the lottery by Oceola Plank of White Sands, Alabama. He had been wined and dined and interviewed by innumerable newspeople and had been sought out by dozens of people who were offering to invest his money. Ocie had refused all offers by saying, "I ain't touching that money until I find out what God wants."

Kate was happy for Ocie, for he talked constantly about God's finding him and becoming a converted man. She had prayed for him ever since he had come to stay with them, and now she felt there was hope.

Jeremy had gone fishing with Ocie, and Kate felt at loose ends. She looked at Jake's closed door and suddenly made up her mind. She had wanted to talk to him and now decided it was the time. She looked over at Cleo and Jacques and said, "A woman has to be strong."

Jacques stared at her coldly. *No, males are strong. Females are weak.*

That's not true, Jacques. Cleo watched as their Person headed for the door and then added, *She's going to see him. I want to see this myself.*

Kate knocked on Jake's door and called out. She heard his answer, "Come on up."

The two cats followed Kate upstairs. Jake was standing by the window looking out at the Gulf. He turned to her and said, "What's going on?"

"Jake, I just wanted to tell you how proud I was that you were able to say no to Avis. Not many men could have done that."

"I nearly didn't."

"I know it was a temptation for you."

"Well, that's over now. In a way it's been good. I've always had sort of a dream that we'd get back together, but I see now it never would have worked."

"Is that true?"

"Would I lie to you?"

Of course he's lied to her, Jacques sniffed. *Males can lie to females. It's part of the way things are.*

Oh, hush, Jacques. I want to hear this.

"I've about decided to leave for a while, Mary Katherine."

Jacques perked up. *Good, the Intruder is leaving. Now I'll be the number one male around here.*

"Leave? Why would you want to do that?"

"I just feel like I need to get away for a while. Besides, what good am I around here?"

Kate went up to Jake and turned her head up so she could look into his eyes. "You can do a lot of good. You can feed the cats."

"Feed those ungrateful animals?"

"Well, then you can take care of Jeremy and me."

Jake stared at her. "I'm not sure I'm too good at that."

"I've been wanting to tell you, Jake, it's meant so much to me having you here. I was so skeptical when we first moved in. But we've gotten to be good friends, haven't we?"

Jake Novak looked at Kate with a sudden burst of insight. She was a confident woman with warmth and strong feelings behind her frequent laughter. As he held her eyes, he suddenly realized that no woman, not even Avis Marlow, had ever affected him the way Kate did. Her lips lay softly together, and she smiled at him now, and he saw the fullness waiting. Somehow he knew that the fullness was a promise of the future.

Kate was watching Jake carefully, and she understood what was happening. Her expression grew smooth and she took in a sudden breath.

Jake put his hands on her shoulders and pulled her closer. "Yes, we have gotten to be friends. Don't you think friends should express their feelings?"

"You mean—like a handshake?"

"No," Jake said, "like this." He pulled her into his arms and kissed her.

Ugh! Isn't that disgusting, Cleo?

Shush, Jacques, it's romantic.

Why is he biting her face?

He's not biting her face, you idiot!

Well, what is he doing then? You can get germs doing things like that. Cats have better sense than to do something that vulgar.

It's romantic, Jacques. You wouldn't understand it.

I've had enough of this. I'm going outside and kill something.

Well, I'm going to stay here. Cleo arched her back and put her eyes on the two in front of her. *I do love feel-good endings.*

THE END

About Gilbert Morris...

Gilbert Morris has been a favorite novelist among readers for many years. His books include the Christy Award–winning *Edge of Honor* and popular series such as The House of Winslow, The Appomattox Saga, and The Wakefield Dynasty. Mr. Morris lives in Gulf Shores, Alabama, with his wife, Johnnie.

If you enjoyed *The Cat's Pajamas,*
be sure and pick up the previous adventure of Jacques and Cleo,
What the Cat Dragged In

In their debut mystery, Jacques and Cleo and their owner—or rather the human *they* own, Kate Forrest, and her son, Jeremy, and her co-heir, Jake Novak—become involved in a deadly murder mystery, with young Jeremy as the chief suspect. But feline sleuths Jacques and Cleo come to the rescue and reveal the identity of the killer.

And coming soon...
When the Cat's Away

When White Sands, Alabama, is chosen as the location for the International Cat Show, cat lovers from all over the world flock to the beach. Jake Novak is disgusted at the idea of people fawning over cats, but Mary Katherine Forrest is delighted.

As for Jacques the Ripper, he is already famous for solving two crimes, and now is ready to win Best in Show.

But when the favorite pedigreed cat is kidnapped, the cat-loving world is shocked. Then when other favored contestants disappear, Jake Novak is hired to solve the catnapping. Jake, the non-cat-lover, isn't too concerned—but he *is* worried when Cleo, Mary Katherine's favorite, disappears. Then, as Jake pursues the case, a murder of one of the cat owners forces him to throw himself into the pursuit of a cold-blooded killer.

As the plot thickens, the friends of Jake and Mary Katherine—Beverly Devon-Hunt, Enola Stern, and Oceola Plank—are drawn into the chase, and everyone joins forces to run the catnapper to a blazing finish.